The Seduction Diet

The Seduction Diet

BRUCE DUNDORE

authorHOUSE®

AuthorHouse™
1663 Liberty Drive
Bloomington, IN 47403
www.authorhouse.com
Phone: 1-800-839-8640

First published by AuthorHouse   09/21/2011

ISBN: 978-1-4670-2598-0 (sc)
ISBN: 978-1-4670-2597-3 (hc)
ISBN: 978-1-4670-2596-6 (ebk)

Library of Congress Control Number: 2011916125

Printed in the United States of America

1. OBEY THE MONEY.

He was face down, arms spread, on an Eastern King bed wearing nothing but a pair of soiled Depends. His skin so pale it glowed blue. Pink drool stuck his lower lip to the black satin bedspread. His eyes were closed. No movement of the lids.

Empty vodka bottles were scattered on rich Persian rugs that covered perfect white marble floors.

A breeze lifted the curtains by the open bedroom window.

It ruffled his Caesar cut crop of walnut dyed hair that had lost its luster hours ago to sweat and desperation and pain.

He didn't feel the breeze. He wouldn't feel anything ever again.

And that was just fine by him.

My name is Tommy Cox. I'm a cop. Malibu PD. A place where dumb money has a chance to live stupid.

I lurk in the gated driveways and moated homes of the rich and famous and the rich and not so famous.

Their beach clubs. Private schools. Restaurants. Bars. Pilate's class. Collagen clinics. Waxing dens. Poodle parlors. Anywhere they spend their money. Anywhere they get in trouble.

The body on the bed belonged to J.P. Buffet. Massively successful diet pill salesman and president and CEO and spiritual leader of Lifethin International, a legal Ponzi scheme in a business they call multi-level marketing.

He sold pills that worked on the hope centers of the brain.

And he sold nothing at all. Because the pills he sold were nothing more than an elixir of guarana, green tea, caffeine, ma juang, ephedrine, sharks tit, and a basal marmalade that didn't help you lose weight, but made your heart beat like a hamster in heat and give you the energy of a 68 pound 12 year old midget high on Red Bull and Hershey's and crack.

Those pills should've been illegal, but they didn't come under Washington's radar because Lifethin would fill the government's foreskins with the one thing that ends hope and that is money.

J.P. Buffet had plenty of money. But he was shit out of hope.

Everybody should have at least one chance in this crap filled life to get as close as they can to striking it rich. But for money to mean anything, you have to earn it. You have to have done the deed, made the thing, thought the thought that attracts the money. Otherwise, you're no better than the entitled spawn and revengeful ex-wives of the money magnets, who think they are due theirs just cause they have the same DNA or are a receptacle for the DNA.

I swore I was going to figure out how to bring wealth down on me. But I was going to have to earn it. I spent a lot of intellectual capital figuring out the angles and the one thing I would not accept was that I wasn't smart enough to be rich. I just needed my break. This is the story of how you get your foot right outside the door of opportunity so that when luck cracks it open an inch, you're there to shove it all the way into the room. And how you have to earn the money to respect the money.

If you don't, the money will drive you crazy.

Being a cop, dealing with the wealthy, taught me that there's one thing that is different about those that *Have*, and that fucking tax payer fueled insight is that when they get in some kind of trouble it doesn't consume them, it's not a moment of panic, the world isn't going to end, and, frankly, in some circles, gaming the system is a badge of honor. A call from their lawyer informing them that they're being sued, held accountable, pointed fingers at for a death, a slander or just an opportunity that would assuredly screw over an entire community of elders, the sick or the impaired is water off their feathered backs. They don't sweat, stay up nights, yell at their wives or kick their mistresses. What they do, what they know they can do, is hire an army of specialists to keep the consequences at bay.

The system was created by them to be gamed by them. The history of money in this country is the story of the big bamboozle.

They created Fortune 500 companies by importing bananas gotten by torturing South American natives to pick them from trees in jungles teeming with spiders the size of a baseball mitt. They spent 18 hour days in air cooled offices drinking gin and whiskey trying to figure out how banana's taste on cornflakes and how much could they charge for the delicacy. Then they showed a couple Jews in Hollywood how hilarious it was when you slipped on the peel, and voila: The banana was born!

The railroads, automobiles, oil wells, computers and even Lunch-ables were created by shifty dreamers who borrowed from the government and then leased or sold the shit right back to them and the government didn't even have time to blink.

But goddamn if that isn't a skill. And so they earned it. They were worthy. They appreciated the wealth.

Everybody else is a tadpole. They have evolved. They have ten times the shelter, ten times the food, ten times the safety, ten times the sex, ten times the love. Shit. Now, all that is left for them to do is to drive everybody they come in contact with crazy, keep them off balance, in a foggy swirl of their vision and genius. Cause if they can convince you of their genius, of the possibility that they're channeling some superior life force, you'll sign a check faster in hopes of catching their train to the money.

Everything I am going to tell you is cobbled together the way a good cop cobbles together a case. It's a 40-30-20-10 deal. That's the percentage mix of fact, conjecture, eyewitness, and fancy. So pay attention. I'm going to tell you about how some people manage to get theirs, while others spend their entire lives waiting under the table, begging for scraps.

And how I finally got mine.

2. LADIES AND GENTLMEN, THE GREATEST SALESMAN IN THE WORLD.

The Staples Center was crowded to the rafters with seventeen thousand diet pill salesmen hopped up on diet joy juice looking for a shot at touching the sleeve of The Man That Made Them Rich.

He could spin tales of happiness that made their eyes wet with the promise of limitless opportunity. It was all multi-level. Which is about as hard a business model to figure out as exists in the world. It meant that you sold the rights to others to sell for you and they in turn sold the rights to others to sell for them and at the end of the day the only thing that got sold was the right to sell.

Multi-level is a bugle cry to cab drivers without a sense of direction. Receptionists who don't know how to use a phone. And divorcees. You have a boatload of divorcees. Women who sucked at marriage *and* divorce. They all made a fortune from the early efforts of one fucked up but uniquely talented man.

J.P. Buffet borrowed the initials from J.P. Morgan and pilfered his last name from Warren. What better calling card was there in business than a cobbled together name that demanded respect and awe. His real name was Oscar Dard. He hated it. He thought it sounded like people swearing at him in Dutch.

His mother died when her intestines fell apart from too much speed, vodka, ice cream and a weak genome. His father disappeared when he found he'd be stuck raising spawn he never really wanted and wasn't sure was his.

And so the kid grew up feral.

Stealing hubcaps is a gateway crime. It leads to stealing the cars the hubcaps are attached to. And so one night that legions of Public Relations Specialists later managed to bury, young J.P. Buffet pushed an old woman from the driver to the passenger side of her Ford Pinto, took off and crashed the car and killed her.

The next five years were spent in a under funded foster home for wayward boys. The only good thing to come out of it was that J.P. Buffet, AKA Oscar Dard, developed a silver tongue so slick it kept him safe in the shower.

He could sell just about anything. When he sold, he felt wanted. When people bought, he felt loved. His first year out of the foster home—when it was obvious no one wanted to adopt an eighteen year old who looked like a member of a Boy Band and would waste no time talking the pants off your daughter—he sold three hundred thousand dollars worth of diet pills from the back of an old Plymouth.

He sold each and every one of them with a tear in his eye as he explained the death of his mother due to diet pills. He didn't mention the vodka, speed, and the bad genome. And he did it by telling people he felt morally compelled to create a diet pill that wouldn't kill you. He was going to help people lose weight for the good of the world. It was complete bullshit, and then people lost some weight because they took his shit and just stopped eating completely. They spent their waking hours chewing on their fingernails and scratching their elbows because of the chemicals in his pills and because their bodies were starting to eat themselves from the inside out. And then a couple of them died. The government took him in and he charmed them too. He told the Senator from Arkansas that headed up the investigation that his belly went too far over his belt. He told the

Congressman from New Jersey from the oversight committee that his double chin was threatening his blood pressure and how he could help both of them with just three green pills and a purple pill a day. Then Lifethin put twenty grand in both their reelection campaigns, and two months later, when the Senator from Arkansas went down a notch in his belt and the Senator from New Jersey's neck was no longer spilling over his tie, Buffet got off with just a tiny fine and a small black eye to his reputation. And the next year, both those Senators quit politics and became distributors full time and were earning upwards of two million a year.

He was purely and simply The Best Salesman in the World.

In America, that made him an Artist. When it comes to selling, Americans are Picasso's and Rembrandt's and Da Vinci's all rolled into one. Beethoven, Mozart, Bach, and The Beatles are culturally on the same plane as Kroc, Kellogg, Ford and Popeil. That's no bullshit. Look it up.

I was lurking in the aisles in the middle of a sea of over fifteen thousand folding chairs on the floor of the Staples Center. The place thundered with the multi lingual hoops and hollers of distributors from every corner of the universe. They were so hopped up on the diet juice and the culture of Lifethin that it wasn't hard to feel like an outsider, an interloper, like I had just stumbled onto an alien space ship and was hoping the little green men wouldn't notice that I wasn't green or little.

I always wanted to see Buffet in action. I had studied his rise to see if there was something I could learn about the art of making money from promises. Every now and then, when I was asked to move by some lackey, I just flashed my badge. I think that's the thing I like most about being a cop. The badge. It told everyone to just leave me the fuck alone.

Elton John was on stage pounding out 'Tiny Dancer' on his red lacquered grand piano in front of a huge LifeThin Corporation banner. It was there to remind him he really wasn't the dinner, just the appetizer.

He didn't want to be there. But his fee of a half a million dollars for thirty minutes of music-just piano, orange wig optional-was agreed to in thirty seconds of negotiations.

The man who created hundreds of memories for millions of people, who sat at the left thigh of Lady Di, was one of the poorest men in the room. He'd spent most of his life not paying taxing and buying custom made glasses made out of diamonds and suits made out of recycled chandeliers. He had a red piano, for Christ's sake. So when the government did come calling with the bill, Elton's pockets were empty. On the suits that actually had pockets at all. The principals of Lifethin, those charged with arranging the entertainment, knew this. So they bid low. Elton bit. But only after he heard that Willie Nelson, another man in dire need of satisfying the IRS, had asked them for a million dollars and they had turned him down.

J.P. Buffet waited just off stage. He was shiny in a sweat, as unnatural substances struggled to find a way out of his body. His eyeballs were dilated. Nice big brown spots that made him look like he had two holes in his head. And they darted and rolled. Upward, side to side, apart. Like he was channeling the ghost of Marty Feldman.

His handlers—Hank Gates (took his name from Bill) and John Welch (took his name from Jack)—waited at his side. When Elton finished the last flourish, Gates ran out on stage, pumped his fists in the air, and screamed, "Are we ready for the show!" to the hordes of juiced up rich and on their way to getting richer diet pill junkies.

They exploded in a multi-lingual "YES!" that was ten times louder than the applause for Elton. Elton slinked off the stage and got a handoff of his check from Welch.

J.P. didn't even acknowledge him as he poured airplane bottles of vodka down his gullet to satisfy the bad genome he inherited from his mother. Gates pumped up the already pumped up crowd, thrusting his fist in the air as he shouted, "Here is your leader! J.P. Buffet!" I could see Welch was worried. He'd seen J.P. in this type of wild-eyed frenzy before. The last time, the old boy wound up in a hospital in Saigon in what passes for intensive care after sitting too close to what passes for a bar girl who shot ping pong balls out of what passed for her cootch and one hit him in the eye so hard he fell off his stool and cracked his head on the floor. If he hadn't been so drunk, it might have killed him is what passes for doctors in Saigon said. Welch and Gates knew their King was on the downward spiral. They just had to make sure no one else did.

J.P. wiped the sweat from his forehead and glided across the stage in his seven thousand dollar Armani suit and perfectly dyed hair, arms flapping like any minute he would make his body leave the stage and follow his brain to the rafters, where he would stand and piss on them all.

And the crowd went wild.

Gates ran over to J.P. and buffered his walking like you would a toddler who was taking its first steps: Arms spread out, not interrupting, but making sure if the little rug rat fell, he wasn't gonna hit his head on the coffee table.

"Get the fuck away from me, Hank!" J.P. scolded as he spun around and faced his disciples and shouted, "I see a million dollar check!"

The crowd roared and stamped their feet. J.P. smiled and sucked in the power. "I see a two million dollar check!" And the crowd roared again.

J.P. rotated his head from side to side, like Ronald Reagan used to do when he gave a speech. Perfect little ninety-degree arcs so he could see everybody, make eye contact with everyone in the room. And come to think of it, he had a lot in common with Reagan. They both forgot a lot. They both were about as removed from the world around them as a human being could be. And they both needed unconditional love and admiration.

"Are we in a spaceship?" J.P. rallied out to the worshippers.

The Crowd roared back a big sweaty Yes!

"Are we ever gonna land?"

The Crowd roared back the inevitable No!

"You guys are great!" and with that, J.P. dipped below the podium, then shot back up with a white cocaine shmear across his upper lip and got a big welcome cheer from the crowd.

He was even sweatier now, coke and alcohol seeping from his waxy pores.

"You guys are great! I love you guys."

They all answered back "We love you too" in their own languages. Spanish, German, Japanese, Italian, English, and Hmong. It was a terrible noise, like the UN being evacuated during a Godzilla attack.

Then, in the middle of the cacophony, J.P. took off his clothes.

First his tie. Then his shirt. He flung them into the crowd, as Gates and Welch were caught between stopping him and hoping this was just a playful stunt that he'd end early. Whatever it was, the crowd devoured the shirt and tie like they hadn't eaten shirts and ties in over a month.

J.P. sailed around the stage, got close to Gates and Welch and taunted them, "Crack whore on my dick. Baby out my ass . . ." Then he pulled off his pants, flung them into the crowd, ripped off his briefs, threw them into the soup too. Gates and Welch rushed out, grabbed JP by his arms and pulled him offstage. The crowd went crazy. And why not? They just saw God's balls.

3. THE KATZENJAMMER KIDS.

J.P. Buffet's mansion squatted on the beach like an elephant hypnotized by the ocean. Everything about it screamed new. It had too much of everything. Too many windows, to many columns, too many balconies, too many railings, too many doorknobs.

It was a wedding cake Mediterranean. Perfectly formed imported rocks were individually lit up to create splendor. It looked like Camelot had Liberace been King Arthur, Lisa Minnelli been Guinevere, and Richard Simmons been Lancelot.

The house didn't get much better inside. The décor was bad imitation Blenheim Palace, which was already bad imitation Versailles.

Big rococo gold framed paintings of the hunt; hounds, horses, horns, gentry, and lions. English Nobles posing with lions. Lions killing bears. Lions perched on cliffs overlooking all they were about to kill, maim or scare the shit out of.

These surrounded a portrait of JP done in the style of the hunt paintings but without the craft. That was lost when art got to be about slicing up sharks and formalydehyding them in tanks. Or the day Pollock splattered a canvas and someone said "genius" and art schools all over the country told their models to cover up and go home, we won't be needing you anymore.

There were camera's everywhere. Part of an extensive system a paranoid J.P. had his security team install. Picture and sound, it kept a running record of all the low points of J.P.'s high life. It was secretly expanded by Gates and Welch to keep a running record of all the legally embarrassing and share holder value damaging details of J.P.'s sordid life.

I was there to question Lou Mellini and Lars Sackman, J.P. Buffet's "minders". Hired by Gates and Welch to make sure J.P. stayed out of trouble in public in addition to the general security a man his balance sheet demanded, they were present the evening of J.P.'s last night on earth. That made them suspects. Guilty of something. And I had been dying to pinch these two for a long time. They always seemed to walk on the dark edge.

Lou was a former Special Forces Op. Could've worked for the department, but these guys always came back a bit too damaged to pay attention to something as ring-a-ding as Miranda Rights. And there was a boatload of jobs for them amongst the wealthy. Not that they liked what they did. Rescuing a drunken, drugged up naked millionaire did not hold the same thrill as securing Fallujah.

Lou's right hand man, Lars Sackman, was a little more mysterious. He was an Afrikaner from South Africa. From everything I've heard about these people, they're the Dark Continent's version of a redneck. He had a fucked up Afrikaner way of talking which was essentially to spit sentences out like he had Tourette's. Half of them ended in a question embellished with a "yes?" He was also a black belt in Kempo and Judo, and got to be a contender in the welterweight division of the Ultimate Fighting business. He had a job once as a personal bodyguard to one of the stars of bimbo pop. But he hit on her—"You like me? Then, we fuck, yes?"—and got fired by the record company so he washed down to Malibu where the rich hire the dangerous to protect their Chihuahua's.

According to Lou and Lars, when the chauffeur dumped J.P. home after the event, he had taken his clothes off inside the limo and run out onto the beach, pulling on his dick like it was a leash and he was taking the rest of his body for a stroll.

"Didn't you guys think to help him?" I asked.

"Deal or no deal!" Lars burped up.

"I'm not arresting you, you stupid shit. I'm just asking questions."

"Deal or no deal, yes?"

"What he means is that we were watching Deal or No Deal," Lou clarified.

"Banker was up to five hundred thousand! She could get rich, yes?" Lars explained. Lou went on to tell me they had been watching a real cliffhanger with a contestant that still had the one million, eight hundred thousand, forty thousand and the twenty-dollar amounts on the board.

She was an unemployed cashier from a Walgreen's in Spokamonk Acres or some such shit place like that. She lost her husband in Iraq, and lost her health care too. And she had two children, who had turned the garage into a meth lab and were getting a little harder to discipline.

"Lunatic hung on," Lou said.

"She was greedy, yes?" Lars asked/said.

Lou told me that the woman No Dealed the half a million, thinking, believing, hoping that inside the case she had chosen was the million. Even Howie Mandell was trying to tell her to take the fucking deal, "He was pleading to her, for Christ's sake," Lou added. But she didn't. She didn't take the deal. The next two suitcases she chose held the eight hundred thousand and the forty thousand dollars. She had a fifty-fifty chance on the million or the twenty dollars. The banker kept his bid at three hundred thousand, she turned him down, chose a case, it turned out to be the million and she went home with twenty dollars. Came out later she had to borrow another twenty from Howie Mandell for the cab back to the airport.

"Money makes stupid, yes?" Lars observed.

I could only glare at these two semi-bozos. "So that's it? Your boss is naked, out of his head, running on the beach, and you're too busy watching Howie Mandell avoid physical contact with some out of work cashier on Deal or No Deal."

"Deal or No Deal?" Lars Touretted, shaking his head, like just saying those words made him happy.

"Lou, tell your fucking monkey to shut the hell up."

Lou led me to the video security room, which was a whole separate wing of mansion. Lou's playground essentially. It was twenty screens, covering every important part of the place, even the guest bathrooms. Lou smiled at that one. That was his lucky strike extra, as he was the one in charge of installing the system. He had cameras on both the toilet and inside the shower, but you could tell it was the shower cam that was his favorite. The control panel on that monitor had its buttons worn down and the screen was a little blurry from fingertips rubbing it.

"We see wife of President shit once. First Lady they call her, yes?" Lars volunteered. Apparently, J.P. had the President and his wife over for a fund raising. It was J.P.'s way of showing that he wasn't just rich, he was important. But the President stayed for only a half an hour, as J.P., though rich, wasn't important. And just to prove it, the First Lady crapped in the toilet and didn't bother to flush.

Lou told me he couldn't show me the tapes of that night. He told me they were the property of Lifethin, and sensitive. "Bullshit,"

I said. That's all I was going to say. This wasn't a fucking debate. I told him if he didn't, his life would get so miserable he'd want to re-enlist. I told Lars if he didn't cooperate I'd send him back to South Africa where he could get a job as a limo driver for the Zulu's.

So Lou played me the tapes. And I kind of wish he hadn't.

The black and white video showed a naked as a jaybird J.P. Buffet tottering down the main staircase. He waved a framed photograph in one hand and slurred, "Where's Mommy . . ." over and over.

He moved like a drunken toddler right up to the bar and stuck a vodka bottle in his mouth and glugged it. Then he screamed into that empty house.

"Where's Mommy!'

He was all alone. Rich beyond his imagination. Cheered by thousands. Loved not for who he was but for what he did and how much it made others.

He didn't have to work anymore. The compound interest alone was enough to float him in style. He should be climbing Everest. Sailing the Indian Ocean. Floating over the earth in a hot air balloon. He had achieved that rarified place in work obsessed American Society. He had plenty of 'Fuck you' money.

But no one to say fuck you to. And no one who would say fuck you back.

And so he screamed, "Where's Mommy!" again.

The third time was the charm.

The next screen showed Lou and Lars running to his rescue. Lou was pushing furniture out of the way to make sure J.P. didn't trip on it.

"Where's Mommy!" J.P. screamed again.

"Calm down, Boss" Lou said as he and Lars drunk-proofed the living room, "Let's call it a night." But there was no stopping J.P. He had given up trying to control his limbs and now they rubbered him all over the room. Lou and Lars did their rock solid best to prevent him from hurting himself and threatening their financial security. This was prime You Tube shit. This was one hundred million hits an hour scandal.

"Boss!' Lou yelled at J.P. to shock him into standing the hell still.

J.P. just looked up and started pissing on the couch. "J.P., that's the couch you're pissing on! C'mon!" Lou pleaded. "You stop the pissing now, J.P., yes?" Lars said.

J.P. started pissing figure eights. "If I want to piss on my own furniture I sure as shit will! I bought this crap to be able to piss on it if I want to. And if I want, I'll piss on you! Yes?" And with that, J.P. started spraying in Lars' direction. Lou yelled to Lars to get the Depends. Which was a good thing, cause with

J.P. heading right at him, if an errand didn't give him reason to leave, you can be sure as shit Lars would've decked J.P. with a champion kick at five feet away and not gotten a splash on him and he wouldn't have cared what the camera's saw, him being a little bit more mysterious than Lou and a redneck to boot.

While Lars went looking for the diaper, Lou did his best to stay out of the way of J.P's spraying. It seemed his bladder hadn't relieved itself in weeks. It just kept coming out. A sure, steady, strong stream. A rich man's stream.

"Hurry up, he's pissing on me now!' Lou yelled to Lars.

"Lou, take me to Boy's Town. Blowjobs all around. I'll buy." J.P. offered as he leaned into Lou.

"I don't play that way, J.P."

J.P. looked up to the camera and gave a little soliloquy.

"Did you ever have a man suck your cock? Huh, Lou? Men give the best blowjobs, cause they're owners. And they know what the equipment likes."

J.P. grabbed the vodka bottle off the bar and let the alcohol run down his throat and his neck and his naked body like it would purify him. Lars ran back in with the diaper and Lou and him corralled J.P., kind of pinned him into a corner, and wrestled to get a foot though the diaper leg hole. "This is usual, OK? Happened three times a month, for sure," Lou informed me, and Lars chimed in, "Four, yes?"

J.P. wasn't going to fight too hard. He'd been through this drill before, and the boys were just making sure he didn't have an embarrassing morning, lying in his own piss soaked mattress with a thousand thread count sheets.

No matter how rich you are, you don't admit to certain failings.

"Wanna win, gotta be thin. Wanna be thin, gotta be thin." J.P. was spewing the shit he'd been spewing for decades until now it didn't even make sense. "Fucking genius, right?"

"Right Boss, Genius." Lou reassured him. "You are genius!" Lars seconded the lie as he tried to get the other foot into the diaper leg hole. "Fuck you! Crock of shit. I'm a crock of shit! Nothing is true. Nothing. All a lie. Hello! A lie. I made millions lying to people. I made millions of lies. Little lies you take three times a day. You know I killed some people? You know I made them die? Me and my pills. Killed them. And did I suffer? Nope. No me. Not J.P. Buffet!"

The filters he could usually count on to stop his inner most fears from reaching his mouth had all been worn away, "Fuck it," he said before going limp and pitching to the marble floor.

"Shit, Lars! You coulda caught him!" Lou said in trying to shift a blameless moment to someone else.

"Fuck you!" Lars fired back.

Both of them ministered to J.P's diapered sack of concrete body and carried him up the faux Italianate-meets-Pee Wee's Playhouse-styled staircase and laid him face down on his bed in the master bedroom.

"Where was his widow?" I asked.

"She never hung around when he had an event," Lou said.

"She goes to a hotel. He always come home drunk." Lars added.

"She afraid of being alone with you two?" I asked, knowing that if I was a woman and my husband was usually three sheets that being home alone a lot with these two fine receptacles of testosterone would make me nervous too.

"I would fuck her. You too, yes?" Lars said.

See?

They say that if life's a shit sandwich, then the more bread you have, the less shit you taste. That's what they say, but there are exceptions. J.P. was one of them. His shit was on the inside, and it kept coming to the surface. Kept being the after taste in his throat. That's why he drowned himself in alcohol and poisoned his blood with coke and his own diet pills. But that's just what I think.

And that's why he was, for all his money, virtually uninsurable. That's why his managers, Welch and Gates, and an army of accountants, publicists, lawyers and the like cut him off from any financial responsibilities. Any ability to run his own life. They made the decisions, they moved the dough. They made themselves rich and he didn't know where anything was, where it was banked, or how to access it. And they knew he didn't care. He trusted them implicitly. They were with him from the beginning. They would take care of him, hell or high water, at the end. Or so he thought.

And now he was dead.

It was Berta, J.P.'s longtime the housekeeper, who found him in the morning. His body was bloated. His intestines had released their last signs of life into his diaper.

Berta had been with J.P. for over fifteen years and two wives. She cleaned after his parties. She cleaned his vomit from the rugs, his piss from the cushions, his powder from the glass tables, his condoms and the condoms of others from every nook and cranny in this grand ol' dumb-as-a-box-of-rocks-bought-in-Colorado house.

Berta lost her brother and uncle in crossing the border to a group of sun poisoned border patrol agents who had just gotten into a shoot out with a local entrepreneur who was running both people and drugs and had a lot to lose. After turning him to pulp, they sated their blood lust on Berta's relatives and shot those boys in the head then smashed their heads in with a rock to remove the bullets and cover the whole thing up. Then they raped her and left her to die in the dust and sun.

But God smiled on her that day and somehow, she lived, and made it across to the Promised Land.

So the sight of a dead, tormented, badly behaved multi millionaire on his bed wearing a diaper did nothing more than make her shrug and whisper a litany of swear words that all ended in "Gringo."

But she was smart, and she knew that with cameras everywhere, she would have to make with the appropriate reaction. So she screamed. To add a little more authenticity, she dropped the vase she was cleaning.

4. THE MAN FROM BELOIT.

The plane from Madison, Wisconsin disgorged its pasty-faced cargo at Gate 6 of the American Airlines terminal about two hours late. It was a parade of cold weather clothes on round corn fed bodies you don't see much out here. They wore pillowed down jackets in bright pinks and greens over bodies that had been super sized by Happy Meals. The sight of a herd of under sunned mid-westerners, who left a place that was twenty degrees below zero and arrived at a place that was eighty-five degrees above, is not to be missed. It was like they had landed on the moon.

They trembled in anticipation at stripping off the down coats and flannel shirts to get into their cargo shorts and too-snug-in-the-belly T-Shirts and diving into that California experience they had watched so much on television and had forced their kids to watch on TV Land reruns.

White folks growing up safe and secure behind white picket fences. Families that got along famously. Mix those memories with the more recent images of Pop stars getting out of limousines with their legs spread, pudenda in plain view for all the paparazzi to see and their faces twittered in expectation. The Internet had given them fresh images of nip slips, up skirts, topless, and no panty. Their ancient memories of the perfect America crossed with more recent images of a place where the debauched washed up to the edge of the Pacific and rolled around in the surf to our amusement, where the talentless children of the wealthy were all too eager to get the attention of the press by flashing body parts, overdosing on cough medicine, or crashing their BMW's into day care centers, and it just made these corned heifers giddy in anticipation.

They would drop two months pay at Universal, Disney, Knots, and even more just walking Melrose and Mom just might get a tattoo.

They would swallow the mapped rumors of where Johnny Depp and George Clooney lived and drive by the spot in their rented Pontiacs only to see a Kentucky Fried Chicken where Jack Sparrow's lair should've been.

They would see more German cars than they could in Germany, more croissants than in France, and more blonds than in Sweden. They would see money. Wealth and tans and teeth and tits that gave Dad a permanent erection the whole time here. Good thing the motel had a cold-water pool.

I love to lurk at airports. I can tell what my caseload is going to be by who comes off those planes. Screw Homeland Security. They don't stop the influx of Russians, the Jersey Boys or the Minnesotan Gang Bangers. They can't stop the Cubans from Florida. They can't stop the scammers who came here because there was so much dumb money and gullible millionaires to be had, and they sure as hell didn't stop all the rich fucks coming here to dig for more money or employ all of the above to help them collect what's owed.

I kept an eye on Lou. He stood at the gate holding a handwritten sign that read "Harry Corvair." And he waited, in his chauffeurs cap and slick black suit; his other role.

J.P. insisted that if he picked up anybody at the airport he'd have to look the part. OK by Lou. With J.P. lying on a slab of cold steel in the coroner's office, Lou still honored the request. His freshly dry cleaned Brioni gave him a busy and satisfying sex life. And the cap looked sharp on his shaved head. To the cougars and MLF's it looked like a black condom with a visor. Exotic.

As the very last pasty pink whale exited the gate, a small man trundled out, blue vinyl roll on suitcase in tow. It's not that he was small in height. It's that his slump shouldered posture made him look like he anticipated getting crushed by the cosmos.

This was Harry Corvair.

He was a small time insurance investigator from a small company in the small town of Beloit, Wisconsin, and even swimming in the shallow end of the mediocrity pool, he felt he was over his head. He grew up slow, sheltered by a domineering mother he adored who wanted him to take over her canine day care and grooming business. And he would've been glad to, as this was a man who loved dogs, except she got sick with a cancer and he had to spend most of his days taking care of the business *and* her, and he was not a man lent to multi-tasking. After two years, she died and so did the business.

He was thirty-five, with nothing to show for it. He met his current girlfriend at a Bed Bath and Beyond. She was buying sheets. He was buying plastic boxes for his mother's belongings. They got to talking while sampling the back massagers in the bedding department. She talked him into helping her install one on her recliner. He went back to her house, strapped the massage pad to the chair, turned on a Packer game, sat down, and didn't get up until the post game interview and by that time, she had already fed him a plate of tater tots and some brats. This is as good as love gets, he thought. She got him a job at the insurance company where she worked. That was five years ago. To Harry, it felt like ten.

This was his first trip out west. Hell, it was his first trip further than Rockford, Illinois. So the sights and smells and lights were all new.

He was here to deny an insurance policy on our very own J.P. Buffet. To make it moot, void, and not worth the paper it was printed on. I couldn't figure out why they sent him so fast. J.P. had really just been zipped out of the body bag. My curiosity was giving me a bit of a hard on.

It seems ol' J.P. Buffet, doing an end run around his handlers to protect the future of his new wife—more on her later—had taken out a life insurance policy in the event of his death. It was a twenty million dollar policy paid from a discretionary fund his handlers allowed him to have. He searched a long time to find a company that would be off the radar, and Beloit was surely off the radar. It might have been the last responsible thing he did. Lifethin insisted the new wife sign a pre-nup, relinquishing any inheritance in the event of J.P.'s death. The two previous wives got a bundle, and they also got some voting shares and were a pain in the corporate butt, so Welch and Gates were extra careful this time, as J.P.'s marriages tended to end before they had a chance to pay off the honeymoon.

The new wife convinced him it wasn't fair. It wasn't.

Was she a gold digger? Aren't they all?

The insurance company's owner, Dick Asher, as dishonest as they come in the Midwest, was glad to take the ten thousand a month fee on the twenty million dollar policy and offer the paper. It was chock full of conditions that would prevent it from paying out. All he had to do was a little investigating of the Malibu police files of J.P.'s arrest for drunken driving, drug possession, surfing, using a skidoo, solicitation of minors, tearing the tags off pillows, turning dry cleaning bags into toys and other sundry and sordid little crimes, and create the policy accordingly.

That policy was as restrictive as one written to prevent taking a pie in the face, riding around in little cars, wearing banana shoes and makeup and fraternizing with midgets would be for a circus clown.

The files on J.P. were kept in a locked vault. The lock was paid for by hefty donations by Lifethin Corp to the Malibu PD to protect the company from any embarrassment J.P. might cause them, and he caused them plenty.

But they could be gotten to. For a fee. Just a taste. They're are plenty of reporters who tasted but couldn't report it due to the hefty donations Lifethin Corp made to the local papers. But for another fee they'd be glad to give a smaller taste of their taste, and so Asher got his. Enough to know how to write the policy.

The front and back doors to the payout were locked. Dick knew it and that's why he sent Harry. This wasn't going to be hard. No use sending one of his more senior investigators. This was a cakewalk. Harry was the icing.

All Harry wanted was to do this job for while and bank the pay. Forty thou a year. A bonus in rare cases. 401K and health insurance. By Beloit standards, he was doing just fine. With a girl named Marsha he was going to marry and dreams of leaving this all behind in ten years and opening a restaurant on the beach in Mexico.

Not that he'd ever been. But he'd seen the pictures.

5. OZ.

Lou had the Bentley parked at the curb outside the terminal. Security let him park there. Not much threat in Bentley owners. No real need to blow anything up. And Lou slipped the guy a fifty and of course he did have the finest chauffeur's suit in the West.

Harry recoiled when he saw it. He was on a cab per diem, and here he was confronted by one of the finest cars ever made. It had deep tinted windows concealing 120 years of automotive know how. He was about to be surrounded by the finest materials that would ever touch his Dockers: burnished wood, titanium, and the soft virgin leather from baby cows that made the mistake of being able to stand ten minutes after being born.

The worst parts of most cities are always around the airports. Los Angeles is no different. The same ugly buildings, dead or dying trees, parking lots, fast food places, bail bondsmen. The same bag people, transients, people only there because they need gas, and others whose faces are fixed in a frown because they just said goodbye to someone and really don't know if they'll ever see them again.

The Bentley floated through it all, oblivious. I followed. Past the oil wells, the crappy franchise family dining joints, the cheap furniture outlets, the drug store chains, the storefront lawyers and colonic clinics and into Beverly Hills, where the city turned shiny and the paint wasn't allowed to peel. The streets got wider. The trees got fluffier. The grass got greener. Nothing was snowed over. No slush or sand gathering in the curbs. Harry hadn't seen colors like this since September, when the Wisconsin winter came in early and hard due to either a freak of nature or the global warming thing. The media preferred the latter. It got better ratings.

He'd never seen vegetation that looked like big versions of the vegetables they never cared for much in Beloit. Trees that looked like broccoli. Plants that looked like cabbage. Grass that looked like string beans. And a bunch of strange low lying ground cover that looked like shiny green Tater Tots.

The buildings resembled the chateaus he'd seen on The Travel Channel, except cleaner and with thicker windows and parking garages.

Everything was better. The roads were blacker. The cars all looked like they just rolled off the new car lots. The sidewalks were empty except for the occasional starlet in painful shoes walking a dog the size of a kitten.

The Bentley turned into the drive of the Four Seasons Hotel.

Parking Valets in matching khaki pants and vests scurried out and surrounded the car like pilot fish. They smelled affluence and tip. An encounter with a major domo. Perhaps they would be discovered. Or perform so well that the Domo inside the Bentley would make one of them his right hand man.

And then, magically, the Bentley door opened and Harry was presented to Los Angeles. VIP's and MLF's and Cougars eyed what they thought was the new big swinging dick in town. When Harry got out of the Bentley, in his wrinkled Dockers and New Balance shoes, his Super Cuts haircut and rubber Casio watch, they could only wonder, 'Is he that rich?'

Harry scouted the untinted world outside the Bentley and gave it all away with his 'Aw shucks' body language. The fountain in this place had more attention to detail then he had in his whole life. The Valet's surrounded Harry's roll on suitcase like it was a corpse no one wanted to take responsibility for killing. Their hands were accustomed to handling finer luggage and they didn't want to spoil the power vibe they got from handling finer luggage.

A professional Valet in Los Angeles can pretty much fuck up my day. They take a sober man's car keys and give them back when he's drunk. They're the biggest drug dealers in town cause it's easy. Every handoff of keys to a known client is a chance to exchange a packet of powder or a small rock of whatever will alter your mood. Management knows this and lets it go, cause every line snorted begs to be enjoyed by three additional cocktails, usually a double each time, and when the customer is really blasted, he's likely to buy a round for the house. Cash.

Valets know more shit than we do. They can smell a cop a mile away. And when they do, they go out of their way to protect the wealthy.

They alert the management that Baron Bazillions ought to just hang a little longer, and by the way there are three thousand paparazzi out here waiting for his Royal Drunkenness to emerge, and by the way there is an unmarked car on the corner because the last time the Baron was on the road he killed two innocent civilians on bicycles and got off scott free and you have no idea how much that pisses us off.

The gaggle of valets came to the conclusion that Harry's tip wouldn't be much, and then one of them would be out of a bigger play with all the other two hundred thousand dollar cars that were rolling in.

But they were trained, goddamnit, to keep up appearances. So one of them took hold of Harry's roll on and dragged it behind him into the hotel, Harry following and noticing for the first time how cheap that thing looked with it's exposed stitching, red wheels and souvenir stickers from the Wisconsin Dells, which is a place in Wisconsin that comes as close as any to being a tourist trap.

Lou told me what room Harry was in. We had a pact. Videotapes of the house on a daily basis and any scheduling info of pickups and drop offs. That was how Lou would stay on my good side. A high profile security guy in this town has to stay on the good side of the police. We can make life miserable for them. And Lou had a record. Just a small mosquito bite of a record. But I could scratch it.

The Widow Buffet had arranged Harry's accommodations and put them on house account. She wanted him to be comfortable. She wanted to soften him. She wanted the transition of signing papers and depositing money to go smoothly, so she booked him into a penthouse suite, which was the twice the size of Harry's apartment in Beloit and was the place the big shots stayed. I'm sure the concierge and bellmen wondered whether this guy was a plant from Travel and Leisure doing a piece on top hotels and acting like a rube just to see if the help would lower their standards. So he got treated like a Saudi Prince.

I stayed there once. In the penthouse. I had befriended a wealthy woman who was between marriages and liked the thrill of slumming with a cop until her next mark rolled in.

I took her out on the town. She paid. At night I fucked her and ate tubs of macadamia nuts from her honor bar and caught up on movies on the pay per view. It lasted three days and was a very calming experience, one we should all have once in our lives. Those nuts cost twenty-five bucks a bottle.

So I know what Harry was feeling. I bet Harry was just like me. I bet the first thing he did was pee on the seat of the toilet, just to mark his territory and take out a little revenge on his surroundings for making him feel even smaller. I know he looked at the mahogany furniture and plush carpet and bed the size of a trampoline and said to himself, "This is gonna be swell."

I also know he knew it was all wrong. That this was a conflict of interest. He wasn't here to give the Widow what she wanted. But he was seduced by luxury and free toiletries and a complimentary Loofah and thought to himself, "What the hell."

He could've taken advantage of his situation. Gone down to the bar, mixed it up a bit. Hell, he might have even gotten lucky. But that wasn't Harry. Harry was here on business. And business trips are lonely affairs. And Harry never got lucky. In anything. So he did what all good attached men do when they go out of town on business. He nestled in, ordered room service, ate on the bed, and called his girlfriend so she wouldn't worry about him.

He wouldn't get through. Cause his girlfriend back in Beloit was taking it up the ass from Harry's boss and didn't bother to answer the phone.

6. LONELY AT THE TOP. NO FUN AT THE BOTTOM.

I know the view from the penthouse, and at sunset it's pretty stupendous. I parked my car across the street on Doheny, had a smoke and looked up at the balcony of his room. Harry was out there, taking it in. From his window, Los Angeles at this moment in time resembled an ambitious dreamer's idea of Paradise. It was all orange palm trees and terracotta roofs and a big cloudless sky open to promise and suggestion and calm. The Pacific Ocean reflected the sinking red sun ball on its sunset black water. It was perfect. A place created just yesterday, untouched by age, undamaged by weather, unaware of a fucking thing, and damned happy for it.

I like to imagine what my quarry is doing, and yeah, Harry was my quarry right now. I would need him, so I would need to know him. He was looking around, and I think I even saw him take a picture of his landscape with the honor bar disposable camera. And he saw me. Leaning against my car. Looking up at him. Our eyes met and we held the stare. Then Harry went inside, and closed the drapes to the light. He had a whole night to find out what Los Angeles was about by watching the local news. In every city, you watch the local news to get a handle on the culture. You find out what's important. In Los Angeles, a story about a cat stuck in a tree next to a 7-11 will take the lead over one about a bomb blast in New York at the United Nations.

I bet Harry was putting himself to sleep watching stories about traffic and Sig Alerts as Viking Princesses with massive chests under Nordic sweaters piloted helicopters over the freeways to keep track of the advancing hordes and announcing to the masses the ebb and flow on the invasion. I bet he stared slack jawed at our car chases as cops pursue criminals at break neck speeds like futuristic posses while the Viking Princess gives the blow by blow report from the helicopter above, her spotlight beaming down on the perpetrator and blinding the other traffic, endangering everybody within a miles distance but helping boost the station's ratings.

He watched our handsome anchormen. Sexy anchorwomen. Weather girls that looked like they had spent some time on the pole and sports guys that looked like they just stepped out of the shower after single handedly winning the Super Bowl.

I knew it was like nothing Harry was used to. First time, no one ever is. He knew he could never survive here. He'd be on a twenty-four seven-inferiority complex.

No. Wisconsin was just fine. People like him. A plain looking woman. A normal job. A take-what-they-give-you life. That way, you could never be disappointed.

Lou Bentleyed Harry to the Buffet Malibu mansion the next day at noon. It was J.P.'s wake. A small memorial to the man, fueled by the finest catering in the West.

When rich people die, the survivors make sure to order a ton of intricately prepared and exotic foods, then for the most part, never eat them. And the richest of the rich always leave the most leftovers as a sign that this most basic need—hunger—has already been met privately, and probably much better.

The uneaten food goes on a truck that takes it to the poor. That way the whole expense gets a write off. And the poor wait on line for the truck to arrive, where, having not eaten anything in days, they are treated to fois gras and truffles and other shit they have no idea what it is or what orifice to stick it in.

And the funniest thing about the whole shebang is that most of the caterers get the feast wholesale at Costco and charge triple what it would have cost at Whole Foods.

But the rich know so little about food, they can't tell. And as long as it was free, they didn't care.

This was going to be Harry's first opportunity to interview the Widow Buffet and inform her of the complications to the policy and the first time I would make Harry's acquaintance, outside the stare down at the hotel.

I was getting prickly with excitement at the thought of jumping into the deep end of a rich man's complicated life.

7. AIR KISSES AND BIG MONKEY DICKS.

Cigars are dicks.

I never understood them. Or the men that smoked them. Except Churchill. But he was English and we all know our brothers across the pond have issues.

The male worshippers at J.P. Buffet's wake used their cigars to impress each other like the Squirrel Monkey uses its penis for dominance. The biggest one creates the most fear and attracts the most followers. And as long as that cigar stayed lit, the owner was the big swinging dick of the moment.

The women were another story. The Mwah Mwahing of air kisses permeated the outdoor deck of the Mansion. Mwah Mwahing is about as empty a social act as there is. No lips touch skin. It's purely ceremonial. It says we are somewhat equal in the pecking order but lets not make it deep as one day I might have to steal your husband, erase your membership at the country club or contribute more to a local charity for a newly invented disease than you and embarrass your surgically uplifted ass into hiding. And it was all mighty fine surgery. Each of these women had been pulled, stretched, plumped, and stuffed to keep them attractive to the husbands who had already moved on to sweeter, younger fare. But they tried. They just couldn't face having to live on a divorce settlement of only half a man's millions.

And who were they gonna find to take up with now that their face and body saving surgeries made them look like brook trout with tits? They were under siege. Their enemy: Younger women.

If it weren't illegal, they'd drown their own daughters.

The Bentley floated into the driveway on a cloud of rose petals. J.P.'s widow littered the entrance with them. She was good at effects, being one herself.

The tinted windows slid down and Harry poked his head out like a mutt on his first car ride. He had to catch himself from not dragging his tongue, but the mansion was about the biggest thing he'd ever seen, not counting the sports arena at Beloit College.

Lou led Harry through the entranceway, past the staircase, through the little living room, into the grand living room, and out onto the deck and deposited him at the plate end of the buffet table while he alerted the widow to Harry's arrival.

Harry scanned the table until his vision dropped out of focus at the far end. There wasn't one thing on that table that Harry recognized. I could tell just by watching him become paralyzed by the endless cornucopia of things he didn't know. And, as a Sunday regular at Applebee's, he considered himself a buffet specialist, so he was really feeling off his game.

He walked the length of the table. There were crab legs the size of the arms on anorexic fourteen year olds, caviar the size of jawbreakers, and more cheese than Wisconsin could ever lay claim to producing in a single decade. There were pastries and cold cuts and dips and fruit. Each food category was piled high on top each other in perfect symmetry and decorated with flowers and ice sculptures so that they resembled miniature floats in the Rose Bowl parade. Harry was choice frozen. Tuxedoed servers stood at attention, tongs ready. Harry came with an appetite. But choice killed it.

"I'll have an omelet." Harry told one of the servers. An omelet he knew. But that tuxedoed and tonged schmuck just looked down his nose at him. "This is a cold buffet."

"Is the coffee hot?"

"Yes," Buffet Nazi answered.

"Then it's not a cold buffet."

If there was one thing Harry wasn't going to stand for it was some Buffet Nazi speaking down to him like he was some kind of yokel. Which he was and knew it but wasn't going let some Buffet Nazi remind him.

The Buffet Nazi and Harry were in a stand off. Until Harry's good-natured side let that asshole off the hook.

"Just kidding. You don't have any scones, do you? I love scones."

Buffet Nazi swept his tongs over a plate of pastries and scooped up a tiny, raison flecked, pockmarked blip of a scone and deposited it on Harry's over-sized plate. Harry stared at that nook and crannied dollop of dough and wondered just how many he'd have to eat to get full. He looked up at the Buffet Nazi with that "You gotta be kidding look" which wasn't going to get him anywhere in Malibu, because out here where money gets soggy, they are truly incapable of kidding about anything.

The rich aren't funny. You give up the muscle when you buy rocks for decoration and spend a lot of time making sure your surroundings are germ free. The poor, on the other hand, are hilarious. It's a matter of survival in the face of overwhelming odds against living past your fiftieth birthday.

"They're organic and dairy free scones." The Buffet Nazi told him, like that was going to make all the difference in the world. It didn't. Not to Harry. He knew scones.

"I love scones. Course, in Wisconsin, they're bigger. Lots of butter. Some cheese. One will carry you the whole day."

"How interesting," the Buffet Nazi said.

When Harry turned away from the table, our eyes met again. He looked at me like he recognized me. But the last time he saw me, from his balcony high up in the penthouse, me down on the street, I had a cigarette in my mouth and to Harry, I was only about an inch tall. Standing twenty feet away from him now, I was taller. Harry didn't put the two together.

I nodded to him. I wanted to let him have his little breakfast alone. I wanted to see what he did while he ate. Did he scan the deck, getting a read on everyone at the wake? Or did he focus on his scone, finding comfort in the pastry? If he scanned the deck, he might be someone who had the powers of observation and would be even more help to me. If he immersed himself in the scone, oblivious to his surroundings, then I wouldn't be able to tread him at all except for the fact that he loved his scones. Unless . . .

Harry sat at a small table in the sun and negotiated his scone into his coffee. The dunked part immediately broke off and dumped right in the cup. He tried to fish it out but it was turning to mash. He dunked again to the same result. Plop. Organic dairy-free balls of wet sand. Soon, all he was holding in the tips of his fingers was one small raisin. He tried dunking that, but the coffee was hot and he burned his fingers and the raisin fell in too. Harry had to commandeer his spoon and eat that scone in its new mashed form.

"They got oatmeal?" Lou said as he looked at Harry spooning in the gruel.

"You can't make things without butter and think they'll hold up to a dunking." Harry shot back not understanding how anybody who called himself a pastry chef didn't know the secrets of butter.

"I hear you. But butter is kind of last century here."

"What the hell is wrong with you people?" Harry wouldn't have usually said that, but his stomach was in a growl. "Everything else about this place is perfect and you can't make a decent scone?" Harry was not to be messed with while hungry. It made him miss his girlfriend even more. That girl could make scones.

Lou wasn't going to pursue this. Harry didn't interest him.

"That's the lady of the manor over there," Lou said as he jerked his head in the direction of the receiving line to a veiled woman seated in a chair, handkerchief dabbing her tears and big hat obscuring her face.

All Harry saw were legs. Tan, long, shiny, sleek. The left one was crossed over the right and the right foot was hanging practically to the floor next to the left. When Marsha, Harry's taken'-it-up-the-ass-from-his-boss-girlfriend crossed her legs, her foot was practically parallel with the ground.

The Widow nodded to the long line of mourners there to pretend to offer condolences. As they did their duty, they'd walk away and talk nasty gossip, jab their cigars at each other or kiss the air.

Their faces were filled with disrespect for the Widow with the tan, long legs. See, they loved the money that J.P. Buffet made for them. And they thought that they could've made more if he didn't have to give so much away to his wives in messy divorce settlements. Now they were concerned that the company would have to make another big payout, and whenever that happened, the company would make some kind of claim that they had a bad year and the payments to the distributors would take a hit. And none of these tycoons was smart enough to challenge that, cause they thought that challenging the company was as good as challenging J.P., and *that* they would never do.

"I guess now is not the right time to talk to her." Harry said to Lou.

"She told me to tell you she'd see you tomorrow. When she recovers."

Harry put down his cup of mash in disgust, "All it takes is a day?"

I was watching the whole travesty from a shaded part of the deck. I had my suspicions. I'd been watching Lou and Lars, Welch and Gates, The Widow and a couple of the tippy top distributors for a while now. Watching them swarm J.P. I knew Lou and Lars got J.P. his drugs. I just couldn't be sure what other cocktails they were mixing him. I found out that Lou and Lars stood to take home three years pay in one lump sum in the event of J.P.'s death. So, there was a motive. Welch and Gates had their reasons too. I just wasn't sure what they were yet. But a lot of people had reasons to want J.P. to die. One of them, the biggest dog on the deck, was Carlos Prima. He was the second best salesman in the world. You'll get a chance to meet with him later when it's his time to dent this story. But with J.P. out of the way, he'd be the first best salesman in the world and in all likelihood, would run the company as its spiritual leader, him having actually sold something and having credibility with the other distributors.

He also had pictures of J.P. in flagrante with a bunch of men in sailor suits on the deck of a gay cruise ship.

None of them would have to do much to help with J.P.'s demise. Speed it along, maybe, but it would be a soft push. A slow prodding. It was just a matter of time before he would fall down a staircase, walk out in traffic, or slip in the shower.

I had tapped the phones in Buffet home and knew how fast the Widow called the insurance company. Shit. She recovered a long time ago. And she was close to Lou. So, there were two motives. And Lars, being mysterious, was along for the ride.

"You the insurance investigator?" I asked Harry and gave him my hand for a real Midwestern like shake, which to my recollection started with a firm grip and ended at the third pump.

"Harry Corvair," he said as we shook. He didn't have a big grip, but it would do.

I had my best smile on. I didn't have to fake it. I liked him immediately. Some people might call him a rube. But not me. As far as I was concerned, there weren't enough Harry Corvairs in the world. This guy was salt of the earth. A real Red Stater. Nose to the grindstone. Cranberries from the can on Thanksgiving Day. A man a pit bull wouldn't attack even if sausages were taped to his legs.

"Tommy Cox. Malibu PD," I said on the release.

His eyes lit up.

I was a real honest to goodness Los Angeles Cop. To him, I was Dragnet. Jack Webb. Seventy-Seven Sunset Strip. Raymond Chandler. Bogart. Hill Street Blues. LA Confidential.

The history of the cop in the twentieth century is all Los Angeles. The history of crime is too. OJ Simpson. The Menendez Brothers. Charlie Manson. Robert Blake. Fatty Arbuckle. Johnny Wadd. Phil Spector. Marilyn Monroe.

Shit that never got solved. Crazy crimes committed against the rich by the rich. Crimes against lonely starlets by Presidents. Heisman trophy winners gone wild. Porn stars with thirteen-inch dicks found with their skulls pasted against the wall by a shotgun blast in a run down hill house.

And we had better names for the crimes too.

The Black Delilah. The Zodiac Killer. The Hillside Strangler. The Wonderland Murders. All New York had was the Son of Sam. And the killer came up with that himself. Can't hold a candle to the The Night Stalker.

LA is a crime-marketing machine.

We sell murders like we sell movies. Catchy titles. Big names. Big money. Multiple stab wounds. Throats cut. Threats written in blood on the walls of toney Hollywood Hills homes. Bodies sliced into pieces with smiles carved into their faces.

When it comes to murder, slaughter, crime, criminals, there's no place like LA. There never will be. It's the natural phenomenon of what happens when you drop bushels of wet, just printed money in a dry, dusty desert.

Fuck. I get misty just thinking about it.

And now Harry was channeling all that history. I was his own personal tour guide to the stories he'd read as a child and watched on TV every night. And who was I to disappoint?

I wore a soft-shouldered Bernini suit and a pair of gabardine slacks that broke on the tops of my Italian loafers and sat there like pudding. I looked like an LA detective should look. I looked like I made more money than I did. To get the respect of the rich, you have to dress at least as good as they do.

Did I tell you I'm not a half bad looking guy?

To Harry, I must've looked like Johnny Depp, who's dick I'd suck and I don't suck dick—but if I had to, I'd choose him. And maybe George Clooney. But Depp has a feminine thing about him, so I might feel a little better about myself.

"You look like you could use something to eat, Harry Corvair." I told him.

"Boy oh boy. Malibu PD!" That was all he could muster.

"C'mon. There's coffee shop ten minutes away. All the Detectives eat there."

8. HARRY, ME, AND SAUSAGE BY THE SEA.

"You enjoying the Four Seasons, Harry?" I asked him as the waitress, a sad faced nineteen year old with a chest that looked like she was smuggling bean bag chairs and who had just appeared on an internet porn site blowing six guys in a motel room in what looked like Van Nuys for four hundred dollars, put a plate of breakfast links and eggs in front of him. "Sure I am. But I have to straighten that out. I think it could be a conflict of interest. And I don't want anything to get in the way of this investigation," Harry said as he broke the yolks and mixed them in with the sausage and made a mess of both. I sipped my coffee and asked, "Conflict of interest?" "You know. Conflict of interest. I'm here on a job. Can't look like I'm going to be compromised." To me, anything that is a conflict of interest is an interesting conflict. It stinks of money. Avoiding it is like shutting the doors on the angels of opportunity. The history of the rich is written in the language of the conflicts of interest. "Leave conflicts of interest to the politicians, Harry. We're in the private sector." Harry eyed the crowd. It was the usual mash up of actors, writers, choreographers, landscape designers, interior decorators and renowned architects. In Malibu, they're known as the working poor. "Okay Harry. No problem. We'll switch the bill to the department." I could do that, if the party under question was offering a service to the force. And I was about to offer Harry the opportunity to offer service to the force.

Harry looked up from his plate, a small stream of yolk at the corner of his mouth. I gestured to it. He wiped the yolk with the back of his hand and pretty much just spread it across his cheek, "But that seems a little unusual too."

"You got yolk on your cheek, Harry," I told him.

I made him nervous. If he was an insurance investigator from Los Angeles or New York, he'd have a certain degree of savoir-faire and gravitas. As an insurance investigator from Beloit, sitting across the breakfast table in Malibu, CA with a detective from the Malibu PD, he had nothing but egg on his face.

"Damn it. I always do that. I love yolk, but I guess it doesn't love me," and he kind of gave a little snort laugh as he dipped his napkin in a glass of water and dabbed it on his face.

"Still?" he asked to see if it was gone.

"To the left."

"Jesus," and he wiped further. "Now?"

"I need your help, Harry." Harry looked up at me like I was the coach of the Dodgers and I just asked to throw some heat in the ninth with a one run lead. "Me? But you're a cop. What do you need with me?" "I think I can trust you, Harry. You're not from here."

Miss Internet came over and poured more coffee in my cup, which pissed me off, cause I had just gotten the mix of cream and sugar just right and she went and spoiled the whole thing due to the fact that she couldn't see too well past her chest. Now, I had to start all over again.

"Harry, LA has about one million less people than New York. New York has over ten thousand cops. LA has four thousand covering a territory the size of Rhode Island. You know what that does?" I wasn't going to wait for an answer, "It makes for a lot of crooked cops. Trying to do more than they can and making less than they'd like. Then you get out here, in Malibu, and these boys see the kinds of money that's floating around and it just makes them mad. So you can't trust them. With information or who's side they're on."

Harry went back to eyeing the crowd. "You said a lot of detectives come here. But these folks don't look like detectives. Couple of them look kind of queer."

I saw what he saw. This morning was an exceptionally queer day at the coffee shop. "Don't ask, don't tell." I told him.

"Yeah, sure. Like in the army," he said.

Truth is, detectives didn't come here at all. Too many queers. But I had to get him on my side. Had to keep his enthusiasm up. I needed his eyes and ears. And the coffee was good.

"I'm feeling some hanky panky, Harry."

Harry pushed his plate away and stuck a toothpick in his mouth. It gave him a prop. If he could've, he would've taken up smoking to impress me. But this was Malibu, and the only place you can have a cigarette is in your dreams.

"What kind of hanky panky?" he asked.

"Don't know, Harry. But something's off with this guy's death."

Harry leaned forward on his elbows, looked around to see if anybody was listening as Miss Internet caught his eye and pushed her boobs together to create more cleavage in hopes of a better tip.

"This is cut and dry. There's no hanky panky. Even I can see that," he said, but he was rubbing his elbows in a nervous tick.

"I don't doubt you can. I don't doubt you can see around corners," I told him to sort of calm him down.

Harry leaned back and said, "This is a slam dunk. He had a substance abuse problem. Alcohol and drugs. The policy took that into account."

"The policy didn't cover suicide?" I asked.

He took his fingers off the toothpick, patted his stomach, and swallowed that little piece of wood.

The next couple of minutes were about making sure Harry didn't choke on it. He was a victim of getting too comfortable with his prop. When the blood in his face drained back into his body he said, "Who, with that kind of money, is going to kill himself? That guy was on top of the world. The policy won't cover you if you killed yourself before the years out, and this is just ten months old. So that's out. Maybe you like it, but that's none of my business."

"What about murder?" I slipped in, knowing full well that this was something Harry didn't suspect at all, but that I was playing around with. If it was murder, the policy gets honored. Twenty million dollars to the Widow Buffet. With a motive to boot.

"Jeez. What makes you say that?" he asked, now real worried and back to scratching his elbows.

"Lot of people had lots of reasons to see him gone. That's all. Not in the usual way. No suffocation or bump on the head. They won't find that. Something slow. A poisoning. Easy to do, right? If he was already dumping that much sludge in his body. Might have been over a year's time. Little bit by little bit. Till it can't be traced. Not by a coroner that gets donations not to trace it."

He looked at me sideways, tapped his fingers on the table, looked out the window, over to the waitress, picked a toast crumb off the table, ate it, grabbed a bag of Gold Fish Crackers from a cup, opened them, spread some butter on them, started munching, then wiped the crumbs off his shirt and said, "Jeeze."

It was a lot to process, and I never seen anybody do it slower. I figured he was still going through a culture shock or jet lag. Then he said, "That's like a show I saw on TV once. Woman killed her cheating husband with radiation from the X-ray machine she ran in his office. He was a doctor, see, and she found out he was cheating on her with the pharmaceutical sales lady, so one night she took out the wall that separated the X-ray room from his office and had a real thin one built to replace it and when she gave X-rays they went through the wall and dosed him. Took about two years before . . ."

"Harry! Focus!" I had to stop him, as I have no time for the inane cop shit they put on TV that makes demands on us in real life. Like you can solve a fucking crime just by finding a hair follicle or that the forensic guys are always the first ones on the scene or that murder scenes are over flowing with so much information it's like a puzzle with six pieces a blind man can put it together.

Let me tell you something. There isn't shit at the scene of a murder that's worth a shit in a court of law. Not hair, not nails, not sperm, not even blood three quarters of the time. The only thing that counts as evidence is if the motherfucker that did it is still there next to the body eating its intestines. Then we got our man.

"That's what I need your help on. I can't find shit out about this. The files are real hard to get to. Lifethin's given the department over two hundred thou the past three years. And I can't be too snoopy, cause the Captain, who Lifethin supported in the last election, will have my badge. Or transfer me to Compton. And I ain't going to work in Compton and fuck up my wardrobe. We clear?"

"I'm not helping you find out he was murdered. That's not gonna help me at all," he said, and I was surprised at his reluctance and new found spine. "I need to see the coroner's report."

"Good luck." I said.

"They have to show it to me."

"They . . . don't have to do a thing. This place is like China, Harry. When they agree with you they nod. When they disagree with you they nod. When they don't know what you're talking about they nod. To make it out here you need to practice *Li*," I told him. He had bluebirds in his eyes when I said that and I could tell he didn't know what that was but didn't want to admit it. So he nodded.

"See? You're doing it right now. You have no idea what I'm saying and you're nodding away. You'll do fine out here, Harry." "This was supposed to be a slam dunk!" "I know. You came out here to get your ducks in a row and all you're winding up with is feathers. So we on?" I asked. "You gonna be Starsky to my Hutch?"

"This was an overdose. That's what I'm here to prove. Not murder. Murder screws up my bonus! I'm not helping you find out about that. You do that yourself and I don't want to know about it!"

"Take it easy, Harry. I'm not gonna screw it up for you. But what if that's what happened. And you stood in the way of the truth for a measly bonus?"

"Measly to you. You people are floating in it."

"And I thought you were one of those midwestern straight shooters. An honest Abe. Guess not. Sorry to waste your time," and I threw some cash on the table and got up to leave.

"I am an honest man. But I have to play this square. For me. I tell you what, you help me get around all the obstacles you say they're gonna put in front of me, and if I hear anything that sounds fishy, well then, I'll tell you. And I want to do what's right. But if somebody tells me that they know who killed J.P. Buffet, I'll tell you. OK?"

"You just be a blotter. A sponge. And you go about your business. Ninety five percent you're right and the fool self-destructed.

But if I'm right, then you gotta do what you're supposed to do as a citizen of the United States," I told him and I knew that the citizen line would get to him. "You keep your ears open. You listen to what they say, how they act when you ask them questions. Just keep me in the loop. I bet you got primal instincts, Harry."

He shoved a whole handful of Gold Fish Crackers in his mouth. He was eating nervous know. He knew he'd have to cooperate with me, being a citizen of the United States and me being the one who's job it was to protect them.

"Anything is fishy, I'll let you know," he said. "But you gotta help me too, OK Detective Cox? I want to know what you know. About people. These people. If this is on the straight and narrow is as plain Jane a case as there comes and you see I'm getting jerked around, you gotta help me, OK?"

"Call me Tommy. And our motto is to Protect and Serve. So I will serve."

This was great. I get a guy inside the organization and all he wants in return is a ride in the squad car with the sirens screaming.

All I needed was for him to tell me whose eyes darted around at the right kind of question and I'd have enough of a lead to follow up on. It was just afternoon and I had done what I considered to be a full weeks worth of work. Good on me.

"This is the name and address of a distributor," I said as I put a slip of paper in the palm of his hand. "Sniff around. Get as close to asking if he thought J.P. was murdered as you can without ever saying that word. Ask who he was with the last night. Ask if he had any enemies. Anybody that might be jealous of him. Ask him about the Widow. Ask them what they think of the corporation. Ask about whether anybody was up for a raise they didn't get. If anybody got fired and pissed got off. I'll dig deep on the payouts. Regular criminals leave fingerprints. The rich leave a trail of money and . . ."

"And what . . . ?"

"Conflicts of interest."

9. VALLEY OF THE DOLLS.

I dropped Harry off at the Four Seasons and went back over the hill to my condo in the Valley.

Ahhh, the Valley.

Where failed dreams took mortgages in the flat lands. On the Hollywood side of the Hills, you had young rockers and hip hoppers on the cusp of fame with fresh, pliant skin to pierce and tattoo. Ten years later, the tattoos were fading and the piercings sagged just like their hopes. They had married their groupies and had a passel of troll-like kids all dressed up like their futures were going be the same as their failed fathers. And here they were, in the Valley. They show up at one of the thousands of Sushi places in Encino, Sherman Oaks or Studio City and nod to each other, as if to say, "Yeah, me too."

I had a respectable condo in Studio City. It was comfortable. I knew I was destined for bigger things, but for now, comfortable was just fine. I had it furnished in a fashion that let visitors know I knew what nice things looked like. I made it look like a room at the W Hotels, which are sort of Howard Johnson's for the hip. Dark wood. Heavy furniture. Shaggy chick. A couple of decent photographs on the wall I got off an Internet site that sold art to bachelors who knew nothing of art.

The neighbor to one side was some Israeli pop star wanna be and the one on the other was a porn star struggling to stay relevant. I did her favors from time to time. Kept her out of problems and kept her fans from bothering her too much. For that, she paid me in blowjobs and an occasional girl on girl show. I know she didn't enjoy the favors much as she really didn't enjoy sex at all, being that she did for a living what nature wants you to do for pleasure. But it wasn't about her. This was about me and my duty as a public servant and some of the perks that go along with that.

Some days, it seems that half the residents in the Valley are either porn stars or strippers. And some days, it seems all the cops in the Valley have permanent smiles on their faces.

Ahh, the Valley.

My Porn Star wasn't home. Which was a disappointment, as I was feeling a little tense. I checked the Internet for a report from a buddy of mine at the crime lab on one of the vodka bottles I grabbed from J.P.'s bar. I had a hunch on the slow poison angle. A little bit in every bottle he drank, making its effects just a little more lethal.

I had it tested for the usual suspects: the cyanides, arsenics and strychnine's. Then we ran it for some of the medical stuff: the depressants, the painkillers, even the appetite suppressants. We figured that with high blood pressure and an alcohol chaser, a good dose of phentermine might explode his heart. But the report came back clean.

Which pissed me off, frankly. I had to pull some favors to get it into the lab without there being an investigation. But a long time ago, my buddy who ran the lab, got caught by a PI hired by his wife in a dirt bag hotel with a hooker. I strong armed the PI to just SHUT THE FUCK UP, as only a detective can, took the guy's camera, kept the roll, and developed the pictures myself. The shit in those pictures would make a pimp in Amsterdam blush. This guy was a fister, and not in the hole that welcomes that sort of thing. Which is why whenever I had a case for him to run a test on, I asked him to make sure he washed his hands. Needless to say, I got a lot of favors done by this guy.

The fact he didn't find anything didn't kill the theory, it just ruled out that bottle. But after the disappointment, I got a little stir crazy.

So I showered, shaved, sprinkled on some cologne, put on my dancing shoes and headed out in an attempt to find another between marriages divorcee who thought so little of herself she would seek the safety of a cop's bed. In the Valley.

Lars Sackman sat with his elbows on the bar and a vodka rocks in front of him. He was in the back room at Duke's, an ocean front family style eatery with a salad bar so long you could get blisters just walking it and food that did not threaten to compete with the view.

Lars wasn't here to eat. He was here to drink and get lucky. The back room was for locals, the lesser folk who lived out here and kept the place humming. The mechanics, the secretaries, the gardeners, truckers, teachers, some middle managers looking to cheat on their wives.

Lars came here a lot. Deep down, he was a tremendous asshole. Sober, he could keep it hidden. But after a couple, the jerk bubbled to the surface. He was a woman hater and he usually wound up insulting the very mark he could've gotten lucky with if he had a modicum of restraint and she had bad eyes and overwhelming reserves of self-hatred.

It was usually after he bought the mark a second drink that he demanded a blowjob. If she demurred even slightly, in that way that said, 'Wait, ask me that after the third drink,' he'd grab her arm and try to haul her outside and force himself on her.

So he spent a lot of nights at Duke's getting his face slapped or plucking parking lot gravel out of his eye.

Lars would never get laid for free.

He was a pink man. And the Malibu sun made him perpetually red and blistery. He had beady blue eyes set against pock marked, acne ravaged skin. His hair was greasy dirty blond, and he never spent money on getting it cut right. And he had a bad case of dandruff, almost to the point of it being a public health nuisance. So, no, Lars would almost always have to pay for sex. And most of the time, even the skankiest hooker charged him double.

He thought tonight would be different. The locals were abuzz about J.P. Buffet's death, a rich man they felt suffered as much as they did but in a much different way. He'd been in here, three sheets to the wind, hanging one handed off the bar, swinging around on his stool like he was on a ship in the middle of a perfect storm, buying endless rounds for everyone, trying like hell to make them like him.

And while he bought, they did.

Lars had taken J.P. home from here a bunch of times. He'd get calls on his cell from the owner or the bartender—*"Come pick up your boss before he embarrasses himself."* And sometimes J.P. was so out of his head, and Lars was so horny, that he'd let J.P. suck his cock. And nobody remembered a thing in the morning.

But tonight Lars was the star. He was close to the events. He told everyone about J.P. and how he died and how he died in a diaper. He told everyone in the bar about a man's sad life and then he slid down the bar and hit on a pretty twenty-two-yearold, just in from Idaho, trying to be an actress, but currently working the bumper cars at the Santa Monica Pier.

And Lars had a mark. And since the whole bar had been listening to his stories up to now, he felt he had copped a piece of celebrity. So this was going to be easy, right?

She told him she was here to meet a producer she met at the bumper cars on the pier. Nice guy. Gave her his card. She showed it to Lars. It was an Israeli name. Israelis aren't afraid of anything or anyone. Anybody who'd spent a good part of their growing years under mortar attack, fighting towel-headed motherfuckers who want to die because in their heaven they get laid big time, had to have a certain crust.

They're the best-trained soldiers in the world. They carved out a shit crazy place on earth to call home. And now, they were making movies by the boatload.

Lars knew the name. The Israeli was a notorious manufacturer of big budget porno. His MO was to "discover" unsuspecting mid-western dreamers and set them up in a "Film". They were so excited they'd show up on the set the next day, not ask for a script, not know what the part was and not care as long as they could be close to the magic. The Israeli had a certain flair, I'll give him that. He actually put some money into these things. No three girls and a guy in a hot-tub-tug-job-and-suck-off for him. No sir. He was a purveyor of costume porn. His most successful was called *King Arthur and His Nights on the Round Table.*

When these unsuspecting damsels showed up on the set, there *was* a set.

A castle or a ballroom or a ship's bow. They were outfitted in corsets, or flowing gowns, or riding pants, or just boots, a snake and a flashlight.

It was glamorous. It was make believe.

Then of course, once he had them in costume, in makeup, under the lights, in front of the camera, it was easy to get them to take the costume off. They would try to object, but they had already fallen under the spell, the cameras were rolling, craft service was standing by, makeup was brushing their face with anti shine powder and pinking their nipples with rouge.

"Act! Bitch! Act!" he would yell in that Israeli accent that rolls one word right into the next and doesn't know how to pause at the end of a fucking sentence.

And that would wear them down.

So they spend the afternoon bent over a cannon barrel, or a wagon wheel, or a horse, and it got easier, and *voila*, A Star Was Born!

"So you fuck on camera, yes?" Lars blurted out. "Maybe you fuck me first. I'll show you stuff you can use." The girl gave him a look and then a "Fuck you, asshole," and Lars didn't see The Israeli.

Lars grabbed her arm, "C'mon baby, you need some acting lessons," and the next thing The Israeli's hand was on Lars' shoulder. Lars turned and did the dumbest thing you can do, which was to get all drunk defiant to an ex-Mossad agent while insulting his new girlfriend. But that was Lars, the tremendous asshole.

"Get hand fucking off me or I break!" Lars spat out.

The Israeli had no intention of 'fighting' Lars. Lars might've even won that contest. No. What The Israeli was going to do was grab a martini glass, smash it on the bar, and jam the stem into Lar's eye. That's how they did it back home. Then, with Lars blinded, and the cops already called, The Israeli would take the girl out of there and disappear into the night. But Lars would be ruined for life, with a glass eye that would prevent anyone from hiring him ever again because you just don't know which eye to talk to and that makes you feel awkward and we do not hire those that make us feel awkward, no matter how capable they are. And shit, with a glass eye, Lars would be just too ugly to get a job in Southern California.

But that wasn't going to happen tonight.

The bartender was shrewd enough to sense the heat.

"Go home, Lars," he said.

"Fuck you," Lars said.

"Listen to the man before you get hurt," The Israeli said. As Lars looked to the rest of the bar, he realized they had their money on The Israeli.

"Fuck you all, yes?" was Lars' last salvo before he stumbled out of Duke's.

He bobbled his keys out of his pocket, dropped them on the ground, bent over to pick them up, and as he stood up again, he didn't see the Louisville Slugger logo coming right at his face.

10. WE MAKE GUACAMOLE IN OUR BODY BAGS.

Harry whistled the theme from Star Wars as he walked up the path to the Ventura County coroner's office. It wasn't an ugly place like most of the places they give over to dissecting the dead. In fact, it looked a lot like something he'd seen before. In fact, he probably had.

You see, one of the producers of the CSI television shows wanted give the coroner's office a little spiff for all the cooperation they'd given him, so he decided build them a new building. But he shaved corners and didn't hire an architect. He just used the blueprints from one of the El Torito's he owned and told the contractor to do the same thing, but make the kitchen bigger as that was going to be where they ripped open the bodies. So that's what it looked like. An El Torito. Harry liked El Torito. Especially on Value Dinner Night.

And when you think of it, it was kind of appropriate. What better place to function as the way station for the dead than a Mexican chain restaurant that counted on getting people in their doors with Sunday coupons?

I was lurking again. I love stakeouts. But not like in the French Connection, where cops in two-dollar rain coats wait outside in the cold watching the crook in a French restaurant eat a four-course meal while the they ate old bear claws and drank coffee from the Greeks.

My clothes were better. My car was comfortable. My Starbucks had foam. And I had planted myself under a Eucalyptus tree, the scent of which was keeping my nostrils open and giving my cigarettes the smell of menthol.

"Harry!" I yelled out of the car, stopping him halfway up the path to Death's El Torito. I could tell he was both surprised and glad to see me.

"Tommy, what're you doing here?"

"You know who you're meeting in there?" and he didn't. "You're meeting Oscar Delpin. And about half an hour ago, two execs from Lifethin showed up, so it's going to be a bumpy flight."

Harry was scanning his brain for some kind of name recognition. Delpin's name jogged him a bit, as it should've.

Oscar Delpin was a celebrity coroner. He gave expert testimony on the death of Suzy Cane, an up-and-coming pop star who was found naked and dead in a trailer park in the Valley. Everybody thought it was an overdose, the way she paraded around town out of her head not wearing panties.

What was it with wealthy young girls, drugs, alcohol and no panties? It wasn't that they forgot to wear them. It was like they all took an oath to get out of cars with their legs spread open and nothing to block the view. Like they thought that the more they did it, the more people would get used to it, and they'd be done with panties forever. And I don't know where I was when young womanhood decided to shave themselves as smooth as a peach, so when they did get out of the car with their legs spread, it looked like they forgot to put their teeth in. Maybe it's gone on for a long time, and it's just me getting old and if that's the case, I don't have much time to make my mark. I've thought about that a lot.

But Oscar testified that it was murder. That pantiless Suzy Cane had been suffocated on the couch inside the trailer in a non-descript trailer park in Zuma. Yes, she was plenty stoned, but that's not what killed her. What killed her was her Dad, Mike Cane. Oscar found semen on the couch. The DNA said Poppa.

Seems Mike Cane couldn't stand his little Suzy's fame, even though he liked the trailer she bought him just fine. She was taking off like a meteor and would have reached the top except for her propensities, and he feared she would forget all about him the same way she forgot her panties. She rarely returned his phone calls, and never left his name at the door of the toney restaurants he wanted to take a lady friend or two. He was just looking for a small ride on her coattails, but he was the past. He was an embarrassment. So, one night, he pleaded with her to come over and have a family parlay to straighten out their relationship. When she got there, he slipped her some roofies and then kept it coming. And Suzy couldn't say no to her Daddy face to face. After all, he had a history of playing doctor with her when she was little. The roofies just made it easier for her to agree to play again. So he raped her. He pulled out of his little girl right before he came and gave a money shot to the couch instead. When the DNA on the semen came back as his, he could've lied and said it was from another time, but Oscar had its age clocked at time of death. After that, Daddy Cane just broke down and blubbered up a bunch of incriminating bullshit. Said he was too drunk and didn't remember much. Said he couldn't get it up anymore, much less come. But the DNA said over wise.

To the press it sounded all-Biblical in its depravity, and in the paper the day after the confession the headline read: CANE *WAS* ABLE.

"Yeah, I know him," Harry remembered. "Jeeze, is he in charge of this?" Harry remembered watching CNN and seeing Oscar on the stand, calmly talking about that sick shit like he was describing the things in his sock drawer. Harry was mighty impressed. So far, he'd met a real live Mike Hammer—me—and now one of those CSI type guys. I told him that if he hung out here longer, he might have a shot at getting adopted by Anjolie Jolie, which went right over his head like a hummingbird.

"I could use some help. Maybe we could do this together." He was outmatched by a CNN created superstar coroner who handled all the hot cases in town. I thought about it. Delpin didn't know me, as I don't get down to the coroners often, being that coroners give me the creeps. I thought it might be good for sport, but I didn't like that Gates and Welch were in there. They'd spot me, go to my boss and raise hell.

"No, you're on your own, Harry. But don't let them rattle you. Don't let them twist you around. And they will try. You gotta put your best poker face on and play your best Banacek hand," I told him as I sent him off and I swear I felt like a parent putting their kid on the school bus for their first day of public school in a bad neighborhood and the driver deep into the gin.

"Keep your eyes on theirs, Harry. The truth is in the eyes."

I sat in my car for a while picturing Harry's visit. I knew that Delpin would have him cool his heels in the Mexican tiled reception area that was probably the El Torito bar and smelled like the chemicals of death or a franchise marguerite. He'd pick up a couple coroner trade magazines filled with tidbits on DNA, fiber investigation, and how Hollywood put the strain on crime labs nationwide cause everybody started thinking that crimes could be solved just by looking to see what was under the cadaver's finger nails, and by the way, didn't coroners all carry guns and make arrests and have more authority in a murder investigation than the detectives?

After about a half an hour, Harry wandered back to the car. He didn't look good. He plunked down in the seat and told me what happened and it wasn't that he scarfed down a bad combo platter.

The meeting took place in a room that looked like a private room they'd hold El Torito birthday parties in but was now Delpin's office. Harry was shocked at what Delpin looked like as he had let some of the notoriety of the Cane case and being an advisor on CSI go to his head. He got some plastic surgery and some cheek implants to lift the sadness that years of cracking open chest plates caused and now looked a lot like the swollen faces he carved up for evidence. Just less at peace with himself.

Delpin recoiled at shaking his hand as he didn't like to be touched. This was common knowledge out here. Delpin had a bad case of germ phobia. He was on a constant amber alert for microbes. If he did get into heaven, he'd sure as shit wipe down the door knobs of the Pearly Gates with Purell.

After the stiff preliminaries, Delpin guided Harry into a room. At the end of a small conference room table sat the two Lifethin execs, Welch and Gates, dressed to the nines in shiny suits that Harry thought looked cheap but cost about five thousand each. Harry noticed they had really nice nails. Clean and shiny. Guys like Welch and Gates get lots of manicures being that their nails get dirty so much on account of their dishonesty.

Harry wasn't expecting an audience, much less two guys with shiny suits, perfect nails and rent-a-smiles, so he was slow coming to the chair that Delpin offered.

"Good day, Mr. Corvair." Gates said.

"Good day, Mr. Corvair." Welch echoed.

After they introduced themselves, Harry got down to business. He went through his documents and what he expected from the coroner's office. But Delpin didn't flinch. He just told Harry they hadn't started the autopsy yet, had no cause of death, and wouldn't start the autopsy for a couple of days. That struck Harry as odd.

"In Beloit, autopsy's are done the day after, cases are closed before lunch," he told them. Delpin explained that their caseload was heavy. They had five killings and two questionable suicides in the past two days and they were understaffed. Plus, he had some meetings with some producers to do his life story as a made for TV movie, so he was swamped.

Harry couldn't help but notice Delpin's eyes as he was telling him this. They were black as coal and dry as cotton and they gave him the creeps. These were eyes that had seen the insides of a thousand dead bodies that died before their time, and for the most part, not by their own hand. Believe me, I know what that can do, because I'd seen a bunch too. Men that have that kind of stare are hard to argue with. Their eyes go dull as if they're trying to protect their brains from the horrors they see every day. Nothing shocks them anymore because to be shocked, you have to feel and Delpin was long past feeling anything.

Harry could only stick to the standards he knew. He reminded Delpin that "It's been four days," and God bless his little mid western soul, as if time mattered in LA. Shit, you invite people over for dinner here you have to tell them to come five hours before you really want them and they'll still arrive one hour late and leave one hour early after informing you they don't eat anything that casts a shadow.

"This is Los Angeles," Delpin told him. It was a phrase that would stick with Harry. A phrase that was supposed to wash away responsibility for time or deliverables. When Harry told me about the meeting, he kept shaking his head saying "This is Los Angeles," over and over, as if he said it over and over it might start to make sense.

"I know it's Los Angeles. I can see that on my plane ticket," Harry told Delpin as he puffed up his chest and demanded the coroner's report lickety split. Delpin might have been all *CSI*, but right now Harry was channeling *The Shield*.

What happened next was pretty much enough to knock you off your bar stool and get cut off mid tonic. Gates started to squirm around on his metal chair like Harry was making him uncomfortable. Harry liked that so he said it again, "And I want to see the coroner's report in the morning, or charges will be pursued by Rockford Mutual." And then Welch started squirming on his seat just like Gates. I told Harry that those two were attached at the hip and might even be lovers, and then Harry said that they weren't squirming around cause they were uncomfortable with him or his prefab speech. They were squirming because they had a belly full of gas.

Both of those boys started farting like a Polish brass band at an Ommpah Festival. They were trying to find a way to squeak them out, but the metal seats offered no cushion for absorption, so their short gusts pounded those hard seats like a soft paddle on a marimba drum.

And all the while they were doing this, together in a sort of duet, they were telling Harry about how uninsurable Buffet was and Delpin just sat there, with his expressionless eyes, while the room filled up with methane.

In normal society, you sort of excuse yourself if that happens, or you don't say a thing, let it pass, and you make sure it doesn't happen again. But those boys just talked right through it, like it wasn't happening at all, or that it was completely normal and why the hell aren't you farting too? Just about all the products Lifethin sold were made with more fiber than you find at the bottom of a gerbil cage. That and other shit that made you feel so bloated you couldn't eat. In between the PHOOFS and PHWATS and the RAT TAT TATS, Welch chimed in with "So your little insurance company policy strikes us as a bit . . . suspect." Then he farted again like it was a symbol crash at the end of the tuba solo of a particularly rousing marching band performance.

So Harry had to defend Rockford Mutual and the policy. He gave a passionate little speech about how Rockford Mutual was "a well respected company in the Great Lakes area and they carefully built the exclusionary clauses against awarding the policy due to suicide, drugs, alcohol, anything risky. No hang-gliding, motorcycling, skeet shooting. No soft cheese or grisly beef. And no raw fish on Mondays. Cut and dry. And I'm here to find out the facts. Just the facts. And you can't fight the facts. They're as real as my nose," he proudly finished just as Gates and Welch let loose again. There is nothing that ruins a passionate speech worse then flatulence on the part of the audience. Except maybe flatulence on the part of the speaker, which is exactly what happened. Harry got gas by osmosis. So as soon as he said "nose" he pooted. Meeting over.

I drove Harry back to his hotel. He stayed pissed and perplexed the whole way.

"Delpin just sat there, his hands folded in front of like he was the principal and I did something wrong in homeroom or something. And the other two, just breaking wind like they just discovered the ability and how much fun it is."

"Delpin's a hard case, Harry. He won't be messed with. Too many lawyers need his approval. They put up a case that counts on the coroner's office report for prosecution and they did something to piss him off, he'll turn in a report that would make the Manson killings look like they all died from choking on sunflower seeds."

"That just isn't fucking right!"

"You're right, Harry. And what did you learn today?"

Harry scanned his brain for a lesson. He didn't have far to go.

"This is Los Angeles?"

"Exactly."

"This was supposed to be easy. This was supposed to be in and out, with my bonus waiting for me back in Beloit. Then, a little house shopping with Marsha, some talk about the future. Hell, maybe I'll even buy a dog. I love dogs. They're loyal. They love you unconditionally. This is getting complicated." And Harry started to feel that maybe he had wandered over to the deep end of the pool in a too tight pair of Speedo's after eating a big greasy lunch

"Harry, it's a health and nutrition company. They got pictures in their brochure of perfect looking people running on the beach without an ounce of body fat," I reminded him, "You can't have the founder dying of an overdose in a pair of diapers."

"It's a diet pill company that killed six people." Harry shot back.

And that's why these guys were so careful. Reporters in town were dying to get at them, run a one-inch tall headline on the front page bringing them down and winning a Pulitzer. In fact, the lead investigative reporter of one of the dailies lost his girlfriend to those pills. Then he had to make a choice: shut up and be a journalist, or teach high school. Harry was shaking his head again, muttering, "This is Los Angeles," over and over. Then he brightened and pulled some souvenirs out of a bag that he picked up in the Coroner's gift shop. He had an ash tray shaped like a coffin and a pad of Post-It's that looked like toe tags.

"They had a suit bag that looked like a body bag," he chuckled.

"Those coroners are funsters at heart," I told him as I pulled into the Four Seasons driveway.

But there was something else that was bugging him. I could tell. He was bubbling indignant.

"What is it Harry?" I asked.

"The whole time, Delpin was picking his teeth."

Damn. The farting I could understand. But Delpin picking his teeth while Harry poured his heart out pleading his case?

That's an insult wrapped in mud.

11. THE MOST BEAUTIFUL WOMAN IN THE WORLD.

I left Harry off in front of the hotel, in a swirl of valets and doormen and fat cats and skinny women. He looked like a guy that just got back from a bender with a Nicaraguan tranny and found out too late that she was from Nicaragua. Then I saw Lou standing there, like he was waiting to deliver a warrant. He wasn't wearing his limo uniform. Now he was in his Hollywood bodyguard black, sans chapeau. Then I saw the car. Her car. The Car.

It was a gun metal gray F 430 Ferrari Scuderia convertible tricked out with just about every custom trinket money could buy.

The tail pipes were coated in essence of chrome, as were the rims of the side-view mirrors, which were the size of half a skateboard. The interior was made out of golden palomino pony skin, which J.P. had procured illegally from some gaucho in Argentina. The gauges were also tickled with chrome and accented with ivory and the shifter was a hand carved piece of burl wood from one of the last craftsmen in Umbria, Italy that knew how to carve it and burnish in J.P. Buffets completely fabricated design of his made up family's coat of arms.

As soon as Harry's foot landed inside the hotel lobby, Lou was there to escort him out. Harry was Dead Man Walking. All he wanted to do was lie down in his penthouse and let the room take over and suck on a Macadamia nut till it grew a sprout.

From the bottom of the chrome-rimmed tires to the top of the window ledge, the car seemed to reach only as high as the top of Harry's ankle socks. The paint was so shiny it looked dipped in oil and there wasn't a soul in that Valet area who could take their eyes off it as it sat under the shade of the hotel overhang, its engine purring in idle.

Even in LA, this was a rare one. It had everything you could want and took everything you had. Lou opened the door and beckoned Harry in and you could swear his body just lifted itself off the ground and poured itself into that car and soon he was snuggled in pony skin and surrounded by so many gauges he felt that this must be what it's like in a rocket ship made by a civilization far superior and way cooler than our own.

Which is exactly the way Italians would like you to think of them.

Let the games begin. I once took some driving lessons from a female stunt driver I hooked up with once who taught me how to do all the maneuvers while she was blowing me. She taught me to be cool under pressure, even though my unmarked Chevy is no match for that Italian whore. I knew I could keep even with them on skill alone and my knowledge of every back road short cut would keep me even.

Lou got in the driver's seat, strapped on a pair of sunglasses that made him look like a fly, throttled the engine and busted out of the valet area to the 'Ooo's' and 'Ahhh's' of the cougars and MLF's. Even the biggest dogs there that day could feel their balls pull way up into their sacks.

Harry had a love of iron parks. The Midwest is full of them. And he was only too proud to tell you that there wasn't a roller coaster in the world that could scare him. But now, with his skull pasted against the headrest and that V-12 engine rattling every bone in his body, and Lou bobbing and weaving in and out of traffic like an avatar in a video game, Harry was scared shitless. Suddenly, that way cool car from the future felt like the used Camaro he drove in high school: all vibrations and roar, obnoxious as hell, boasting automotive bullshit, with the brains of a red neck Nascar driver hopped up on Budweiser, cough syrup and curly fries.

Which is exactly the way you should think of Italians.

I followed, weaving when I could, keeping them two to three cars ahead, but never losing sight. On a turn I saw Harry stick his head out the window and barf. But that car is so aerodynamically designed, none of the vomit stuck to the side. Instead, a rivulet of chunks splattered the big black Escalade behind them.

Trouble.

The Escalade belonged to none other than the four-time Grammy nominated rapper Sissy Phus, and he had a temper that a white man's vomit on his spit polished Escalade would ignite. The Escalade sped up and went bumper to bumper with the Ferrari. Lou maneuvered, but the traffic got thicker, and now we were all stopped in a gridlock. One of Sissy's Peeps got out—a big motherfucker, bald and stupid, who spent a bunch of his youth in stir and stayed healthy by stealing everyone else's cornbread. He was dressed head to toe in nylon running shit that made a shooshing sound when he walked. He walked his big, bald stupid self to Lou's side and started screaming, with his hand jabbing the air like it was a gun and by the way, you know he had one and would use it, him being big, bald and stupid.

Let's not forget that Lou was trained in the exotic art of being able to remove another man's spleen without him knowing it, and so the back of Lou's head just nodded calmly. But the Peep kept it up, and now the cars were honking and when you're pissed and cars honk, you get even more pissed. I have seen and heard of highway altercations that started up with someone blocking a couple of cars to calmly ask for directions, and pretty soon, someone has shot somebody and backed up over the body. If I were king of the world, car horns would beep on the inside of the car just to keep everyone honest.

I got out of my car and took out my badge.

"Hey, Bubba Rub," I yelled. I didn't know if that was his name, I just named him that cause he looked like a Bubba Rub, and anyway it worked cause he looked up from Lou, saw me, saw the badge, swore a whole bunch, which, on any other day, I would've busted him for, and walked back to Sissy's Escalade and shut the door.

Through their back window, I could see Sissy yelling at him, and you know he was saying 'Shoot the motherfucker,' but Bubba Rub just nodded his head 'No' and you just know that guy wound up the next day at the Drive Thru window of an In and Out Burger serving combo's and cokes in his regulation In and Out branded polo shirt.

Harry poked his head out the window and saw me nod at him. He smiled at me and I could see he thought he was going to be OK. He had a guardian angel.

What happened next I know from all the mansion security videos—sound included—that Lou turned over to me on a daily basis. I needed to watch what went down in that house. I had to watch the widow and the staff. And the only person that knew where all the cameras were was Lou. He put in extras. Seems he had a real interest in watching the movements of the widow too. He had a camera in every possible place she could be naked in that house. It was a disgrace and I told him so. Then I watched those videos myself and I watched her dress and undress and dress and undress and I so I didn't threaten Lou with illegal surveillance. I gave him a testosterone hall pass. We are all voyeurs. And I don't trust any man that turns his eye from the unguarded actions of a beautiful woman's private moments.

Lou deposited Harry in the kitchen of the Buffet mansion while he went to rouse the Lady of the Manor.

Harry looked like a midget in there. Everything was huge. The refrigerator was the size of a three-thousand-dollar-a-month New York studio apartment. It had two doors on it, made out of a shiny black lacquer so reflective Harry could see the pores on his nose in its surface. The stove was the size of his Hyundai back home. The sink looked like you could bathe in it while you did the dishes.

He didn't dare touch a thing. Probably didn't want his fingerprints all over the place. Everything was too perfect to touch. Fingerprints on these surfaces would've been sacrilege.

The rich have the best kitchens. They don't cook. They hardly eat at home. But they had some damned fine kitchens. The kitchen is the last place in a rich man's house he can out do the other rich men in his circle. It's a depository of technology and style. J.P. had computers installed in the refrigerator doors, telling whoever ventured in there what was in it and when it was time to buy some more and whether the cottage cheese was plain or pineapple. He sprinkled the room with accessories that only the instruction manual knew how to use. Accessories like a shitake mushroom peeler in case the shitake mushroom skin was too tough. Or an heirloom tomato seed extractor should he have a need to separate the tomato from its seeds. He had bottle openers larger than the bottle it was meant to open. Coffee makers that looked like copper ocean liners that could roast the beans, grind them up, steam the milk, and import the illegal immigrants to clean the cups.

After what seemed to be an eternity in the land of the large, Harry inched his way into the living room. He figured that in a house this size, maybe they had forgotten he was here. So it was time to get noticed. Make an odd sound. Rattle an ashtray. Scout for evidence. Something out of place. A telling picture. A fragment of a moment that would unlock the truth of what happened in that ugly, big house.

But there was nothing. Zip. Just pictures of J.P. with presidents and movie stars and athletes and shiny perfectly skinned people Harry didn't recognize at balls and charity events and red carpets and other places Harry would never experience.

He plunked himself on the couch, and got his papers ready. Ms. Buffet would have to be talked to sternly, no bullshit, no wavering. She wasn't gonna get any money. Period. "Sorry Ma'am, but those are the conditions, but shit you'll be just fine, and hell if things get tough you can live in the refrigerator."

Outside the living room windows, he could see out to the deck and the back of a deck chair. Lou hovered over it squirting lotion in his hands and applying it to a person in the chair. Harry could see the person's hand, waving around in the air as Lou applied lotion to unseen body parts. Then, Lou handed the person in the chair a sheer as gossamer wings cover-up, and a leg shot out and a manicured foot touched the fine Teak wood of the deck.

Harry sat all business like with his paperwork, putting the last page on top of the first then removing it and putting it last again. Busy work for a nervous Nelly.

He didn't want to seem too anxious. He kept thinking, "What would George Peppard do?" so he didn't notice when the French doors opened and in slid a long lean, tan and lotioned leg.

The leg of Jadonne La Rochelle Buffet.

Eastern money has the Debutante Ball and you have to born into that. Western money has the Beauty Pageant and all you need is looks and ambition. After her parents moved to Texas, Jadonne La Rochelle started winning swimsuit contests in the twenty-year-old category when she was only twelve. She swept one beauty pageant in all categories of looks, talent, and brains. She had an ability to walk the catwalk in baby oil, a thong bikini *and* talk about world peace in a way that would've given Henry Kissinger a woody.

Her parents knew what they had in their daughter. There was gold between those legs that all men would covet. She would be their meal ticket out of a bad luck life. So she became their project. Her birth certificate was her business plan. And Texas is the state to start that business. The competition was tough, because in Texas, all the ugly girls get put in straw baskets and are floated out into the Gulf of Mexico.

But Jadonne had something more. She was more than beautiful. She was blessed. All the girls of Texas are God's creatures, but Jadonne was the one he tinkered with the longest. The one he sweated over most. The one he was most proud of. The one that made him say to himself, "It's good to be God."

"You must be Mr. Corvair" she said in a voice that was a mixture of milk and honey and Cointreau and her question danced on the air and rested outside Harry's ear like a flock of butterflies.

Harry looked up, and his world changed. It was like he was Pope Julius II seeing the ceiling of the Sistine Chapel for the first time. He took her all in. High cheekbones. Raven hair made silky shiny by hours soaked in egg and beer and the placenta of baby seals. She had emerald green luminescent eyes that practically blinded him to her perfectly formed lips.

And then, there was the body.

Untouched by surgery. Designed by God if God were some geek gamer who only dreamt of getting laid. Long, smooth and sun kissed.

She wore a hint of thong bikini that was held to her by a thin gold chain that dripped into the crack of an ass that looked like the fresh morning pastries on display in the window of the best bakery in Paris.

Her bathing suit top was the size of tanning-booth glasses that struggled to contain perfect round orbs topped by peanut like nipples that stood at attention and could probably pick up the signal of every sporting event in the country. In high def.

From the video, I could see Harry wipe his eye. He was tearing up. It was all too much for him. His brain wasn't quick enough to process the detail and richness of the information. I bet he felt like Pocahontas the first time she saw London. Overwhelmed by things he didn't understand and didn't know existed. He tried to keep his eyes glued to hers, but he couldn't, as the rest of her body was whispering, "Here, Harry. Look here. Now, look here, to the gap in my thighs and the soft fleshy patch between them."

Jadonne extended her hand. Her fingers slid into and over his hand and his palm undulated in the sensation of her flesh on his. Then, she released a blinding, crescent moon smile and Harry's brain shut down.

"Jadonne La Rochelle Buffet," she told him and it was all rainbow mist in front of Harry's eyes. What seemed like a year later, Harry spoke up, "Harry Corvair. Asher Life and Casualty. We wrote your husband's policy from Rockford Mutual," he said.

Jesus. Asher Life and Casualty. Rockford Mutual. Harry Corvair. Names that sounded so sounded so pedestrian when they followed the poetry of a "Jadonne La Rochelle Buffet."

"String beans!" she said, her teeth like the keys on a piano playing Harry's favorite tunes. It didn't matter what she said. Harry's brain was somewhere on a dingy in the Bermuda Triangle, sharks circling, no helicopter in sight.

"Hericots vers! Harry Corvair. String beans in French. Get it?" she asked.

Harry smiled not knowing what the hell she was talking about. With her voice coming at him in longer sentences he felt like falling on his back, spreading his legs, exposing his belly to a rubbing and pounding his tail on the carpet.

Jadonne circled the couch like she was going to turn it to butter. "I'm part French. My great great great grandmother was part French and part Ottawa. She married a Chippewa. A member of Pontiac's tribe. So I'm part French, part Ottawa and Chippewa. Can you tell?"

Tell what? Harry thought to himself. That's all he heard. 'Can you tell?' Can I tell you what? That you're the most beautiful thing I have ever seen or that has ever been seen that ever existed that can't possibly exist? I am not worthy to be in your presence I hope my ugliness doesn't take away from your beauty I should just kill myself right now as I will never see anything as beautiful as you and my life is over.

"Yes." Harry answered. Slowly he guided his brain out of the Bermuda Triangle and back to shore. "I'm from Wisconsin. Pontiac was from Michigan," he said and right after he said it he didn't know why. What the hell did that have to do with anything? Who the fuck cares? Shut the hell up! There's a floorshow going on and you are witness to splendor.

"God, I love a man with knowledge," she said. Harry was thinking about what other historical pieces of nonsense he could send her way. Anything for Jadonne to say she loves a man that has what she thought Harry had.

If I'd been there, sitting on his shoulder, I'd have reminded him to tell her that Attila the Hun was thought to have been a dwarf. Or that Eau de Cologne was originally used as a way of protecting yourself against the plague. Or that during the reign of Elizabeth I, there was a tax put on men's beards.

What happened next is that Harry got back to himself. Marsha's chubby face came into his head and he imagined it sitting on top of Jadonne's torso. It took over Jadonne's gestalt. And his ardor started to die. He was committed, dammit! To a woman he'd known since high school, who said she loved him. It is common knowledge that the poorest unfortunate starving bugger in Africa, when confronted with a plate of prime rib or a plate of the maggot gruel he was used to, will choose the gruel. It's what he knows. He is safe in the decision. And so it was with Jadonne. The primest rib in the world of ribs versus Marsha, the usual gruel.

If he only knew that dollars to doughnuts Marsha was getting it slipped to her for the fifth time today by Harry's slime ball boss Dick Asher.

"I'm going to get a glass of wine. And you?" Jadonne offered.

"No, thanks." Harry said, and right after he let the 'No' out you can bet he tried to catch the 'thanks' but it was too late. The light from Jadonne's glowing green eyes cast the room in disappointment and Harry had another chance. After all, he didn't want to upset her. Not yet. What he was about to tell her would be very upsetting. He was about to disappoint The Most Beautiful Woman in the World of the past one thousand years of recorded history.

"OK," he said, giving in to the offer as his knees shook because right then he thought he forgot the skill of drinking. But no, he reminded himself, swallowing liquids and breathing air and sleeping are like riding a bicycle. You never forget how.

"Great. I hate to drink alone," she said as Harry watched her walk away, the ocean breeze lifting her sheer coverall up over her perfect ass, and if she had asked, he would've stomped the grapes himself.

Harry went back to shuffling his papers, calming himself, trying to remember the reason he was here. He ran through it like a checklist. In and out. Deny the policy. "Sorry Ma'am, but it's all right here in the fine print." Back on the plane. Get the bonus. Buy the house. Have some kids. Save some money. Sell the house and open that little shrimp shack in the Baja. Harry's Corvair's Spicy Shrimp Lair. Die looking at the water slap the sand. The vida loca, adequately lived.

Jadonne floated back into the room, two glasses of a frosty Napa chardonnay in her immaculately manicured hand.

"Here you go, Mr. Corvair. Can I call you Harry? I find it so much easier to relate to people when I call them by their first name. Everything else is so sterile and impersonal. And I like to get personal," she said as she leaned over him, giving him a show of her breasts that were in a loose partnership with gravity and handing him the glass the way Eve must've handed Adam the apple and changed American history forever.

She sat down, crossed her legs and parted her cover-up to reveal a knee as smooth as a Bernini sculpture and Harry's brain went back into the rough waters of the Bermuda Triangle, dorsal fins circling the dingy. It took him three whole tries to force a voice from his lungs, up his throat and out of his mouth.

"Ms. Buffet, I have to ask you a few questions. I hope you don't mind," he said, trying to stick with the plan, say the words, and *remember* why he was here.

"Toast," she said as she teased his glass with hers. He met her glass and was about to toast when she said, "You have to look me in the eyes. It's good luck." And she glued his eyes in place with a stare that turned his intestines to porridge as they toasted and she sipped the wine while Harry kept his glass frozen in the same space where they started the toast.

"Drink. You have to take a sip after you toast or it doesn't count," she said as she took another sip and pressed Harry into doing the same. He did. It was the best wine he had ever tasted. Cold and crisp and a bit fruity yet creamy with a hint of oak and hope.

Harry put down the glass and started back on the papers, "Ms. Buffet . . ."

"Jadonne," she said, "*Jay-donne*. It means 'I give' in French."

Harry picked up the wine glass and sipped, but this time didn't taste a thing. His olfactory senses were camping out in his eyeballs and dick and his brain was waving for rescue from his dingy in the Bermuda Triangle to the helicopter circling overhead. If she taught French in high school, the whole world would be speaking fluent frog.

But he had discipline, old Harry did. And so he plowed on.

"Jadonne, Ms. Buffet." But that sucked cause it played back in Harry's head as "Eebee, Mee dee bee." Harry had to take a breath. One two three four. He heard himself think. He knew he could talk. One word in front of the next. Slow and steady.

"First, my deepest sympathies on the death of your husband." And with that, her eyes welled up with tears. They gathered at the bottom of her eyes and stayed there, her lower lid and perfect eyelashes holding back the deluge and all Harry saw were two emeralds undulating under clear warm salt water.

Then one of her eyes let go its inventory and a tiny diamond shaped tear trickled down her cheek and made a small splash on her knee and she said, "I loved him as much as he would allow himself to be loved," in a little girl land voice. Harry tried to pull the top off his Bic pen, but his hands were all flop sweat and it wasn't coming off.

"Deedle reeble ruse rugs?" was all Harry heard himself ask her. In his head, he had it all worked out. "Did your husband use drugs?" was supposed to be the fucking question. But the left side of his brain was turning to mush in her presence. It was like he was having a stroke. Consonants, syllables, vowels, all a jumble.

He asked it knowing full well that the autopsy would provide him with answers. What he was trying to establish was fraud, and he hated himself for it. But a bonus, a house, and a shrimp shack pushed him forward. But he didn't like asking that question. Not with a woman he alternately wanted to fuck *and* to nurture. Not with a woman *and* a little girl. So his brain twitched and lurched around in his skull and the result was, "Deedle reeble ruse rugs?" And she understood what he asked perfectly.

"Maybe a long time ago. In his fourth marriage. But not with me. We had sex. That was our drug. Every orifice. Every nerve center. Every sensation a human being could give another. Our body's were our entertainment center. Oh, J.P.!" and she let it go, all tears and little girl shaking.

"Yey danderstand," Harry said instead of "I understand." He didn't cause he was dancing with her every word and she was way in the lead. Sex. Orifice. Nerve. Sensation. Give. Body. Hopeless. At times like these, when his mind was all confused or scattered, Harry returned to the sanctity of the Civil War diorama he remembered seeing as a child in Gettysburg. All the soldiers and horses and generals and smoke and death absorbed him so much, the noise in his head stopped. This must've been one of those moments as Harry was just staring at her empty eyed, trying hard not to image her every orifice made slippery with pleasure. It would be too much for him. It was too much for any man.

She looked up at him to see if she was having the desired effect, then cast her eyes to a designer tissue box on the coffee table and used all her skills as a ventriloquist to get Harry to pull one out and hand it to her. She dabbed her eyes ever so gently. But her makeup didn't run. She wasn't wearing any. She didn't need to. Marsha needed to. Marsha spent years in the bathroom in the morning and came out looking the same.

"He had a reputation you know." Harry said.

"All great people do," she said as she blew her nose and even that was sexy.

"I mean, with substance abuse." Harry said, keeping it all on track, forcing his mouth and brain to partner up a little better.

"Harry, let's have dinner," she said. "I'm so tired. All the crying. So many details. The shock. You understand."

"I just have a few more questions," he said, not believing what was coming out of his mouth. The Most Beautiful Woman in the World just asked him out to dinner and he was talking insurance. Damn you, Harry, he thought to himself, you are disgracing your brothers in gonad.

"There's something about you, Harry. Something I trust. I'm half Ottawa. And Chippewa. The Great Lakes tribes were in Michigan. You're from Wisconsin. See?"

No, he didn't. But it didn't matter. Harry's brain was back on that diorama watching Jadonne have sex with him and yelling his name. Harry's name! Harry Corvair. Oh Harry! Oh Harry! You're so deep! So big! Oh, Harry, I've never felt this way. No man has ever made me feel this way!

And there was Harry, in the middle of his daydream, in the middle of Jadonne, screaming back, "Bime Curling, Agad!"

"Berta!' Jadonne yelled, snapping Harry back to now. Berta came shuffling around the corner, feather duster in hand.

"Give Mr. Corvair the keys to the Ferrari," she ordered.

"No, no. I'll take a cab." Harry said.

"Nonsense. It's just sitting there. Why not go in style?"

"Jadonne, having dinner with you can be construed as a conflict of interest, but seeing how upset you are, I can make an allowance. And I don't want to be rude. But the car, that's just not professional." Harry said as he shuffled his papers back into the briefcase completely out of order.

"The last honest man. That's so sexy. Seven then. I like to eat early. Berta, call Mr. Corvair a cab," she said as she got up, sauntered over to the grand staircase, got into one of those handicapped chairs on the railing, pushed the button, and started sliding up the stairs, legs crossed, perfect hands folded on her perfect lap.

Harry was a vision of perplexedness. She didn't look handicapped. Did he miss something? Did she have a wooden leg? A heart condition? Was there a bum bone inside her perfect hips? Would he be denying her the money to take care of her condition? Could he be such a cad? He wanted to run alongside her, hold her hand, comfort her, tell her he would do everything he could he make it turn out alright, but that would be a lie. And it saddened him to no end.

The pitiful expression on his face as she slid up that wall in her handicap chair reminded me of all the times I watched those late night charity raising commercials about Dikembo and his little brother Motumbo, who lost their parents to the genocide in Darfur and little Dikembo had to raise his brother all by himself. Had to feed him and wash him and mother and father him. And it was all too much sometimes for little Dikembo and they never had enough to eat and won't you adopt him and his little brother? Send just twenty dollars a month, and we'll send you a picture of him and his brother and a little letter from them thanking you Big White Bwana, sir. I could be brought to tears when I saw those commercials and now Harry Corvair, sweet innocent Harry Corvair, had the exact same face on.

"I try to limit my climbing. Varicose veins. You understand," she told him as she rounded the bend in the staircase and was gone.

12. LET'S MAKE A DEAD MAN FLOAT.

Dead bodies are nature's messengers. They gather debris that turns into information. They wash up—on time—to tell us what we've been lying about or what we don't know or what was hidden or what we hid.

I've seen bodies with water bottles in their mouths, remotes, cell phones and even Ipods stuffed up their asses. I've seen bodies cocooned in soggy Starbucks cups, wrapped in bubble pack, and stuffed inside truck tires.

The ocean is a real prankster when it comes to human bodies. Like it was getting back at us for all the times we pee'd in it.

It's harder to eyeball the cause of death after the ocean is done with you. Pollution police work hard. The crappier the ocean gets, the harder it is to figure out how a person got done in. Whether you've been dumped there by whoever it was snuffed you out or you took it upon yourself to try to walk to China, you won't resemble anything near what you saw in the mirror last time you looked.

That baseball bat did some serious damage to Lars Sackman's face. Collapsed it in half, so it looked like his mouth was munching on his eyebrows. Television cables were wrapped around his neck. He got entangled in the pier, and it took the tide smashing him against the supports to cut him loose. And, crazy as this sounds, it wasn't like he was uglier.

I stood at the edge of the gathering crowd. Surfers and beach bunnies, warm bodies, barely dressed. It felt nice in the middle of this mosh pit. My nostrils were filled with the smell of coconut butter and young sweat. The cops had taped off the area, but beaches are a tough place to control a crowd. You can push people back, but the sand just slides them forward again.

This wasn't my case, but I loved watching the uniformed rookies acting all official in front of the beach bunnies. Like they had a chance. On a cops salary. I was talking to a fresh-off-the-flesh-conveyor-belt-bottle-blond, brown-eyed bunny in the tiniest of bikinis. I explained Lars' wounds and how old they looked and what could have made them and some of my personal experiences with ocean defiled corpses and she was being my best student with some of the swellest 'really's!' and 'gosh's' and 'oh my God's!' My head and hand hurt like hell. Being in the young, hormonally thick air was doing me good. I felt like a vampire. Coconut butter was my blood.

I had had a hard night. After I struck out trying to conjole a divorcee into the Chevy for some high school back seat sex, I went home and knocked on the porn star's door and invited her over. She was all agitated. Her producer had told her she owed him one more money shot, but he was a slow payer, so she told him to get lost. And he was a known carrier, so she didn't want to pay it off in a fuck. But this calibre of slime ball are hard wired to get what they want especially when it came to second class citizens like women. And some of them are dangerous. Some of them have mortgaged everything and wind up backed into a corner barking like a mad dog and that's when they get dangerous. And sometimes bodies wash up on the beach.

I was in mid-blowjob at my place when he came banging on her door. I could've stopped it then, but, like I said, I was in mid-blowjob, and to a pro like her that's like the second act and she's rushing to the third and the big explosion. His hollering and banging echoed all through the little Mediterranean styled courtyard the condo guys had built to make the inhabitants feel they were living somewhere in Europe instead of the flats of Studio City.

He smashed her door down and ransacked her apartment. You could hear the shit he was throwing around bouncing off the shared walls.

"I just painted the place, that motherfucker!" the porn star said.

"Keep going." I told her. She had developed a nice rhythm, "I'll send somebody over to touch it up."

"Aren't going to stop him?" She asked.

"One thing at a time." My pleasure came first and this was a hell of a second act and good second acts are rare.

After I got off, I gave my porn star a cup of tea and a shot of tequila, put her in my bedroom, let her watch The History Channel and locked her in. The guy had made a lot of racket, but since everybody in the building knew I was a cop, no one called the cops. That would be like sitting at Baskin Robbins and having a Cold Stone Creamery cone delivered.

I went over. I could've just flashed my badge and that might have been the end of it, but that blowjob threw a lot of testosterone in my system and I was feeling a bit of the warrior.

I opened the door and found myself face to face with The Israeli. Damn. I was hoping for some fat little double chinned Jewish guy in a shiny shirt and a hairpiece. Instead I got tall thin Jewish guy in an Armani suit, lots of his own hair and a square jaw with little bulges of jaw muscles that telegraphed just how pissed he was.

The worst part of this was that he owed me money. I had invested in one of his movies about six months earlier. Twenty thousand out of my retirement that was supposed to pay a hundred-grand back three months later. But then he disappeared and the movie never got released. When I tried to track him down, I was politely told by the Israeli mafia to lay off, forget it, to write it off on my taxes. Twenty fucking grand. My attempt to make a killing doing nothing.

The reality was that he was back in Israel setting up a border raid on Lebanon to fuck with Hezbollah. And it was all hush hush. My attempt to make money in the porn business took a back seat to the tangled politics of the Middle East. Just my luck.

He was screaming at the top of his lungs and I could tell he was pretty coked up. He had forgotten that I lived in this building as it looked just like all the other faux Mediterranean wonder palaces that lined the back streets of Studio City and housed his other starlets. I don't think he even recognized me. I had to remind him. I had to remind him about the twenty-grand. He said I was crazy, that he didn't know me and where the fuck was the porn star, that little cunt, and I had better stay clear of him if I knew what was good for me.

So I nailed him in the head with a coffee pot. He went down on one knee and I nailed him in the head with a thick glass ashtray. He went down on two knees and I nailed him in the head with a lamp. He went down to one elbow and I nailed him in the head with a marble statue of Buddha that the porn star had on the mantle for no reason I can figure out.

That did the trick. He flattened on the carpet real nice. I put him in the back of my car and drove him to his house in Burbank and cuffed him to his electric meter. I grabbed his wallet and liberated it of its cash. Five grand. OK. Now he just owned me fifteen. But I got to thinking about how this asshole never intended to pay me back.

That he thought all cops were patsy's. All American's were patsy's. That an American cop was the patsy-est assed combination of patsy you could get. He was protected by his own and who knows, maybe even the State Department, so he could think like that. And I got to thinking that when he awoke, and recalled my name, it wouldn't matter that I wore a badge. This was a bad man. The two most dangerous groups in Los Angeles now were the Russians and the Israelis. They were both stone crazy. They even scared the Gangstas. And every cop knew that any run in with them would have to come to closure in our favor if we valued picking up our pensions.

So I bashed his head in with a brick. It was what I had to do. It's not a fair world. It's as lawless as I have ever seen and the criminals are different now. They have bigger guns than we do, no regard for the badge and nothing hems them in morally. You can't arrest them because the law or money will let them right out. And then they'll come looking for you. And then you will die. But not fast. These boys liked a bit of torture, coming from an area of the world that was fond of beheadings and knew their psychic impact. So I did what I had to do. And I can just imagine you thinking me a brute. I accept that. But, if you were in my position and you knew what I knew and seen what I'd seen, you do the same, I promise you. No matter if you never did a violent thing in your life. No matter if you never stepped on a bug or kicked a dog or pushed a crying baby from your lap. You would've taken him out as a matter of self-preservation.

So I hit him one more time for good measure.

My hand was cut from the ashtray after I smashed it against The Israeli's hard head. Sergeant Lucas, who would always be a Sergeant, saw me and my bandaged hand at the edge of the crowd and decided to talk to me, probably so he could meet my student, whose name I found out was Kari. She was from Arizona. Phoenix.

"Tommy, keeping busy?" he asked, his eyes trying to stay on mine but you could tell they were really wanting to rest on Kari's ample chest.

"Not as busy as you," I answered and shook my head at him cause I knew what he was thinking and he should be ashamed and all, being a public servant and Kari being one of the public he was serving.

"What happened to your hand?" It was wrapped pretty well, the porn star having come from Nebraska out to Los Angeles to get into nursing, and Lucas needed something else to focus on, being that Kari's breasts were heaving under her bikini top and the coconut oil made the sunlight undulate on her orbs with each heave.

"Nothing. Banged it up fixing my front door." I said.

Lucas was going through Lars wallet, making a show of it, making sure Kari the Undulater was mesmerized at his police technique. He flipped through a couple of dollars, credit and Costco card, driver's license. Then he held up a small picture of the Widow Buffet, topless, taking a shower. He let out a low wolf whistle and showed it to me.

"I know him. He worked for J.P. Buffet. Security and favors." I said.

"I know. One step ahead of you, Tommy."

"You guys are good. That's all I got to say," I half smiled back at him.

"Miss," he said as he tipped his hat to Kari and sauntered back to Lars body and pushed it body with his foot. It was pretty much into a rigor mortis phase. Lucas kicked it again, gauging the hardness of the corpse by the sound of the thump to his boot. Kari kind of leaned into me on that. She was getting excited.

"What's he doing?" she asked.

If I wasn't a man with morals, I would've probably taken her to get some frozen marguerites or whatever bottle blondes from Phoenix drink, regaled her with more cop stories and then given her a thorough pat down.

"Seeing how long he's been dead by how hard his body is," I told her.

"Wow, is that how they tell?" God bless her little heart.

"No. He's an asshole. He's doing it that way because he thinks it'll impress you and he has a tendency to hit on women at crime scenes. Right, Sergeant?"

"I busted him six years ago." Lucas said. "Drugs. Minor shit. Got off though. Connections. Now he's security. Damn. We got it all wrong, Tommy."

"Yeah? He ain't kicking you right now, is he?"

"Well, no one's gonna miss him. He's just an oil spill. We'll mop it up."

"Not even worth filing a report." I said.

"No, we'll file like we file them all," he said, making sure that if Kari said anything about this afternoon, it would be how responsible the police acted.

But it was bullshit. Lucas had no family to speak of. And the people he knew were all in the same business. Which was keeping out of each other's business.

This was no rush. Trying to find out who murdered Lars "Sack of Shit" Sackman would take precious time away from making sure some tycoon didn't off his wife so he could run away with his secretary, or his wife off him cause she found out he was going to off her and run off with the secretary.

Then, we also had to keep our eye on the secretary.

So, no, Lars would go John Doe. If anybody stepped forward, we'd get on it. For about a week. Then he'd go back to missing. Fuck it. He wasn't rich. He didn't pay for the right to die dignified.

"Want to get a drink?" I asked Kari.

"Sure," she answered and slid on a flimsy little beach cover-up.

"I'm at the Malibu Inn. We can go there. My room has a patio."

Bingo. I still had it going on.

I took her arm, led her out of the crowd, then turned to Lucas, just to kick the body a little.

"We're going to get a drink on her patio. Want to join us? Oh, that's right, you're on duty."

I didn't even bother to look back and see what his expression was.

13. SHINING THE EYES OF PEACOCKS

I wheeled by the mansion just in time to pick up Harry. Kari the Undulator was sweet, but no porn star, and I'd been spoiled. She was like the demo's they have at car shows. They look great, but there's no engine inside.

Harry was cooling his heels waiting for a cab, and my contact at the cab company called to tell me what time the call came in. So here I was, grinning my grin as Harry came out of the house, with his suitcase in front of him to hide the boner that is the inevitable result of a meeting with Jadonne La Rochelle Buffet.

Lou got the call from the boys at the station. He went to identify Lars' body and to answer some questions. Like, who killed Lars? Which was as good a question as you could have. And Lou was the best person to ask. I told him that for now, I'd vouch for him, might even give him an alibi. But only if he kept doing what I wanted him to do, which was to slip me those tapes and shut the hell up about it. I needed to keep him thinking that I was on the edge of not being his buddy, of turning him in, of planting some evidence to make his life difficult. I also knew that Lou would make it through the interrogation just fine even if he did do it, having been trained to withstand torture and all in Iraq.

Did I think he killed Lars? Maybe. Maybe no. I don't fucking care as long as it didn't involve J.P.'s death. But he sure as shit was in line to be asked. As were Gates and Welch. Anybody who worked with him, paid him, or knew where he spent his off hours. Including the widow. These were people of interest.

At this point, the only person who wasn't a suspect was Harry. And that's only because I didn't believe he could swing a bat that hard.

"Tommy!" Harry said when he saw me.

"Get in. Time for your next appointment."

Harry had made a call to Carlos Prima just like I'd told him to. He called under the auspices of a private investigation, and Prima had no problem with that, claiming in his thick accent to "Want to help as much as I can in these tragic times," or some such bullshit like that. I gave Harry a series of questions, ones that are sure trip up somebody if they had something to trip over.

As I drove the way over to Prima's Beverly Hills mansion, I briefed Harry on Prima. I could tell his mind was still spinning with a sexual diorama of Jadonne engaged in a multitude of acts with Harry, cause he kept drifting. He told me all that he remembered about his meeting, mumbling through a bunch of it, and not in linear order. I had to make sense of that. And I bet he was trying to push her out of his head and calm his wood with images of the Civil War, Gettysburg, the battle of Little Round Top, Lincoln's Address. But Jadonne's image was just too powerful.

It was the peacock time of day. When Los Angeles looks its best with the sun setting big and orange over the ocean, and the male peacocks, if you were rich enough to have any on the premises, opened their feathered tails to attract the female in a last ditch effort to get a date for the night.

Carlos Prima was rich enough to have a whole herd of those beautiful and dumber-than-shit birds. Prima had been with J.P. from the beginning, through all four wives, through the drugs and alcohol, even bailing J.P. out of the tank in Boy's Town when J.P. got arrested for giving blowjobs in the bathrooms of clubs that run shoulder to jockstrap on Santa Monica Boulevard.

Prima was the shining example of newly acquired bad taste money. His mansion stood on a lot in Beverly Hills that once had an original craftsman built by Charles Greene. He razed it and built a tribute to his own fat bank account. What they call a McMansion, and that does a disservice to the clean and utilitarian lines of an actual McDonalds. It was covered from property line to property line with statuary. Greek Gods, mermaids, horses, dogs, angels, and Roman senators made of poured white plaster from molds that Prima designed himself. The mermaids had water wing sized jugs, the Roman Senators had tented togas, and the baby angels were hung so huge they looked like they were tethered to the earth.

They were specially crafted to cause outrage amongst his snot-nosed neighbors. It was bad enough that a diet pill salesman was living next to them, but he was a foreigner to boot and he paid them back for their intolerance with visual blight.

It pissed them off so much that they were not above smashing one of the statues in the middle of the night. Or having their help do it. And for everyone they destroyed, Prima replaced it with two. With even bigger dicks or tits.

As manicured and pouffed Welch and Gates were, they had nothing on this guy. This guy positively glowed. His eyebrows were sharp as a rapidiograph's line. His face smoother and tanner than a black baby's ass.

Prima grew up in a shitty part of the dustiest dirt-poor outskirts of Mexico City. No hope. No future. Unless you call rolling old ladies and caring for mongrel fighting dogs a career. One night, he snuck into a Lifethin event at a local hotel, thinking this would be a lucrative moment to practice his superb pick pocketing skills and saw J.P. preaching the benefits of diet pills and hard work and gullibility and you would've thought he saw Jesus. He signed up right there and then and went on to be Lifethin's second best salesman. J.P. got him tutored and styled and voila, a rich man was born! Prima loved that man. He loved a lot of men, but that man he loved the most, so when Welch and Gates told him J.P. was gone, he got so distraught, he went out and smashed the plaster horn off a Unicorn sculpture on the front lawn. Then he went and replaced it with two fresh ones, but not after flipping off a neighbor.

Prima had a manservant named Tchak. He was Vietnamese and usually wore a neck to floor satin Nehru house coat with little Lifethin logos embroidered into it, even when Prima took him out to Mr. Chow's for ginger redolent diced squab and crispy garlic noodles soaking in hoisin sauce till perfectly soggy.

Prima picked him up from a Lifethin event in Bangkok five years earlier, paid for his sex change and brought him back to work for him and provide him with the peculiar entertainments Prima had a penchant for.

Tchak had both a pussy and a dick, but in reverse order, the dick behind the pussy, which allowed him to actually fuck himself while Prima took him up the ass.

When you have the money, you can do the most amazing things to the human body. To top it off, he wore false eyelashes and his hair was pomaded into a Tin Tin point and he was in the process of binding his feet for Prima so he walked real odd.

I told Harry as much as I could about what to expect, especially from Tchak, as I didn't think he had encountered too many he/shes were he was from and they can be shocking to the uninitiated, especially when they're Asian.

Then I dropped him in front of Prima's house and told him I'd meet him at the hotel. I was on to other things. Back to the Malibu and a one on one with Lou Mellini. A person of interest. He got through the questioning at the precinct just fine. Of course, it was Sargeant Lucas that did the honors, and he'd be no match for Lou. As stupid as Lou was, Lucas was stupider. He didn't know how to press or pursue. He was from a family of cops and firemen, so he got preferential in the academy. He might as well have drawn the pirate from the back of a matchbook to get his badge.

All the security videos in the world couldn't give me the vibe I was looking for. That certain energy in the air that tells you right away whether a person is guilty or innocent or whether there's something hidden in the basement or buried under the house. That's why I needed to head to the mansion. See Lou. Take his temperature. If he was shook up by Lars, something was up. Lou didn't give a raw shit about Lars. J.P. hired him separate, probably cause Lars would let J.P. suck his cock, so he was a friend with benefits. But if Lou was shook up by Lars death, he either had something to do with it or thought he might be next.

Lou had car detail duty on the Bentley. The rose pedals still littered the driveway, dead now. Masked into the asphalt. Sort of symbolic. Jadonne was leaning out the window, dressed in a camisole that is not the kind of costume you wear when addressing the houseboys.

Most of the staff had been let go already. This place was usually humming with plant primpers, car polishers, rock maintainers. Buffet had about ten working for him full time. Even had a guy that smoothed out the beach sand three times a day. All gone now. They were Lifethin payroll. And that payroll just evaporated. And so the rose pedals rotted.

But Lou was still there. Berta too. And Lars was dead.

Curious. Made sense though. Want to keep your job longer, knock off the extra paycheck. And the place did need security. There was lots to rob. The most valuable thing was leaning out the bedroom window in a lavender camisole top, which is the kind of clothing that officially signals the end of the mourning period.

I'm not saying Lou killed Lars. But I look for motives, and steady employment is a good one.

"Don't forget to detail the inside." Jadonne teased Lou. She punctuated it by giving him an eyeful of a breast that was close to sliding out of the camisole. That's when I rolled in, having watched the proceedings from behind one of their imported boulders in the front of the house.

Jadonne laced up and closed the window. Show over. I pulled up to the Bentley and rolled down the window.

"You let go of the detailing staff?" I asked him.

"Company fired her driver after J.P.'s death. Company's gonna change a lot of things," he said. He didn't like my being there. He didn't like me period, but right now, we were meant for each other, me and him.

"Maybe already has. Your boy Lars can't swim too good."

"What are you saying?" he asked.

"That your boy Lars can't swim too good."

"I already answered that shit. Even took a polygraph. Passed. With colors."

"Wow. A polygraph. Impressive."

Lou started rubbing that car in same place in a circle, over and over.

"I'm on your side," he said. "I'm cooperating with you. Even though I don't know what you're looking for. Even though I don't like you much, or trust you at all. And I didn't tell them anything about the tapes, or you and me. OK? We OK?"

People just don't respect the police like they used to. Used to be, a cop came questioning, you'd be like a dog with its tail between its legs, hoping like hell you weren't going to get a beating. Used to be, they'd invite you to come in, have a cup of coffee. It's not like I remember those days, but I have heard they existed. Which always made me wonder whether I was out of my time. Which always made me want to make that killing so I could live well without having to be part of the flow.

"All the same, kind of odd your boy washed up," I told him.

"Not my boy," he said.

"You ever play baseball?" I asked him.

"What are you saying?" Lou asked, which pissed me off. If there was one question I hated more when I was dancing an interrogation it was, 'What are you saying?' cause then you have to clear it up and that's no fun or you have to keep the answer obtuse and that's hard.

"What am I, speaking fucking Ukrainian?"

"Whatever Lars was doing he was a free agent." Lou said.

"He was swimming." I said.

"Am I under arrest?"

"You want to be? I can do that. I'm a trained professional at arresting people," I said, letting this conversation flow to where ever Lou stumbled with it. But he was cagey. Smartly paranoid. He knew that cops could be the bigger criminals, and ever since I got to Malibu, about the same time he started working for Buffet, which was about the same time Buffet married Jadonne, me and him have always had dry eyes for each other.

"Was he dealing? Like dealing to J.P.?" I asked, throwing my line into the water. "Am I under arrest?" he asked, wringing the soapy sponge he was washing the car with like he wished it was my neck.

"Seems you've gotten mighty friendly with the widow. Seems she's gotten comfortable with you." I was pushing it. Lavender camisoles was essentially how Jadonne dressed most of the time. This is a girl whose skin never got used to fabric and rebelled against being covered at all. But still, I wanted to let him know I was keen on his act. I would sniff out anything between them, anything that would put a clock to the untimely death of her husband. If there was a scam brewing, I'd suss it out. I kept a close watch on the house at night. Watching for Lou hanging too close, any sort of romantic entanglement, any sort of motive to off the tycoon and scram with the widow and the money. Or just the widow. Or just the money.

Harry was the fly in that ointment. If there was a plan, it just got monkey wrenched. Harry was either the wrench or the monkey. Harry sniffing around made everyone run for cover.

"Am I under arrest?" was all he said again. "Cause if I am, I'm gonna call my lawyer." I smiled, winked at him, and said, "You don't have a lawyer."

I'd gotten all I wanted to get. Which was to tell him I had my doubts, that I'd be wanting more from him, that my eye was on him and that I could still make his life miserable. I had to keep those tapes coming. I was in the house and I smelled the smell. I just didn't know where it came from yet. But Harry just being here was raising it to an awful stench.

I looked up to the Widow's window. She was peeking out, pulling the errant strap of her camisole back up over her creamy brown shoulder. And I swear she smiled at me. Must have been the unmarked car.

Chicks love unmarked cars.

I made it back to Prima's house just in time to watch Harry trundle out, looking even more confused than after seeing Delpin. He got in the car and just shook his head.

"Goddamn it!" he said. "Goddamn these fucking people."

Harry gave me the complete download. He told me about Tchak, "What the hell is that!" and how Prima offered him a job as a Lifethin distributor because he knew that outside of Philadelphia, Milwaukee had the fattest people on earth, and how Harry could work that region and make fucking millions. Which, up to now, was probably the truest thing anybody had said to Harry since he'd arrived.

I looked down at his shoes and saw about an inch of peacock crap on them. And I know peacock crap cause a long time ago I'd been to Prima's house for a party and had stepped in some myself. It's nasty stuff and there is no avoiding it and it can stick to your shoes and harden like concrete.

"Harry, you mind?"

He looked where I was looking and got out of the car and scrapped that shit off his shoes, which takes a interminable long time, peacock shit being what NASA used to secure parts of the Shuttle together.

"He's got about a hundred peacocks in there. That's got to be some kind of violation. Why don't you just go in there and bust him for humane society stuff?"

"Get in, Harry. I'd just as soon bust him for bad statuary than too many peacocks," I said, eyeing the truly horrendous arrangement of statues with erections and strippers tits on his front lawn.

Harry got back in and told me how he asked Prima about the possible hanky panky. Did anybody have anything against J.P.? Did he know whether J.P did drugs? Drank too much? Owed somebody something? And how while he was asking the questions, Tchak kept answering for Prima in an accent that you could cut with a noodle:

"Ayboty luf JayP!" and "JayP no dugs!" and "JayP no dink!" and "JayP rit man, no o noboty!" until Prima waved his hand at Tchak to shut up and Tchak ran out of the room crying like a little girl, "Mist Carlot no luf Tchak no ma!" and how his voice made such a fucking ruckus Harry thought he was visiting a kennel for small dogs.

"You know he's got a chair in there he stole from the French Government. Used to belong to King Francois . . ."

"Francois Le Premier," I interrupted him, knowing full well about the chair, which is why I went to his house for that party. Did a little moonlighting for an insurance guy a long time ago. He got hired by the French Government to inquire about a rumor that some dip-shit pill salesman in the U.S. had purchased a stolen and rare chair from a fence. Chair was worth about two hundred thou, but more importantly, was part of a set of six. Prima was the pill salesman. He had the chair. And he paid me twenty grand to say he didn't. Fine by me. I have no soft spot for the French and a cop has to supplement their pay, and I'd rather do it this way than escorting some pantiless pop star to a concert.

"Guy has pictures of Buffet all over his house, like he was married to him or something," Harry said, but there was no married couple in the world that had that many pictures of them on display at once.

The house was a shrine to Buffet. Buffet was Prima's God and "God's don't commit suicide, Mr. Corvair," was what Prima told him, "A man worth five hundred million dollars does not kill himself." And that's when Tchak came back in the room, after changing out of one silk mau mau into another one embroidered in Lifethin logos and yipped, "Fy hun milwon dolla no kill kill!"

"And that's when I got the speech," Harry said, looking more annoyed than I had ever seen him. "That's when he took me outside to that fucking peacock toilet!"

I was trying like hell not to laugh, but it was hard. I lit a cigarette to stuff in my mouth and insure that if I did laugh I was going to burn myself. I knew the scene. Prima's back yard was the size of a Par Three fairway and the lawn was an ocean of peacocks. It didn't matter to Prima and Tchak if they got their shoes muddied with P-Crap, as they just threw the shoes away for the help to fish out of the recycling bin. But these were the only shoes Harry had and Harry only had four pairs period.

"I told him money doesn't buy happiness, that's why it didn't matter how much Buffet had, he could've still committed suicide," Harry said. "Thought I'd never hear the end of it. How 'yes it does' and 'that's news to me' and 'look at me am I not happy?' and 'are you happy?' and how I could be happier if I was working for him. All the time with that houseboy following us with a white umbrella with those logos on it saying, "Mistah Carlot appy man," and "You not appy," and "Money make eyeeboty appy."

And sure as shit, Prima was a happy man. Harry had met and seen a lot of folk out here that weren't happy and had big money. Delpin wasn't happy. Gates and Welch weren't happy. Lou wasn't happy and everybody at the hotel didn't look too happy. No one smiled at Harry. No one gave him a have a nice day.

LA used to be a lot happier, back in the day before the Northridge quake and the Rodney King riots and the saturation of mobile phones and the traffic jams that had you bumper to bumper for an hour when you were going just half a mile.

But Prima? No. That was a happy man. He had a mega mansion, chairs that the government of France would pay dearly to get back, a lawn full of well-hung white plaster sculptures that pissed off his whiter than white neighbors and a Vietnamese towel boy who knew all the secrets of the Orient. And I'm not super sure about this, but I bet he was selling peacock shit to NASA at a premium and I know that sounds crazy but there is some crazy shit that goes on and all you have to check for is the fact that there were no remains or parts at the supposed crash site of United 93. And when you know that, you just doubt everything in the world.

No. Prima? He wasn't just happy. And I bet, even though he was good at looking sullen, that since the death of J.P. Buffet, he was ecstatic.

Harry told Prima that rumor had it J.P. used drugs and then Prima told Harry that rumor had it that Prima was an asshole and that he resented Harry coming to his house—his cathedral is what he called it—and accusing J.P. Buffet, his God, of being a lesser man.

Then he took it a step further and ragged Harry for insinuating that Buffet was a man at all!

"I told him law is law. Contract is contract, and when contracts aren't honored, the whole damn country risks unraveling and pretty soon we're no different than those other godless countries where people run around with towels on their heads and explosives around their bellies. I'm just doing my job, Mr. Prima, is what I told him."

I thought that was a nifty little speech. But it was pretty much wasted on Prima. He'd been buying law and laying waste to contracts his whole life and if it hadn't been for him and his money, Tchak would've been one of those towel heads with explosives around his belly.

"You know what he told me?" Harry asked, then didn't wait for an answer he was so pissed off at the memory, "He told me to get another one. Job, I mean. A better one. One that pays me a hundred times more then what I'm making now. One that will make me happy. One where I'm my own boss. A master of my universe. A universe of my own invention."

"What did you tell him, Harry?" I asked, cause up to now I hadn't said a thing because I was shutting down the urge to laugh my ass off at Harry's escapade by clenching my teeth together and pinching the inside of my thigh.

"I told him if he didn't tell me the truth I had people that would find it out and he'd be in big trouble, is what I told him," and Harry shifted uneasily in the seat at that one, not knowing if that was the right thing to say and how I would take it as he meant me and wasn't sure volunteering me as an enforcer was the right thing to do. It wasn't. But I was tearing up too much to get mad at him.

It wasn't so much that he went Tony Soprano on Prima. It's just that Harry couldn't carry that off. When you know bad people, you don't tell anybody. You just hint at darkness. You have to have the darkness in you too. You had to, at one time in your life, been a bad person, or are willing, suddenly to become a bad person. And Harry and I both looked down to his freshly scraped number four pair of shoes and knew he wasn't a bad person and wasn't on his way to being one.

Prima didn't buy it. He just looked out over his flock of fucking useless but beautiful peacocks and told Harry, "Beautiful birds, yes?" and then went on about how peacock feathers shine the eyes of God and how they can only give him three or four years of full plumage and then they die but give him so much beauty in those years and Prima approached Harry and put his hands on his shoulders in a moment of phony sincerity and went on about how Buffet *could not give anymore*. And now he must worship the feathers Buffet left behind, whatever the FUCK that meant, and Harry didn't know either. But he wasn't finished. He went on about how he had to make sure they are cared for, the memory of them, so that we may continue to shine the eyes of God. I could tell Harry was putting the klempt in verklempt with that little speech, cause my groin hurt just trying to follow it.

"Jesus, Harry. What happened then?" I asked.

Harry was staring out the window to the other homes he would never have a chance in his whole life to visit much less own. He was staring out at the Mexican gardeners and Inland Empire pool boys going about their chores.

He was staring out at a woman walking a dog, ear phones on, lost in some fucking god awful tune a woman her age shouldn't listen to, in perfect pastel sweat pants and top, wearing more jewelry than Harry had ever seen at all the jewelry stores in Beloit, with a butt carved smoother than the French carve butter.

"Gates and Welch showed up. Prima went to talk to them. Gave me his card and told me to think about being happy. That he could make it possible for me to be happy." Harry rubbed his forehead hard. He pushed his brow all over his face, like he was trying to massage his brain through his skull.

"Probably can, Harry." I squeaked out between my teeth. "Probably could make you a rich man?"

"You laughing at me?" he asked, probably because I was sort of purple by now and tears were streaming down my cheeks.

"Would never to that, Harry. Just having a migraine."

"Do you have a phone? I want to call my girlfriend."

I gave him my cell and watched him dial and watched him wait for an answer, which didn't come. His little Marsha was probably under Dick Asher's desk right now giving him a blowjob. Harry's mouth went into a frown and he closed the phone and handed it back to me like he was handing me the liver of a small dog.

"Want a cocktail? Judging by the sun, I'd say it was Happy Hour. At the Four Seasons, that means they add a dollar to every drink," I said, trying to cheer him up.

"Yeah, sure. Just one."

And we drove back to the hotel in silence; Harry's forehead resting on the car window, letting it bounce on the glass at whatever little pothole or bump was in the road.

He should've been home by now. He should've had the report attached to an email that would be sitting in Dick Asher's inbox. He should have checked out of the hotel and been in a cab back to the airport and on the six o'clock flight to Madison, with a puddle jumper the next morning to Beloit where the recent weather report had the skies overcast and the temperature at seven degrees with the wind chill making it feel like thirty below.

And now he was feeling like the trophy was slipping away. He was in a game that wasn't played fair, by people with so much money they didn't fear the rules. Not the cops, not their neighbors, not the law, not the government and certainly not a lowly insurance investigator from a place no one here had any interest in visiting or hearing about except to sell diet pills to its super-sized population.

I took great care to go slowly over the speed bumps in the road, what with Harry's head thump thumping on the passenger side window. He'd been through enough speed bumps these past two days, and I feared for his brain.

14. AND ON THE 7th DAY, GOD SPANKED THE MONKEY.

I've never seen anybody nurse a beer like Harry the night after his difficult day. He made it last. Right down to the last bubble. He was hunched over the bar with his elbows locked on the rail, nose right above the opening of his glass, the early foam dried to the top of the glass and already gone crusty.

He didn't notice the three cougars looking his way. Or actually, looking his way the minute I walked in from the men's room and pulled up next to him. Pants that drape draw a lot of attention. If you learn one thing reading this, it's that you gotta have pants that drape. But I sure as shit hope you learn more than that. This is a goddamned how to on how to get rich. This is Instant Wealth for Dummies. Pay attention.

It was the money hour, the agent and producer and screenwriter hour. Made men, almost made men, men on the first step to being made, and men who were made then got unmade. And the cougars figured they might have a shot with one of them before their looks threw in the towel completely. These girls had hope. Seriously damaging, dangerous hope. The kind of hope you spend the rest of your life regretting because it made you take roads you should not have taken in cars you can't afford. These girls weren't going to get a part in a movie. Or an agent. Or a favor. They would get fucked in one of the open Four Season's rooms that the concierge always made available to the agents in hopes that one day they'd get that agent to bankroll their own restaurant. The rooms were for free, and if the concierge was smart about it, he'd turn down the agent's offer of a tip.

These girls would get fucked and maybe even humiliated by guys who were always late coming home for one reason or another that their ever thankful wives did not question them about. And sometimes the most desperate of them might threaten to expose one of these boys. But then a wad of bills would appear, or a car, or a down payment on a condo in West Hollywood, and they'd disappear. That's how it's done in Los Angeles. That's how a lot of money is made. How a lot of property gets owned. And how a lot of restaurants get opened.

Of course, unless they fucked up and chose to shack up with the screenwriter, in which case it would be them that would do the humiliating. But that's what you do to writers in this town. And they're OK with that. They can get a million dollars for a eighty page screenplay that has more white space than the Antarctic about a dog that talks and solves crimes for his blind master who is a top detective who lost his eyesight in a car crash the very first day he picked the dog up at the kennel AND SOMEHOW THE DOG KNOWS THIS AND LEARNED TO TALK BECAUSE OF IT. Or some shit like that. And for the most part it only took them two mornings to write.

Anyway, right now, agent and producer bait were looking at me. And I was looking at Harry. And Harry was looking at the last bubble in the bottom of his glass.

I gestured the Bartender for a drink. "Gin and tonic." Harry looked up from his last bubble and said, "I'm just trying to get my ducks in a row."

"And all your winding up with is feathers." I countered as the drink came and I swirled it in the glass and took that first end-of-day cool cool sip.

Harry rolled his droopy shoulders like he was adjusting the weight of the world from the left one to the right and then back again.

"I'm getting the royal run-around. No one says what they mean around here. No one means what they say. I'm just trying to do my job. A simple job. Why the hell did you think Prima was gonna help me?"

"One of the things you have to learn, Harry, if you're gonna help a member of the Malibu Police Force, is that you chase down a lot of promising roads that wind up dead ends." I used the whole phrase—Malibu Police Force—to make Harry feel the gravitas and honor I was bestowing on him. It worked. He nodded, looked straight ahead, stopped rolling his shoulders and I think I energized him a bit.

"And it's the same damned discipline you need in insurance investigation," I kept going. "You and me, we're not so different. We hunt the unknown, the hidden, the denied. We uncover the lies, expose the truths, and till the soil in hope of creating a level playing field." Shit, I was real pleased with myself right now. The words were doing their damage. I needed a resurrected Harry. An invigorated Harry. The Widow still needed to be dealt with, as did Lou and who knows, I might even have Harry take a crack at Gates and Welch again, but this time with a wire. In fact . . . .

"I think I'm going to get you a wire," I said and seemed that it was right on the 're' of 'wire' that Harry spit up a mouthful of very expensive beer all over the bar. The cougars and MLF's turned away at that, as no agent or producer could ever be astounded to the point of spitting up their beer, so that must make Harry a writer, and so they weren't interested.

"Jesus, Tommy, wires are for criminals and informants."

"Since when did I become an informant?"

Just what the hell did Harry think he was doing if not informing me?

"You want your bonus? Your house? Your restaurant? You wear a little wire."

"This is all going to far! Too fast! Christ, a wire! Those things get discovered, all hell breaks loose."

It was television and movies again. That was the problem. All those scenes of guys with wires getting discovered and getting killed for wearing them. It was the whole rip the shirt open and slam them on the hood of the Buick shit, then shoot them in the head and bury them in the end zone of the stadium.

Or the guy getting so nervous with flop sweat he shorts the wires and electrocutes himself.

I have never seen any of those situations nor have I talked to any cop who has either. That's fucking screenwriter bullshit, probably from the same idiot who gave us the Talking Dog Detective series.

"Harry, we don't even use wires anymore. Just a small wireless device no bigger than an iPod shuffle. You could swallow the thing and shit it out the next day and use it again." I wasn't sure about the shitting part, but I wanted Harry to wear the piece, and as he got closer to the widow, I sure as hell wanted to hear it first hand.

"I got a dead guy dumped in the ocean with his face caved in and somehow he's connected with this trinity and your help, you being in places I can't, is going to save me a world of dead ends. So, do we wear the "iWire" or not."

Harry ordered a shot of whiskey.

"That's not how you get my cooperation! A guy was killed and you think he's involved in this and you want me to wear a wire . . ."

"No bigger than an iPod shuffle."

"It's still a wire, Tommy! It records what people say when they don't want recorded what they're saying." The shot came. Harry downed it and spoke through the burn. "That guy Lars got hurt cause he was an asshole."

"If that was a prerequisite, this whole town would be empty."

Harry looked to the cougars. After the way he threw back that shot of whiskey, he looked more interesting to them. Like maybe he was the screenwriter, and he just doodled an idea on the cocktail coaster and I offered him two mill for it. But their eyes still drifted over to me, trying to figure out the connection between us. And tonight my pants were draping exceptionally well.

Harry gestured for a refill. He was trying like hell to be less of a rube. We were developing a whale and pilot fish relationship. I was the pilot fish. Harry the slow moving and relatively harmless whale.

I toasted Harry and turned to the cougars. They toasted back and crossed their legs, but not before giving me a flash. Harry caught it. Thought it was for him.

"I'm not interested," he said.

"Oh, they're way way past your per diem."

Harry's beer came. A slice of lime hanging on the edge of the glass.

"Why the hell do you people put fruit in your beer? Ruins it."

"Cause of the sun, Harry. We scurvy easily." Harry didn't know what to make of that, and to be honest, neither did I.

Harry pulled out a small picture of Marsha—his little potato of a girlfriend from his wallet, which was a leather laced thing that looked like something you make in high school shop class after you've mastered the Popsicle stick pencil holder.

"And this is why I'm not interested. My Marsha."

I looked at the photo. Shit, those cougars had boils better looking than her.

"She good in the sack?' I asked, knowing full well Harry might just clock me for the disrespect. He didn't. He just took the picture back.

"Shut the hell up. How dare you!"

I was baiting him for sure. And I knew after he'd seen Jadonne, he wasn't looking at that photo of Marsha much. I could see it in his face when he showed me her picture. His eyes had been tainted. The fluids in a man's eye expand for beauty, and Harry's had nearly popped out of his head.

"Do you believe in original love?" I asked him.

"What's that?"

"The one that sticks with you. The one you'll always regret letting go of. The one that had you when you were shaping your idea of what love was going to mean for you for the rest of your life. Original love. Every woman after it has to measure up to it. And they never do."

"Well, yeah. It's what me and Marsha have." he said. "We met in high school. She's been with me through thick and thin. She's a loyal one. Loyalty is all you can ask for, right?"

"From a dog."

He leaned back in his chair, spun his beer around in his hands.

"It'll get all warm you do that." I told him.

"I thought you and me were friends," he said in a hurt puppy voice.

"How'd you do with the Widow Buffet?" I asked, cutting to the chase.

"She's something, I tell ya," and he whistled to himself.

"The kind of woman God jerks off to."

"That's an awful thing to say. That really crosses the line."

"I don't have any imaginary friends, Harry. Don't believe in nothing but me and the natural forces, not God and not country. Makes me sick when people sing the national anthem at ballparks. Fucking mythology, all of it. I die, I turn to dust. That's why we have to get what we need now. So, I'm asking you, how'd you do?" and I ordered another gin and tonic.

"Fine." he said, "She's a nice person."

"Harry, I saw the picture of your girlfriend. We both know what Jadonne looks like. And you not showing interest is like the manager of the Yankees sticking with a scrub pitcher when he can trade up for a twenty game winner who also bats three fifty from both sides of the plate and is willing to join the team for a scrub's salary. So are you soft on her, or are you one of those mid-western fags that goes to church on Sunday cause you like when the priest puts a wafer in your mouth and you can taste his thumbs when he pulls his hand away?"

"Fuck you, Tommy. I have a job to do and she's part of it," he said, mighty proud to stand me down. He spun around to take a look at the cougars in the corner.

They were gone. Nobody was interested in them. They had to move on to a more promising bar, with easier conquests.

"A man can appreciate beauty without wanting it for himself." Harry said.

"That's what museums are for."

"Sometimes I don't know what you're talking about."

"Ever think of stealing a painting?" I said as Harry threw a twenty on the bar. The bartender picked it up, looked at it like it was a turd and told Harry the bill was eighty-six-dollars. Harry blanched.

"It's the limes," I told him as I covered his bill and left a twenty for the tip. "Look, I think somebody put J.P. under for a reason. Might have been your policy they wanted. Don't know yet. But you keep snooping, asking the questions. I'll cover it from the other side. Keep them all nervous. They aren't good at being nervous. Somebody's going to make a mistake. Somebody's gonna spill. I can make my mark. Big case. Big cop. I'll option the screenplay and cut you in for twenty percent of the net."

"I wrap this up, there's a bonus in it for me," Harry threw in. "Fifteen grand. That's a down payment on a house," he said all home owner dreamy like. "That's the start of my future. Then, we sell and head down to Cabo, open a bar. Right on the ocean. That's the dream," he said.

"Then help me protect it." I told him. Harry stared into his beer like he was looking for a bubble to burst and help him make a decision.

"When it's original love, does anyone cheat?" he asked.

"Sometimes. And then it's broke forever. It mostly happens when the man gets stupid. Men always get stupid that way, Harry. It's in our genes. Ambitious men always think they can do better. Sometimes the woman takes you back. Most of the time, if they're worth a shit, they don't. But they'll be in your life your whole life, no matter the pain you caused them. They just won't trust you ever again. And you'll regret it and the day you find out you're dying, whether you're married or have a passel of children or a bushel of best friends, they will be the first people you call to tell. Because they are the only ones you want putting coins on your eyelids."

Harry's mind was racing, his eyes darting back and forth, probably watching a short film in his head of his little Wisconsin dumpling doing things with his boss he never thought possible.

I shook his hand. "No hard feelings about what I said. You need to get a tough skin. They're gonna jerk you around royally."

I showed him out to the valet. "Let me buy you dinner," I offered. All of a sudden he got big eyed on me. A sure sign he was about to tell me a lie.

"I'm meeting an old high school buddy. We're going to grab something."

"OK, Harry. I'll drop you off."

Harry got fidgety. Another sure sign he was right in the middle of the lie. "He's gonna pick me up. I'm gonna get ready." Harry said as he turned back to the hotel as he rounded the end of his lie.

"Getting ready for a high school buddy? What, like, dressing nicer?" I was enjoying this. Harry was looking for his next out.

"Nah, just gonna wash my face . . . ."

"And call Marsha. Original love, right?"

"Yup. Like clockwork."

"And she won't answer again, will she?"

Harry's shoulders drooped again.

"You don't have any high school friends in L.A., Harry."

"I might."

"Nah, if you did, you wouldn't say 'I might.' I'm the only friend you have in L.A. Isn't that right, Harry?"

"Yeah, you kind of are."

"You're going out to dinner with the widow, aren't you?"

Harry spoke to his shoes, "Conflict of interest, isn't it?"

"Not if you wear a wire."

15. THE DATING GAME

When Jadonne went out with a man, she was going out with all mankind. She is a woman of little makeup, no surgery, perfect genes and no upkeep. It drives other women of wealth and means to distraction.

She wasn't a gal's gal. Every gal knew that when their boyfriends or husbands saw Jadonne they'd be thinking of Jadonne when they were making love to them. Come to think of it, these days most gals would be thinking of Jadonne too, just to quicken the orgasm.

When she walked through a place, you could hear the sound of faces getting slapped. If she walked through a Chucky Cheese, mothers would slap their little boy's faces, then turn and slap the fathers. If she walked through a church, you'd hear priests slap the choirboys.

She had one talent. One reason for being on this earth. She was beautiful. Organically, range and cruelty free beautiful. Every last cell in her body was untouched by science. To men of great means, that was as close as they would ever get to God's true labor. She pleasured their eyes and egos. In first class, women of great beauty were no luxury. They are the air. They're put on the planet to help these men compete. They are absolutely necessary in the pursuit of wealth, and they invigorate the capitalist system better than a tax cut.

All women like Jadonne want in their lives was to sip at the trough for as long as it can last, and to be rewarded for their service when it's time they were retired and put out to some condo off the beach, where they could spend their alimony on useless younger men who fed on their fear of getting older. They say the saddest ten years of a woman's life are between thirty-nine and forty.

There was a whole new army of impossibly beautiful creatures emerging from the ooze and Jadonne was heading to the Cliff of Old News. Not that she was old. And she sure as shit was better looking than three quarters of the new ones. But she had been around. She had already divorced her way into millions. And spent it. She made the stupidest investments in the world.

She had a weakness for three in the morning direct response commercials. And she wanted in. So she invested in developing her own line of products. But instead of a George Foreman Grill that drains the fat, she developed a grill named after a minor lightweight fighter from Panama that kept the fat in. What happened were grease fires in the kitchens of the idiots that bought the Manitas Pacqoima Fat Cooking Grill and payments in out of court settlements with each and every one of them. Plus, Pacqoima lost every one of his last ten fights while hawking the grill. Some say he lost those fights because she slept with him and made his legs weak. That's what some say.

She bought gemstones from Thailand that turned out to be glass. Seeds from Brazil that promised to grow a type of sugar cane that could be made into fuel but that turned out to be cactus. She backed a toaster that promised to not just toast the bread, but squirt butter on it while it was toasting. More grease fires ensued and more out of court settlements were granted and pretty soon whatever divorce monies she had won for her hard work in staying married to rich assholes was gone.

I'm not saying she was dumb. Far from it. But creating a new product in a world where everything has already been invented is hard. Maybe that's what attracted her to J.P. Buffet in the first place. He made it. He was over the wall. Maybe that's what attracted me to this case, too. A man died who did what I wanted to do and was incapable of doing. It's a humbling thing. And I am not easily humbled. So I owed this guy his due. I was going to find out why this boy died.

I drove Harry to the Mansion. Told him I'd drop him off and lurk somewhere close. Told him to play it cool, not to notice me, act like he didn't know me. I taped the iPod shuffle sized transmitter under the flab of his right breast. He kept touching it, thinking about it, feeling sheepish about going to dinner with Jadonne. Feeling worse that she might say something incriminating and I'd be all over her.

This wasn't cheating on Marsha, he said over and over to himself. He hadn't done anything wrong. He had his suspicions about Marsha. His doubts. But then the concept of original love seeped back into his brain he almost told me to turn around.

He looked out on the ocean. The Pacific Ocean. Surf boys and surf girls were zipping and unzipping wet suits and Harry liked watching that. It was sexy and innocent. And they were so fucking pretty, all of them. And then Marsha's face appeared and then Jadonne's image crawled in on Harry's brain and elbowed Marsha out.

Jadonne. She's just a job. She's what Harry needed to get to the bottom of this. She'd spill. They all do. She'd say something incriminating about her relationship with Buffet and Harry's left brain would record that and take it back to Asher, who would hire one of his lawyers to make the policy stand. Since when does insurance pay out these days, anyway? That's what his left-brain told him. And Harry was all about the left-brain. The left-brain is the 'keep it simple' part of the brain. The best part of the brain. The right brain is the demon.

His right brain was like a vagabond starved of water. Jadonne was the first sip it had in weeks and it wanted another one bad. Harry rolled Jadonne's sparkly image over and over in his head and only stopped when he realized that we weren't moving anymore. We were at the mansion.

"You're on your own, little buddy," I told him.

"I should've brought flowers, don't you think?"

"Conflict of interest, Harry."

I coasted away slowly as Harry went to the front door and knocked. Berta opened the door with a look in her eyes that saved her from the more physical act of shaking her head in disapproval.

Another victim. She didn't care much for Miss Jadonne. She thought she was trash. But Berta herself wasn't too far from the sociological dumpster, so she kept her mouth shut.

She let him in just as Jadonne was placing her perfect ass on the varicose vein saving chair to slide down the length of the staircase. Her legs were crossed and the skin on her knees was nice and shiny and brown.

She wore something loose and sequined that looked like second skin. She shimmered. Her chestnut hair surrounded her walnut tan face and she smiled that crescent moon smile and Harry nearly fell to his knees. Then both his right and left brains chimed in together in a complete betrayal: *Fuck flowers. You shoulda bought jewelry.*

"Hi, Harry. I'm so excited!" she would gush.

And Harry would open his mouth, but nothing would come out.

Harry's "wire" was working just fine. The sound was loud and clear, with very little of the scratching you get from a wire that's rubbing up against a shirt. It was a marvel of modern technology at about ten-thousand-dollars per.

I followed Lou as he drove the Bentley towards a restaurant perched up high on a bluff overlooking the ocean that I knew was a favorite haunt of Jadonne. She'd go there when J.P. was at a convention, which was about once a month. She had a house account, and liked to sit at the bar and get hit on by thirty or forty men a night, then leave in the Bentley, after having excited them all to the point that they were tripping over each other in the men's room trying to jerk off to her memory.

I could hear Jadonne in the car playing the perfect hostess. She offered Harry a drink, Harry turned her down. She begged him to have a drink as she didn't like to drink alone, and Harry gave in. Then POP, the cork popped out of the bottle of champagne that Jadonne kept in the ice bucket for any emergency.

"Champagne?" she asked.

"Sure. Why not. I don't drink Champagne much. I'm more of a beer man." Harry said, like that might be some small turn off to her. Some way to hint to her that he just wasn't in her class, so let's keep this about business.

"I know you are. Honest men are beer men," she responded. "To our first date," she said and I imagined them about to toast, but the tinkling sound never came.

"Wait a second. This isn't a date," Harry said.

There was a long pause in the conversation that filled up with sadness. I imagined Jadonne staring out the tinted window working on getting a tear to well up in the corner of her eye. She had perfect control over her tear ducts and had mastered the art of being able to cry at will. Which, in Los Angeles, is a highly desired talent.

"I'm sorry. I screwed that up," Jadonne said. "I always screw things up. I didn't mean to be forward. It's just been a hard couple of days. And then you showed up and you don't want anything from me. You're not like the others. You're not even from here and you don't know how refreshing that is. People here, they just aren't honest. They use you. They never tell you the truth. They speak in code out here, Harry. 'Yes' means no. 'Sure' means no. 'Maybe' means no. 'No' doesn't mean anything at all."

"I know what you're saying. I've talked to Tommy about it." Harry said as he gave in and toasted her.

"Who?" she asked.

"Detective Cox." Harry answered, kind of surprised she didn't know me.

"Oh yeah, the nosy cop." she shot back, voice flat as a pancake.

A couple of curves later I could see the silhouette of Lou driving the Bentley, his head darting to the rear view for what I assume was to catch a glimpse of Jadonne's cootch. Jadonne offered plenty of opportunities.

She didn't wear underwear too often. Cramped her style. It was suffocating to her. But unlike the Pop Queens who never knew how to get out of a back seat without flashing their goods for all the paparazzi to see, Jadonne was a pro. Her pussy would be viewed only by the privileged and paying few. But the tease was the game. And

Lou was up for it. He registered every shift and cross of the legs. He took some speed bumps at high speeds to see if it would jar her legs open. But she was good. She was a pro at pussy management.

"No. He's a swell guy. He's helping me out." Harry said.

"With what?" Now she was curious.

"Oh . . . just how to get around. The lay of the land. Los Angeles. What to see, what to do." And I guess Harry thought that was a pretty good save.

"He's a tourist cop?"

"Christ, Harry, move it along," I said to myself.

"This is business, Jadonne. You know that, right?"

"Of course, Harry. But we can pretend? Right? Just for a little while?" she said. "I suffer from a lack of self esteem. That's all," she added, "And this town doesn't help."

"How can anyone like you suffer from that?" Harry asked.

"Anyone like me? What does that mean?" For a creature like Jadonne to say she suffered from low self esteem is like Ali saying he couldn't jab, Montana doubting his short pass, Jordan wishing he could dunk, or Martha Stewart forgetting how to make a doily. Jadonne knew full well what Harry meant, but she played it. He was a man. And to Jadonne, men were as simple as playing Crazy Eights.

"We never had much money, growing up. My father beat me as a child. And did other things . . ." There, she did it. Put herself in the victim column. But Harry still didn't get it. Back in Beloit, abused children just shut the hell up as they were abused to do. And then Harry gave her the obligatory late politically correct reaction.

"That bastard!"

"You're speaking about my Dad, Harry."

"I'm sorry. I didn't mean to . . ." he didn't finish his thought. I thought maybe she put her hand on his knee and every hair on his body stood on end.

"I know. I know. I don't want to talk about it. Maybe one day."

"Sure. OK. To our first date." Harry said as he toasted her for real now.

"Oh, thank you, Harry." Jadonne toasted him and even over the iWire I could hear the mood lift. I could hear the Mmm's and Hmmm's as they sipped the champagne. I knew that what Harry really wanted was a cold beer. That would have made this moment perfect for him.

The Bentley turned off the PCH and took the high road up to the restaurant. I took a short cut to the service entrance. The low road. I didn't want to make a grand entrance. I didn't want Lou or the Widow to see me. The detour threw the transmission off a bit and I started to get static and fuzz. But it sounded like Lou had put some kind of 'world' type mood music on the stereo. Which is a word hardly capable doing that machine justice. It was a ten-speaker sense-surround deal with a special doo hickey vibrator buried in the seats that measured the beats and bass of a song and vibrated those beats into the asses of the passengers lucky enough to have their asses in that car. I bet that Harry had drums and panpipes and the voices of Oprah's African Girl's School choir led by Bono vibrating right through his balls. And I bet his whole body was quivering so much he didn't even notice Jadonne's perfect little finger making little half circles on his knee while singing along to Bono's cover of KoomBaya.

16. I PUNCH LOU IN THE NOSE JUST FOR THE HELL OF IT.

I was seated in an unlit section of the bar with an eagle's eye view of the valet drop off behind the bar and if I spun around one eighty, I got an eyeful of the full restaurant and every Big Swinging Dick in it.

I was reading the paper—The Sunday Styles section of the New York Times keeping tabs on the room like an anthropologist for The Discovery Channel.

The Sunday Style section is all wedding announcements from the offspring of important people. I liked this section better than any section of any paper, even sports. I liked looking at the pictures, seeing if they looked like the newly weds should be together, seeing if they had love in their eye or whether this looked like a marriage to keep the genes pure.

I wondered what the offspring of these people would look like. Would the children of two good-looking people be good looking, or would their mutual good lookingness cancel each other out? And who would stay together? And who was marrying for money and who was marrying for original love?

I'd write couples names down and run them through the computer about two years later. About fifteen percent were already divorced. If you ran the names seven years later, it went up to forty-eight.

I wondered if being in the Style Section was akin to being on the cover of Sports Illustrated. A curse. The evil whammy. That athlete on the cover of SI was sure to have a shitty game the next time he played and these folks were all heading into big expensive and public divorces just for being in the Sunday Styles section, where their plain looking children, handsome summer homes and yapping little dogs would all be divvied up.

I could see the Bentley roll up to the Valet stand from the bar window. Lou lined the back passenger door up perfectly with edge of the red carpet that snaked out the entrance. Lou was good. He knew how to do the details.

Tip hungry Valets rushed to open the door on the near side. Harry's door. I saw Harry get out and check out the perfect leafy entrance and red canopy and the Valet's gold brush epaulets.

Lou waved one of the Valets off from Jadonne's side and opened the door himself. She came out, slow and careful, Lou close to her. Too close. I could tell he was pressuring her. Real aggressive. Smiling as he leaned into her. She didn't like Lou up close and personal. She had to squeeze past him, almost had her breasts pressing up against him, almost shared a little too much air with him. There wasn't anybody to discipline him now. If he could share her air, who knows, maybe she'd let him share more. He did it like he knew some secret. Like he had something on her. All three of them—Lou, Lars, Jadonne—all had something on each other. It's what happens when you live at the ocean with too much time on your hands and all your needs have been met and you're too self absorbed to bother spending your idle time helping the starving children in Africa.

"You're out of line, Lou," she said straight to his face, fearless, standing him down, like she had some secret magical power and all she had to do was switch it on and turn Lou into a nervous little girl in a tutu with the lead in Swan Lake.

"I know what you're doing," Lou said, sort of under his breath to stay out of Harry's earshot. But the device picked it up, loud and clear, even though Harry only had eyes for the view from the cliff of ocean and more ocean.

"I'm having dinner, Lou. So it's good that you know what I'm doing. Cause if you drove me to a restaurant and didn't know I was having dinner, I'd be a little worried about you. I would've had to go back to my original impression of you, Lou."

"And that would be . . . ?"

"Funny, J.P. dying on your watch," she said. She could go beautiful to ballistic in no time flat. These two people didn't like each other. They didn't like each other at all.

Jadonne shifted past Lou, and Harry and Lou locked eyes, and Harry burned a look at Lou. As dangerous a look as Harry could muster. Lou just tipped his hat at him as Jadonne offered her arm to Harry to cradle.

"What was that about?' Harry asked her as he did.

"It's about a lack of respect. I'm getting it from all sides, Harry. Since J.P.'s death. It's tearing me apart."

"It's not right what he did." Harry said with all the bravery he could muster. He was feeling especially protective of Jadonne. And now he had her arm in his and it was like he was carrying some kind of special package to somebody very important.

I watched them as they entered the restaurant and walked into an arena of eyes, all glued on Jadonne, her arms locked in Harry's, pulling him close, as if to protect her from the glue.

I watched from behind the newspaper as the maître 'd nestled Jadonne into her seat, then tried to get to Harry before he pulled the out the other chair for himself. Harry didn't have any idea of protocol, and his simple little act of seating himself gave pause to the alpha males in the room. They didn't know what slot to put Harry in. Was he a Rube or an even Bigger Swinging Dick without a care in the world what the world thought of him? They'd seen that before. In their hero's: Bill Gates, Warren Buffet, the richest of the rich, in their Wal-Mart cardigans and Ford Taurus's'. And there was Harry in his Target jacket and Payless shoes. And they nodded to him, hedging their bets, and thinking maybe they could catch Jadonne's eye.

It gave Harry the creeps.

"Why they all looking at me?" he asked her.

"Because you have the look of a man that walks with confidence. You're not trying to impress anybody. That's power."

Harry looked around the room and all he saw were eyes: the women, the alphas, the wait staff. A bottle of champagne magically appeared. The cork was popped and the champagne was poured and the bottle was spun into an ice bucket and the waiter placed a napkin on his sleeve and said, "I'll bring some water. Sparkling or flat?" Harry looked to Jadonne for the choice. She was sucking on a breadstick.

"I know. Bad manners. I do it all the time with the breadsticks here. I like to get them soft before I bite." The waiter looked at Harry for the order, his mind racing to what that moist breadstick meant in the larger world of metaphors.

Jadonne closed the deal, "Sparkling."

"I know what you mean. I like to dunk stuff in my coffee. Soften it up. Makes it tastier." Harry said.

"Me too!" she gushed. "We have so much in common." She lifted her glass and toasted him. Clink! And the eyes in the room watched them both.

I stepped outside to grab a cigarette and saw Lou standing by the Bentley talking on his cell phone and I wondered to whom? The company? Telling them he was keeping tabs on the widow, reporting her adventures? His bookie? Telling him he was close to getting some money in so he could pay him off? Who? Wasn't a friend. It looked like business. He was wiping the windshield down here and there, plucking eucalyptus leaves from the wipers. I searched my pockets for a light, but had nothing. This was as good an excuse as any to torment him.

"You're pretty attached to that car." I said.

Lou saw me, and put away his cell. "Well, if it ain't Officer Krumsky."

"Oh, Jeez, Lou. That's funny. God, you're hilarious. Officer Krumsky. From West Side Story, right? Fuck. How do you think of that shit, Lou? So spontaneous."

"Alright, alright," he said, now embarrassed he tried for a second to be a smart ass. "I didn't bring any new tapes with me."

"Gotta light?"

Lou flashed a gold Zippo. A classic. He flipped it open and lit my cigarette, knowing full well that if a single sparked ash hit the foliage it would start a fire that would torch the hillside and send the denizens into a frenzy of packing and spending days in a luxury hotel while they called their insurance providers to get more than what they paid for their mini-mansions while the fire department put out the flames.

"Nice lighter," I said. It was.

"Little gift from the widow."

I snagged it from him. It had J.P.'s initials engraved on it. I pocketed it.

"That's not yours to take." Lou said.

"Consider it evidence." I said. Lou didn't argue. He didn't like where he thought I was going.

"You got it nice right now, don't you? All alone with the widow. Hubby's dead. God knows why. And you have his lighter. His car. Smells a bit, don't you think?"

"I'm helping you out. The tapes. I'm not spilling nothing."

"You always open her door like she might let you fuck her against it?"

"What are you driving at?" Lou asked.

"I'm not. You are." I answered. "She must be hard to turn down, she asks you to do something for her."

"I can handle it."

"Do you?"

"Do I what?" he said real dumb like and that pissed me off.

"Are we back to that? You not knowing what the fuck I'm talking about?"

"She's a tease man. Walks around in shit that's barely there. Doesn't take much imagination to see where the clothes end and she begins."

"Nice scenery. That can change a man. Make him do things so he can keep on enjoying the scenery. Right?"

"She knows what she's doing," he said in a way that told me he thought he was done with the conversation, but it wasn't his to end.

"Do you?" I asked him.

"Do I what?" and that just sent me.

I wacked him with a short left to the tip of his nose, just enough to cause massive amounts of pain, not to break it but to bend him over and make him tear up like a Catholic High School girl who just found out she was pregnant by the priest.

"Fuck!" he screamed, all bent over holding his schnoz, "You fucking broke it!" I grabbed him and held him up, real careful.

Lou would kill me in a bar fight. Like I said, he was Special Forces. He could remove a man's eye, roll it around in his mouth and stick it back in the socket without the poor sucker feeling a thing.

But I'm a cop. And you just don't hit cops. Not in Malibu. They erase you from the social register but quick you do that.

"Why you humping me?" he said through his hand.

"Cause you might know who killed Lars and you won't tell me. And I gotta know. I just gotta know, Lou. My bonus depends on it. I crack this and the captain promised six silver bullets with my name on them. That's an honor, Lou. And I don't get honored much."

"Such bullshit," he said as he spat some blood on the black top.

"Who? Was that a name you gave me?"

"I don't know who killed Lars. I don't care. He was a fuckup. I warned him about his friends. I warned him about his big fucking mouth. I didn't do nothing!" The pain in Lou's nose was starting to wear off, so he was feeling close to normal and a little bolder. "And I'm not fucking the widow. Even if she'd let me."

"Louuuuuu . . . . ?"

"OK, I would if she let me."

I reached into his pocket and pulled out a fat gram bag of coke. "Lookie lookie here." I said, waving the bag like a toreador in front of the bull. "That's not fucking mine!" he said. And it wasn't. But it's a great old trick and works every time.

"It is if I say it is. Here I am, face to face with you and I just fucked you. I can do twice as much damage with more time and distance. You know that, Louise. I can call you Louise, right? Cause right now you look more like a Louise than a Lou."

Lou straightened up like a man wrongly accused. He looked around the parking lot, saw the Valet's were watching, not really knowing what to do, as they knew me and how I could be. But I kept my tab paid and tipped well. So they were fans.

"I'll ask around. Maybe something will turn up," he said.

"OK. But Louis. Stay away from the widow. You're farting way higher than your asshole. And she's got enough problems than to fraternize with a suspect," I told him, pushing him into a nice little corner.

"Since when am I a suspect?"

I put the gram bag in his pocket, and patted it for safekeeping.

"Since right now. Consider it a gift from the department for all the juicy shit you're going to give me."

Lou reached in his pocket and pulled it out and was about to hand it back to me when I popped him again in the nose. He buckled over again and I stuck that gram bag deep in his pocket like it was a rare button that fell off his suit and told him what was obvious, "Now you're really gonna need it. Just to fight the pain."

The appetizers were long gone by the time I came back from educating Lou. There was an empty bottle of Cristal upside down in the bucket and the waiter was pouring a fresh popped one. Jadonne never shied away from a flute of that over bubbled shit, but the truth was, she didn't drink much. But the man sitting opposite her would drink his and her share just fighting the nervousness of being with The World's Most Beautiful Woman. And she would say stuff that would make your heart race and your dick hard and so you had to drink some more just to even out the adrenaline that was flooding your veins in the hope that tonight *you might be lucky enough to wind up with this woman* and you really couldn't believe your fate.

Jadonne knew to sip little long sips. And you kept steady with her, but you drank more. She took in less than a hummingbird and you were hosing down like an elephant during a drought all the while dreaming of taking her to bed or just seeing her naked. Her mind, on the other hand, was on you being too fucking drunk to do or remember anything. And that's when she had you. When she called you the next morning and asked if you were OK and you asked if you did anything you should be ashamed of and she told you, "No, you were cute," that was when you checked your credit card balances and went and bought her something expensive. That's how it worked. And it always worked that way. 100% of the time.

She told Harry about her past. He could've sworn her words formed themselves as they left her mouth in minty little puffs and drifted over to him so he could breathe them in. "I did makeup for awhile. Some fashion. Some special effects. That's where I met Rick Knox," she told him.

Harry knew the name, "The movie actor? He's swell."

Rick Knox was big news in the red states. He was an action star from the Ukraine. A real dumb cocksucker. I had several run ins with him myself. He liked to drive too fast, drink too much and do both with sixteen year olds girls. They were the only creatures he could hold a conversation with, being that he was primarily monosyllabic and informed only about himself. He spoke about himself in the third person. "Rick Knox doesn't do this. Rick Knox believes in this . . ." that sort of celebrity shit where at some point in your life you've become a bar of fucking soap.

"That's what I thought. In the beginning." Jadonne said. "I mean, he was handsome, made good money, well, for awhile, great money, I mean, not J.P. money, but it was sexy, you know."

"You went out with Rick Knox?" Harry asked and then rattled off a bunch of Rick Knox actioners: *Those Are the Knox!* and *Knox Out!*, the comedy he did with Mel Brooks, *Bagels and Knox*, and his most recent actioner, *Hard Knox*.

Jadonne averted her eyes to her champagne glass like she was about to confess a great sin. "I was married to him," she said and I could tell that almost knocked Harry off his chair and I bet it was because now he wasn't just sitting with The Most Beautiful Woman in all the World, he was also sitting with a celebrity by association.

"Wow, that is something." he gushed and here's where I bet his mind was traveling. I know cause I know men are essentially little boys and I bet his mind flashed to the times he watched a Rick Knox movie at the multiplex and how now, in some metaphysical way, by virtue of him sitting across from her, he felt connected to Rick Knox. If he saw Rick Knox, say at a Home Depot buying extension cords, he wouldn't be tongue-tied. He'd say, "So, we have a mutual acquaintance, Rick!" and Rick would say, "Rick Knox has no acquaintances, only fans." and Harry would say, "Jadonne La Rochelle!" and Rick Knox would smile like he did when he blew away the African Dictator and his midget guards in *Knox Out!* and then he'd shake Harry's hand and they'd go out for a beer and maybe a pastrami sandwich. And I bet Harry liked that feeling. It was full of hope and promise. It made him feel shiny. It made him feel important. And he was. He was sitting opposite The Most Beautiful Women in the World. He looked around the room, and the other women all smiled at him when they could without their husbands and sugar daddy's seeing them. They smiled at him and he knew why. It was because, in his way, he knew Rick Knox.

"He beat me Harry. All those tough guy roles. Let's just say he stayed in character long after the cameras stopped turning," she said. "He never hit me where it would show, just the upper arms, upper legs, back, shoulder. Never the face. It didn't take much for him to fly off the handle. If I didn't get him something, or do something he wanted me to do—like take it up the ass. I don't like that, Harry. I won't do it. Not for any man. No matter how much I love them. It's not right. It's not natural. You understand. Don't you?" and as soon as she finished she went back to putting her lips on the champagne glass and Harry refilled his.

Now I could tell he was pissed. He didn't really hear her talk about taking it up the ass, or how she seemed to be preparing him against disappointment in case that's what he wanted to do with her, which it wasn't as you could bet dollars to doughnuts Harry just wasn't a giving it up the ass kind of guy. I am. But that's another story.

No, Harry was back at Home Depot in aisle twelve with Rick Knox. This time, in this dream, when he told Rick about knowing Jadonne and Rick smiled, Harry hit him in the head with the shovel he picked up in Gardening. And when Rick begged his forgiveness, and asked him to go have a beer and a pastrami sandwich, Harry turned him down. He'd spit on him is what he'd do. And the patrons and salespeople in the Home Depot all looked at Harry, because right now he was a bigger action hero than Rick Knox ever was. And then Harry returned his eyes to Jadonne as he snapped out of his revenge Home Depot fantasy to tell her, "Then I'm done with Rick Knox. I'll never go to see one of his movies ever again."

Fucking A, Harry. Fucking A.

She smiled at that and said, "Then there was J.P. He was different. He had more money than the first two. But he didn't have the attitude. He knew it could all go away in a second. Like the time those four people died taking the pills and Congress went after him. Just like that he could've been ruined. And it affected him. Not the deaths. But the fact that he could be out on the street in a moments fuck up. He was troubled. The money came so quick. And he knew it wasn't built on anything. It wasn't like he made something that could last forever. Like a car. Or a TV show. A really great handbag. I just can't believe he's gone." Then she looked down into the bubbles of his champagne flute and all Harry could say was, "I'm sorry."

That was all the encourgement she needed. She kept going, this time with more butter and violins. "He didn't leave a will. Just that policy. It's all I have." She shook her head and sipped again and this time Harry downed the champagne so fast it watered his eyes and he poured another because he knew he was nearing his rough patch of truth and he sure as shit wish he had a beer, cause drinking good champagne really fast means you always taste it with your nose.

She went on. "He wanted me to be cared for. He didn't want me to have to get married again. He said I'd have enough money to invest, live carefully, maybe take a job at a charity helping kids without . . . things. Or pets without homes. Homeless pets. Pets that roam around outside, no one to take care of them. Pets that forage in the trash, or kill other pets."

"Those would be wild animals," Harry corrected her. Or illuminated her. Or informed her. He didn't even know why he decided to talk. She waved him off.

"He told me that I would have the time to give back to the world. Like he never did. Sure he gave. But he never ladled soup at a soup kitchen, or delivered turkeys on Thanksgiving to the turkeyless. He knew he couldn't trust the company to do the right thing. They blamed me for breaking up his second marriage."

"Did you?" and Harry felt like shit the minute he asked that. "I'm sorry. That's out of line."

"Christ, no. His second wife was a lesbian. Sort of a late bloomer. She even came onto me once. But I don't do that either. I mean I have. But I don't get my identity from that. I'd do a threesome though. Two girls and a guy. Or two guys if the guys didn't mind. What's the matter, Harry?" she asked, and I could see Harry's whole demeanor change at the talk of threesomes and lesbians and sexual equations that were threatening to short out his sheltered synapses.

She brushed her hand up the side of his glass and brought his eyes back to her. "Harry, that policy will come through, won't it? There isn't a problem, is there?"

I could see Harry try to swallow on that one. He had a lump in his throat the size of a marshmallow. The Turkeyless would not be getting their turkeys this Thanksgiving, and Harry was to blame.

"Well. There could be." Harry said in a warm putty kind of way. The way his shoulders slumped it was like all the bones in his body had turned to gush.

"And what does that mean, Harry?"

"It means we won't . . . might not . . . award the money."
There. He'd said it. The can was open and the worms came crawling
out. Jadonne put down her glass. It was too much for her. Her eyes
welled up. The tears were building and building on the lower lid,
threatening to flood the rest of her face in a deluge of fear and pain
and cool, clever manipulation.

She was playing him like a Stradivarius. She could smell
guilt. This wasn't exactly new news to her. She knew cause of death
might come up and spoil her party. So she was prepared. I wouldn't
have been surprised if she had had her tear ducts filled with saline
solution.

"What will happen to me, Harry?" she pleaded, stretching
the 'me' real long and pitiful like. "The company owns the house,
the furniture. Everything. J.P. was right all along. They'll just throw
me out. I'd need an army of lawyers to challenge them. And I can't
pay. I've tried to deal with lawyers on a commission. They all agree
if you sleep with them. Let them fuck you up the ass. Shit! Harry.
It's not fair!" and the tears just came right down her face, practically
pulling her lashes off, and splashed on the table cloth and Harry
didn't know what to do, hand her a napkin or call FEMA.

Jadonne's face was covered in her napkin when the waiter
approached with the bill. She told him to put it on account. The
waiter looked at Harry like he was some kind of heel, making The
World's Most Beautiful Woman cry. In public. In a place she was a
regular. Before it got completely dark. And he said, "I'm sorry Ms.
Buffet. But the account's been closed."

Harry saw she was lost. He saw she didn't have a clue what
to do. "It's OK. I'll take care of it," he said as he pulled out his arts

and crafts wallet and set out to make it all disappear, per diem be damned.

"I can't fight them alone, Harry" she said, biting on her smooth, tan knuckles, "You see what I'm up against. I'm afraid to go to the store. I keep thinking that they'll just clean me out, furniture, everything, by the time I get back. And this is just the beginning."

"Where I'm from, a man pays the bill," he said sort of like John Wayne might have said it if John Wayne had ever made a western set in a ritzy restaurant high atop the cliffs of Malibu.

Then Harry picked up that bill, not taking his eyes off of Jadonne's, looked around the restaurant at the other alpha males watching him rescue his damsel, and Jadonne just glowed, "Oh, Harry, where is your halo!" That made Harry smile like a ninth grader who just got a blowjob from his way too hot for high school teacher. Then Harry looked at the bill. He tried to not react. He tried to be like John Wayne when The Duke was confronted with an entire tribe of war painted whooping Apaches on the ridge and all he had was one bullet in his Winchester and no water in his canteen.

"Seven hundred fifty seven dollars and eighty six cents," he said under his breath and I had to strain a bit to hear it in my earphones.

It hit him in the sternum, knocking the wind out of him. His mouth opened and closed like a trout that was yanked out of the stream and left to die on the dock. *Seven-hundred-fifty-dollars-and-eighty-six-cents.* At this point in a man's restaurant life, with a bill he can't possibly pay and a woman he desperately wants to keep impressing, you go kind of deaf. All the background sounds drop out and all you hear is the low hum of the blood in your ears as your heart pumps crazy panic and somewhere deep in the thickness you hear your dark little soul asking, "What the fuck you're doing in a place you have no hope of being able to afford? You stupid stupid little man."

Jadonne asked him what was wrong, but nothing came out of her mouth. The room swirled and his shoes felt tight.

I counted the Cristals. Three bottles. Two appetizers. Poor Harry. He was sitting there with a bill in his hand that was upwards of two and a half weeks salary after taxes and 401K are taken out. A bill that was as high as what his Doc charged him for a total yearly physical with X ray and lab work and finger up the ass. And he hadn't eaten anything more than a couple of sprigs of salad and a basket of bread.

The Waiter'd seen this before. "The Cristal is two hundred fifty dollars a bottle." And Jadonne said, "I had no idea. Did the price go up?" And Harry was still gulping for air and he let his card drop on top of the bill and let the waiter carry the card like a dead rodent into the back of the restaurant.

About now Harry's hearing was coming back. And people were talking about him; "The man that made the beautiful woman cry," "They must have a troubled relationship," "What the hell is a woman like that doing with a guy like him," And, "Must have a lot of money." And, "I don't think so the way he turned white at the bill."

I bet Harry's mind drifted back to aisle twelve of the Home Depot and this time Rick Knox was kicking the shit out of Harry, laughing his ass off and emptying sacks of peat moss on Harry's head which is why he didn't see the waiter come back to the table and ask him for another card.

Harry didn't have another card. Harry was a one-card man. So, it was time the Calvary came in to save The Duke from those mean ass seven hundred fifty dollar and eighty-six cent Apaches.

I sent a busboy over to Harry's waiter with a note in his hand and watched while he gave it to the waiter and while the waiter whispered in Harry's ear.

Harry came over to the bar, leaving Jadonne at the table, surrounded by eyes.

"Give me the bill," I told him.

"Christ, Tommy, it's good to see you. I had no idea . . ."

"What, did you think you were drinking Pabst?"

I took the bill, and flipped it to the bartender.

"Put it on my tab," I told him.

He didn't like that. This was too high. And my tab was nonexistent. It's a hypothetical tab. It's a tab that says "I drink for free and I won't bust you for hiring illegals in the kitchen or serving underage prom queens." It says, "You stay open." It says "I won't follow you home tonight and plant a bag of meth on you and bust you and send you to jail for a week where you will take it up the ass if you survive at all."

"I'll pay you back. Soon as I get my bonus. Promise, Tommy."

"Don't worry about it," I told him. "Consider the fee for getting me information. I'm liking what I'm seeing. I'm liking how all these bozo's are bumping into one another, and I like that it seems to all happen around you."

That made him feel like a champ.

"I'm just going to get Jadonne home," he said. But when he turned back to the table, she was gone.

17. DID YOU HEAR THE ONE ABOUT THE STRIPPER AND THE SNAKE?

In my expert assessment, Uncle Snatchers—*"100 beautiful snatches and 1 ugly one"*—was the best gentlemen's club in town. It's where the porn stars danced to make some extra change, promote their new releases and meet aspiring producers that would spend the entire night slipping twenties in their G-strings while promising them the lead in the next big facial-rama.

The business had changed for these girls. The Internet had swooped in almost overnight. There were just too many amateurs willing to do it on camera for a couple hundred dollars. They had all had the requisite boob jobs. They all strived to achieve the perfection advanced by their boyfriend's video games—the Lara Crofts, the Claire Redfields, the Jades—and would do just about anything to be on camera and uploadable online. They'd count the hits they got like it was a huge compliment that some kid in his garage wearing nothing but a pair of off white tidy whiteys had pulled aside the pee flap so he could jerk off to them while they took a money shot to the face. It was even better when these amateurs could charge for the experience. Some of these girls were making a hundred thousand dollars a year and all they had to do was fuck their boyfriends and a few of their fraternity brothers.

Women's lib was soundly defeated somewhere around 1998 and was just a quaint memory a mere two years later. The new girls didn't care at all. Getting paid to do it on camera was very liberating to them. Or else there was a whole generation of women that were getting abused by their fathers. I'd like to think the former.

Uncle Snatchers was also where I had another "tab." And the perfect place for Harry to get his mind off Jadonne. Especially when Starr was on the pole.

I'd known Starr for five years. Busted her twice for prostitution, and once for drugs. But she was OK. She'd done about six films before she realized it was safer on the pole. She kind of specialized her way out of the porn business. She didn't do girl on girl and you have to do girl on girl. And she wouldn't do anal and if you don't do girl on girl you have to do anal. And she wouldn't take a money shot to the face and you have to take a money shot to the face if you don't do girl on girl or anal.

She came to California to be an actress. She was from a well to do family in Shreveport, Louisiana. Her life changing moment was when she was living in a dog-eared section of West Hollywood in a cookie cutter stucco apartment building upstairs from a snake handler who supplied serpents to the movie business. Coming home one day after a series of lousy auditions, she went to pee and next thing she knew she was in the grips of a boa constrictor that had found its way up the pipes of the building and into her toilet. She wrestled with it until she could grab a carving knife from the kitchen and slice away at it until there was nothing left to choke her.

The handler screamed bloody murder when he saw his prize snake hanging off Starr's shoulders like strips of jerky hung out to dry. He was supposed to take it to the Valley that afternoon to be in the title sequence of a six-tissue jerker called 'The Boner Constrictor.'

She was pretty out of it at that point. Getting attacked by an eight-foot boa constrictor will do it to you. The snake handler took advantage of the situation and gave her a shot of anti-venom that made her woozy, sweaty and horny. Then he brought her to the porn shoot and offered her up in exchange for him not being able to deliver the film's namesake. When she came to, she was doing two guys on a set that looked like a barn.

And, for some reason—probably the anti-venom—she got off on it. And she got paid. Five hundred for the first guy. Three hundred for the second. Eight hundred for essentially one hour's work. She never earned that in the legitimate theatre. And that's how she wound up fucking for the camera.

When her Dad found out it was his own little girl he was jerking off to -apparently, 'The Boner Constrictor' was his favorite - he cut her out of the will and wiped her name and face from his memory. Then in complete and utter shame, he shot both himself and his wife and bequeathed his entire estate to Jerry Falwell's Ministry. He left his little girl alone in the world thinking she caused it all. But that's not the saddest thing. The saddest thing is that her name is really Starr. Two 'r's.

Harry and I sat in my usual booth. He wasn't appreciating Starr's talents as she slide, upside down, legs in a vice grip around the pole, and then scissored them open and twisted them behind her ears and grabbed the crotch of her thong by her teeth and pulled it aside for all the world to see. It was a neat trick. One that would've ruined the concentration of a Russian chess champion on Ritalin.

But Harry wasn't engaged. He was still off with Jadonne, pouring Cristal he couldn't pay for with a woman he could never really have.

I needed him here. I ordered a round. Beer and tequila. Switch Harry's high. Bring it home. Get his head out of the Jacuzzi and into the trailer park.

"Here's the key. Something that turns over in my mind and takes me all kinds of places," I told him as I washed down the tequila and waited for him to follow, "He was wearing Depends."

"Old folks diapers? He was just forty." Harry said as he struggled through the pure alcohol vapor of the tequila.

"If it was a suicide, then he knew that when you die, you leak, and he would prepare for that," I said.

"Not a lot of dignity in dying, is there?" Harry said as he watched Starr sit at the edge of the stage with her legs at six o'clock and right at that moment, looking deep into her snatch like it was an old time radio and he was listening to Roosevelt discuss the Pacific Theatre, he was thinking there wasn't much dignity in living neither.

"But if it was drugs and alcohol and accidental, why would he put a diaper on? He wouldn't be thinking straight, right?" I said.

"If he killed himself, then he's out of the policy for sure. And that's that!" Harry said, brighter now that Starr was kind of fancying him and that was mostly because he was with me. The best thing you can be at a strip club is a cop, because no one wants any trouble and the ladies cross the line just to stay out of trouble. Then I laid it on him, "But he had a head injury. A bad one."

Harry finished his tequila and grabbed his beer, "You telling me there was some kind of hanky panky?"

"Why would the murderer wrap him in a diaper?" I asked.

"Maybe he was getting ready to kill himself and got murdered before he had the chance. Wow. That changes things."

"Back door was open," I told him, "And there was sand on the kitchen floor. Not from Lou or the other one. Different shoes. And they might be stupid and dead, but they wouldn't be sloppy."

Jadonne had a pretty tight alibi for that night. She was shooting a photo spread for the upcoming Christmas party invitations. J.P. liked her to dress up like an elf. She had the photos to prove it. She made a fine elf.

"The coroner could tell you the cause of death, goddamnit! I'm not buying the whole deal. He was drunk and he died. Period!" Harry was getting a little fired up. He could see his payday going out the window at the same time he watched Starr sliver up the pole.

"Why do women do this, Tommy? Why do they exhibit themselves in public like this?"

"Because, Harry. Men are a mystery to women. They can't do what we do."

"Which is what, exactly?"

"They can't sit elbow to elbow with a complete stranger at a bar watching a ball game on TV and strike up a conversation like they knew each other for fifty years. They can't pee standing up. It's revenge really. That shit angers them. They show us all they have because they know if we touch it without their permission we go to jail and then there's one less of us to make them angry. They're just trying to drive us mad."

"Is that it?" he asked.

"And the money's good."

I needed him back on my page. I'd done enough philosophizing for the evening.

"I might agree about the suicide. Or an accidental death from overdose, if everyone around him didn't have a reason to want him gone," I told him, "And prying the truth out of the coroner is going to be hard. Impossible for me. But easier for you. Me, they'll slap on the wrist for getting too close. You, they have to deal with."

"I need more time," he said, looking into Starr's nether regions. He was scheming now. He would have to call Dick Asher and get some money wired. He wanted another day with Jadonne. Just one more. One more minute in the presence of her beauty. "The boss isn't going to like this."

I reminded him the boss wasn't going to like paying out that policy. That's when Harry's mood went morose. "I think she's cheating on me, Tommy," he said as he went into that state where the Cristal and beer and tequila mix together to cause a perfect storm of regret and suspicion. "I've known about it for awhile. I trusted her. Now I don't know what to do."

"Marsha?" I asked like I didn't know and wanted to be dragged into this gently.

He went on to tell me about his suspicions. About how she was always on the road with Dick. How they went to client lunches at least twice a week but there were never any receipts and they always came back hungry. How whenever he wanted to make love she wasn't in the mood. How they hadn't done it in four months.

"Original love," he said.

"It's a killer," I said. Then I told him he needed to find out for sure. I told him I could arrange that. He asked me how and I told him not to ask, but that in less than thirty-six hours he could know for sure. But he shook his head. He didn't want to know. He couldn't handle the truth.

I pushed a shot of tequila Harry's way, which he pushed back at me. He was starting to get so melancholy I thought he was melting into his elbows.

"C'mon, Harry. I don't like to drink alone," and I raised my glass in a toast, *"Salud, amor y pesetas para disfrutalas!"*

"What does that mean?" he asked.

"Health. Love. Money. They say it all the time in Cabo."

And we drank.

And Starr winked at Harry.

And I winked at Starr.

18. HARRY CORVAIR, AMAZON SLAYER.

When Harry awoke the next morning in his deluxe penthouse suite at the Four Seasons, he was covered in hair. His room was torn apart like the Homeland Security just found out he'd rented 'Lawrence of Arabia' at Blockbuster. The Honor Bar had been dishonored. Little liquor bottles were scattered all over the carpet like there might have been a midget's bachelor party the night before. The sheets were in small twisted balls. Candy wrappers stuck to the mattress.

Altoids were all over the place and Harry even had to pluck one out of his ass.

And he was covered in hair.

Starr emerged from the bathroom in nothing but a towel, showered and fresh, drying her hair, which was now very short, almost hardly there. Without her makeup and in the light, she looked like a woman who might have been attacked by a boa constrictor while peeing. Which as you know, she was. The hair loss was due to the anti-venom, which she kept taking way too long after the first episode because it gave her a tongue that was longer and more skilled than Gene Simmons. It's not that she was bad looking, but she was hard and sad. Without makeup on, her eyes were dull and her lips were bent in a permanent frown. Like a snake, come to think of it.

There is not doubt in my mind Harry was frightened and he probably pulled one of the balled up sheets over him and tried to put the puzzle of the night before together as Starr dropped her towel and slid on a pair of baggy jeans and a tight t-shirt and arranged her majestic breasts just so and greeted him, "Hey lover, how you feeling?" then started plucking the hair off of Harry and sticking it to certain areas of her scalp and voila, she had long hair again.

Harry looked down to his southern parts and saw he was naked. His dick didn't look like his dick. It looked like he had rented it out for the night to someone who returned it with two flat tires and an empty tank.

Starr pulled a wallet out of his pants and took a not-so-small amount of his hard earned and way over his per diem cash, "For a cab, OK?" Harry nodded and Starr smiled, stuffed the cash in her pocket and started to moisturize. Harry smashed his face into the mattress and right into a Reeses Peanut Butter Cup.

Then the phone rang. It was Marsha. She was pissed.

The phone felt like it weighed thirty pounds and was made of guilt. She screamed at him and cursed him and made him feel like a slim bag, which wasn't hard right about now.

And don't you know that the first thing Harry said to her was something along the lines of, 'Hey Cupcake,' which is about as guilty a greeting you can give to a woman you have not talked to in 48 hours, half of which was spent with a stripper with extensions. When your woman is mad at you, don't call her a pastry.

She fired back with the requisite 'Don't Cupcake Me' and Harry did his best to explain that he was on the case, that it was complicated, and that he wasn't getting the answers he wanted, but that he was working with one of Malibu's finest, and they were getting closer.

She told him that Dick was thinking of hiring somebody else to do the job and that it probably wouldn't be too hard to find somebody better than Harry. Low blow.

Dick was always threatening to fire Harry. He would've appreciated a bit if Marsha would've stuck up for him. But she wasn't the sticking up kind of gal. She called them as she saw them, and if you sucked at what you did, it didn't matter how much she loved you.

"This is my case. My bonus! Everything's riding on it. You and me. The house. Our dreams! Cabo! The restaurant!"

"You bet it is," she said. "And you better not screw it up!"

The phone went dead. Harry slumped against the headboard of the King Cal bed and looked to Starr, moisturizing in a mirror. She saw him looking sad and told him that he was great last night. The best she ever had. That any woman would be lucky to have a man like him, and that he was so big he hurt her, and that she must've come five times, and that she hadn't had it so good since she spent the night with Rick Knox. She said he reminded her of a wild Mustang the way he snorted from his nose when he came. She called him Lover and Stud and Sex Muffin.

And all of a sudden the room didn't look so bad. It looked like a battlefield where Harry triumphed in an epic sexual encounter with a Queen of the Amazons and he won, dammit. He'd won.

When she left, she left a matchbook from Uncle Snatches with her number on the back. Tribute. The spoils of war. He had been as good as Rick Knox.

When she left, she took all the energy of the moment with her. Her lies were shallow and temporary. As long as she was there, she could fuel them. The moment she left, they just disappeared into the carpet, ready to get vacuumed up by the cleaning crew.

And Harry had no memory of fucking her. He remembered stumbling in the hallway. He remembered not being able to find the key card to his room. He remembered Starr giving him a private show. But that was all he remembered.

Harry got up and took a look at himself in the mirror. He looked bad. He looked small, pale, doughy and insignificant. He looked at his dick, hanging there, like a spaghetti noodle you throw to the ceiling to see if it's cooked. Then, he heard a knock at the door.

It was Jadonne. "Harry, are you in there?"

Harry went into hyper speed to clean up his little battlefield. He tore up Starr's tribute, flushed it, and threw the sheets and towels in the closet. Grabbed up the candy wrappers and liquor bottles and threw them in a drawer.

"Harry! Open up," Jadonne pleaded.

"Be right there!" he answered. He was all exposed nerves now. In one night, he felt like he'd cheated on two women. And in a way, he had.

He threw on a bathrobe and opened the door.

Jadonne wore a tight fitting cream-colored doe skinned top with little perforations in it that let the walnut color of her nipples show through. She had on formfitting riding pants made of satin and knee high boots made of defenseless baby animals. Her hair was pulled back, revealing the perfection of her heart shaped face. A pair of black sunglasses shielded her eyes and set off her ruby red lips perfectly.

Starr was now a distant memory. Jadonne had etch-a-sketched her out of Harry's brain.

She slinked past him, shoulders hunched over and walked to the open window and just stared out. It wasn't hard for Harry to see she was upset.

"What is it? What's the matter," he asked.

She pulled off her sunglasses, and revealed an oh-so-tiny shiner below her eye. A tear tumbled out of it and slid down her cheek. Then she put the glasses back on. Show over.

"Jesus! What the hell happened?"

"Nothing," she answered. He pleaded with her to tell him, got her some tissue to dab her eye, and a bottle of water out of the honor bar to soothe her.

"No one can help me, Harry," she said about as forlornly as that line could be said. Harry wasn't going to give up. He was the amazon slayer, after all.

"Let me try," he said.

Jadonne told him it was Lou. She told him that Lou was watching her for the company. That the company was looking to get her out of the house, throw her onto the street, and she really didn't have any protection. They wanted to know if she was cheating, as then they could embarrass her, claim she was an adulteress, had no right to nothing and had sullied the memory of J.P. Buffet. Lou told them about their date. He told them that more happened than did. They got into a fight. She threw an ashtray at him, and he hit her. The video cameras saw her throw an ashtray. They didn't see Lou hit her. Harry asked her if she called the police.

"Harry, it's Malibu. Women get beat up all the time. Most of them don't mind, as long as they can recover with jewelry." That didn't register one bit with him, so he dialed me up to see just how far warped common sense law enforcement had gotten out here in Egypt by the Sea.

"Tommy will know what to do. Lou can't get away with this," he said, holding the phone in his hand. Jadonne sat on the edge of the bed, covered her face in her hands and said, "I don't trust your cop. I don't like how he looks at me. And I think he's working for them too." She was getting suspicious of her own shadow. I don't blame her. They were coming down hard on her now. She was a money threat, and the wives knew things about J.P. that could destroy the business. So it wasn't above them to want to figure out a way to make her go away. Permanently.

Harry excused himself and put down the phone. He needed to listen first. Get it all. Write it down. This was good. This was rich. This wasn't going to help him with the policy, but it was exciting. And it didn't take much more than sixty-two channels and an NFL package to excite Harry.

She told him about the stories J.P. had told her. About the financial shenanigans and about how the pyramid was starting to collapse. And how as it's a multi-level marketing organization, if there were too many at the top making too much, then it ruined it for those just coming in. She told him how two of the top distributors died real mysteriously in the past two years, making room for a couple of newbies.

Harry was starting to feel like he was getting in over his head. But he was in over his head as soon as he got off the plane at LAX, so this was déjà vu.

"They flatten the pyramid. Get rid of the big earners, and the money drifts down. Keeps it going longer. And now, J.P. is gone . . . ." and with that she let loose some more tears. Harry handed her some tissues.

She took his hand, and held it while she dabbed her eye under her glasses, rubbing her thumb over his knuckles as she blotted out the fear and sadness. It was a rhythmic rubbing, stroking, prying between his fingers, riding to the nail, circling, then sliding back down to the knuckle. He was way way over his head.

"Stay with me, Harry. I'm all alone. I need a man. A man like you to make me feel safe," she told him, "Let's go for a drive. Be with people. It's safe around people. You can get a haircut."

Harry had no idea where the idea of a haircut played into this, but he thought that maybe in her sadness, she was just word associating. But he had to ask, "A haircut?" She blew her nose and sniffled, "It's just that you'd look better with some styling."

Indeed he would. A little styling never hurt anybody. Harry was looking way too small, pale, doughy and insignificant right now. It was time to get some styling. It was time to look significant. She could mold him whatever way she wanted. He would be putty in her hands. If she wanted him to get his hair cut like Phil Spector, he'd do it. She could dress him in a clown suit, give him a foam arrow and stand him on a corner of Ventura Boulevard with a pair of her thong bikini's in his pocket and he'd sell a hundred condo's. After all, he was as much a pleasure maker as Rick Knox.

"Was there a woman here last night?" she asked, looking around the room that looked like it was cleaned in record time. "It smells like a skanky woman in here."

Harry panicked. He started moving random items around, stacking newspapers and magazines, straightening out the television remote to line up perfectly with the edge of a lamp.

"A haircut! Yes! I think I'd like a haircut. Freshen up a bit. Let's go, shall we?" and he ran into the bathroom with his pants and shirt and in two minutes flat was ready to go, the iWire safely inside his pants pocket, and he didn't even know it.

The Valet pulled the Ferrari up and opened the door for Jadonne.

"Harry, you drive," she said. "I'm too upset." Harry froze up. This was way too much car for a pale and insignificant man like Harry. You know he was wrestling with the whole idea because the next thing she did was coo, "C'mon. It'll be fun. You'll love it. I'll teach you. I want to watch you drive."

Fun. Love. Teach. Watch. The words swirled in Harry's brain, reducing his choices to zero.

19. DRIVING MISS JADONNE.

More on the Ferrari.

As I said, there was no more beautiful and no less practical car. Any model. Any year. They had evolved as a car about as much as Italy had as a society. Sleeker, but no less argumentative, temperamental, or impulsive. And fully confident that no matter what they said or invented or did, it was fucking brilliant.

The engine sat right behind you. It's pipes and pistons rattled through the seats like a massage chair switched high on all functions: Swedish, Thai, and deep tissue. This one got eight miles to the gallon, city; thirteen, highway; High test. It needed tune-ups and filters and oil changes every three months. It needed brakes and clutch and tires every six. It needed more than gas and oil and antifreeze to run. It needed money. It was the most beautiful woman you ever had demanding you fuck her harder, deeper, faster, weirder and making you buy the finest jewelry and clothes for her because you knew you could never satisfy her in the sack like she wanted.

And right now, Harry was the worst lay it ever had.

He jerked it down the tree-lined boulevard of Mediterranean condos, backing up traffic and getting nasty stares by people incredulous that somebody like Harry would be allowed to drive a car like that in a democracy.

He struggled with the clutch, popped the gears, fumbled with the Ferrari's G-Spot, and still got noticed by several women walking dogs the size of kittens and a couple of cops wondering whether Harry was drunk or just bought the car.

Jadonne had Harry turn off the highly competitive boulevards and into the Hollywood Hills. "Ease it in, Harry," she told him as she put her hand on his knee, offering an instant jolt of goosepimples up his leg and to his balls. "Feel the clutch. It's a living thing. Work it softly. There's no traffic on this road. We're all alone. Press it down to the floor, let it up soft and slow and let the balls of your feet press the accelerator. Pretend your feet are hands; your toes are fingers. Clutch and gas, together. Let it drive you. Fool it into thinking it has control."

Harry followed what she said, following the noises of the engine, hearing it go quiet, moaning contented, then breathing heavier, to a full moan, and the vibrations went soft and soothing, and the car seemed to turn to butter, oozing them up the road.

"See what I mean. Don't get in its way. It does what it wants. It wants you to help it along, is all. Because, after all, you have the key."

Harry smiled. "Yes, I think I do" he said.

And Jadonne patted him on the knee. "Pull over there. I'll take it from here," she said. "I like this road. I want to go fast."

Jadonne knew how to drive that car. Different from Lou. When Lou drove it, Harry's teeth chattered. When Jadonne drove, everything was soft and smooth and gummy.

She took him on the Grand Tour. Up the ribbon of Mulholland Drive with its vistas and oversized mansions. The wealth of nature and the ego of man battling high above Los Angeles in a contest of wills.

He saw old and new money homes, huge lawns with no one on them, big shiny cars with no one in them, and sprinklers misting rainbows twenty feet into the air with no one to turn them off.

And then he saw, galloping down the middle of Mulholland Drive, in the middle of one of the biggest cities in the world, a five point buck. Huge. A trophy deer for sure, as big as any he'd seen in Wisconsin—coming right at them. Oblivious to the Ferrari heading toward it. It was used to the snarling grills of the Escapades and Tundras so much so that the flash of chrome was deer shorthand for danger. But to that deer, the low slung Ferrari looked like the road was undulating, and it couldn't process that, being a deer and all who, after all, are creatures with bones growing out of their heads.

"Jesus, where did that come from," Harry asked as Jadonne kept right at it, foot on the accelerator and that deer came at the Ferrari, with a look in its eyes that was dumber than shit, not understanding the situation at hand.

"Jadonne, slow down." Harry yelled, but she kept it steady.

And the deer kept it steady in a full lumbering gallop.

"JADONNE!" Harry screamed.

She slammed on the brakes just as the deer reached the car, its front legs cut out from underneath it, like a clean ankle tackle on the open field that hurts no one but stops the play. It crashed right onto the hood, torso first, full deer jaw landing on the sheet metal with its lips practically kissing the front windshield. It was alive, unhurt, but shocked for sure. It had no idea why the road hit it. And it stayed there, completely out of balance and unable to pull its legs together to lift it off.

Harry turned to Jadonne to see what the hell she might be thinking. There was no emotion in her face. Stone cold she was, with the deer lying prone on the hood of her temperamental Italian Sports car, drool pouring out of its mouth and a bubble of bloody snot in its nostril.

For a moment, Harry's world was still. This was a new side to a woman he had put high up on a pedestal of desire and physical perfection. It was like pulling back the curtain on the Wizard and seeing he was flesh and blood. That's how much she fell from the pedestal. That's how much he was Dorothy in this adventure.

But we are slow to blame beautiful women and quicker to forgive them.

The deer struggled off the hood, righted itself and galloped away like nothing happened. "Why?" Harry asked her. It was a simple enough question. He just wanted to know whether running over deer was a local pastime during the weeks they were low on gossip.

"It has to know it can't run here like that," she explained. "If you go around them, they think that's the way it is. It's not, and some movie producer asshole in a Hummer will take it as a badge of honor to kill that thing and hang its head in his entertainment room as a trophy that he'll say he bagged with a bow and arrow and a tube of Chapstick. And that asshole, because of that story, will get the backing to make another motherfucking lousy Rick Knox movie. I spared that deer. I spared us all."

Harry looked back through the tiny slit of Ferrari back window and saw the gray tail of the deer descend off the hill and back into the semi-wild and he saw the method to her wonderfully benevolent madness.

"Are you having fun, Harry?" she asked him, getting his eyes back to her.

Harry was happier than he thought he ever had a right to be. "Are you hungry Harry?' she asked.

"I am that Jadonne."

"I like it when you say my name." she said as she shifted into gear and steered the Ferrari on the asphalt ribbon of Mulholland Drive as the rust smog brown air of the San Fernando Valley spread out beneath them, and Harry started building another pedestal of worship for her to place her exquisite and mythological ass on.

19. RICK KNOX IN "THE ASSHOLE KNOX!"

Rick Knox's was getting a little long in the tooth to be jumping off of the back of a ten wheeler onto the hood of a speeding Mustang that sailed off a bridge and crashed into the ocean just as he leaped onto the deck of a speeding yacht while snagging its flag from the mast and tumbling into a Jacuzzi filled with a topless woman whose tits he'd cover up with the flag to get a PG-13 rating while chugging a bottle of rum and puffing on a fresh lit cigar.

He'd done the exact same stunt seven times now. Only the machinery and location changed. And as his last two movies did less than the first two, Rick couldn't command the outrageous salaries anymore. Nor could he act like such a jerk on the set. He used to demand sex from script girls and make up girls and extras and the caterer. And they all complied. Before they did, they'd have to sign a legal document stating that they would tell no one about him needing to use a penis pump to get it up. Due to his steroid use in his body building days, he couldn't use Viagra, so he had to bone it up the old-fashioned way.

But you couldn't tell he was on the downside of his career by the looks of the billboard announcing his new movie. It blighted the landscape of Topanga Canyon worse than a combination laundermat, abortion clinic and bowling alley.

There was Rick, fifty feet high, torn T-shirt, muscles rippling, sawed off shotgun over his shoulder, gold bar in hand, tattooed and sweating, with a woman in a thong bikini hanging on his leg like a kid from Darfur does to a loaf of bread while Fort Knox burned in the background.

Above the whole calamity was a headline set in burn in hell Helvetica Bold: RICK KNOX BUSTS FORT KNOX IN "HARD KNOX!"

Jadonne passed this billboard plenty of times. This was her favorite road when she wanted to get away and take the Italian out for the afternoon. And you just know it must have kicked her ass, her ex up there thirty feet tall with a Playmate at his knee that she knew he'd fucked.

Harry admired the artwork, then turned to Jadonne and said, "Must be hard on you. Seeing his image everywhere."

"The man who beat you at least once a day? I'll say. I gotta get out of this town," she said as she let that last thought linger. Harry lingered on the beating part. He couldn't imagine a man wanting to beat Jadonne. It would be like squashing flowers or stomping on kittens. So wrong.

"Where would you go?" Harry asked.

"I don't know. Maybe home to Michigan. Or Mexico. Cabo. Somewhere like that. A place on the beach, a little beer and lobster restaurant, plastic chairs, no TV, fisherman's nets everywhere and a souvenir T-shirt I would design that would make the place a funky legend. I'd serve scones. The best on the planet. Places like that, Harry, they only need one specialty. Lobsters the same. Beer is beer. But the scones. They would be all mine."

"I love scones," he said.

They were both smiling now. She was smelling her scones. He was eating her scones. People would come down to Cabo from all over the globe just for her scones.

Harry's eyes watered up. He felt warm all over. Like when his mother tucked him in after heating his pajamas on the radiator.

He was making scones in his brain. He was making scones with her. He was serving warm scones in plastic baskets. He was pouring the beers. He was wearing a pair of board shorts and a shirt of her design and the place was crowded to the gills. Jadonne tended bar. She'd wink at him and let everybody there know that Harry was her man and that he made her happy.

He had the dopiest grin on his face and was starting to lean into her like she was pulling him to her with the magnet of love.

"What?" she asked as she thought his leaning meant he wanted to tell her something special.

"Nothing. Just nothing," he answered as he sat back up straight as she turned the Ferrari into a gravel parking lot of *The Inn of the Nihilist*, a hippy, woodsy, arts and craftsy café with a deck overlooking a small picturesque waterfall and a lactose intolerant and peanut allergy free menu that vegans loved but a rabbit wouldn't touch.

They wandered inside. It was empty. The air was cooling down. Jadonne took a seat at a table by the somewhat dilapidated railing of the outdoor deck. Harry picked up the menu and scanned the prices. "No Cristal," he told her. She giggled at that. They ordered from the menu, which to Harry's amusement, was made out of birch bark.

Harry ordered a meat loaf made out of pinto beans, mushrooms and switch grass. It came in the shape and color of a meatloaf but that's where the resemblance ended. It tasted like a newborn's first poop smells. He had a bite than filled himself up with pita bread made from hearts of palm and bee pollen.

But it didn't matter. Because his appetite was filled just by watching Jadonne talk. She munching on a gluten free breadstick that were baked in a compost heap oven. She twirled them in her mouth, moistened them, made them soft. Harry tried to remember if he ever saw her eat anything else and he couldn't. She just drank and sucked on breadsticks. And that was fine by Harry.

She filled him in on her life. How she got here and how come after two lucrative divorces, she had no money.

"I lent my Dad money for a doughnut franchise and then that damned no carb craze happened," she told as she swirled the breadstick in her mouth, "Have you ever tasted a no carb doughnut?"

Harry struggled with the meatloaf mash and tried to talk through a mouth full of whatever. "That didn't catch on too well in Wisconsin. We're the cheese state, so that means there's a lot of support for crackers."

Jadonne kept weaving a trail of alimony tears, and Harry was all too happy to let her go on. Her voice was music to him. The perfect pitch, pronunciation and a slight innocent lilt at the end of her thoughts, which made her more childlike, more a victim of this big bad world.

She talked about bad investments and lawsuits from those who were burned by her toasters or cut by her patented knives. What she didn't tell him was just how expensive it is to keep an A-lister's engine steam-cleaned. There was hair, nails, loofah scrubs, thousand dollar tubes and jars of magical and useless skin creams, boob jobs, Botox and collagen injections, face peels, spray on tans, private trainers, spiritual beauty advisors. Hell, some of these specimens even had their assholes waxed.

The newest rage, even with the men, was to take off all the pubic hair. Run it bald. Shave it smooth twice a week. Not me. I like a little pubic hair, on myself and others. It reminds me that we came from apes, not bowling balls.

But all this fuss could run up to thirty, maybe forty grand a month. Not that Jadonne did all of that, she didn't need to. Like I said, she was a natural beauty. And that drove other women insane. Which was why Jadonne had no girlfriends to speak of. She wasn't what they call a gal's gal. She was more a man's gal. A married man's gal. And that drove women even crazier. Women, when they first meet each other, immediately take visual inventory of the other women's strengths and weaknesses. It's what they do to compete. They'll look at their feet and if they're wearing shoes they don't envy, they go into the freezer as a competitive threat. Same with clothes, hair, makeup, and jewelry. If the other woman isn't wearing anything they want, they can't have anything their man wants either. That's where most women get it wrong. A man in an unhappy relationship always wants strange. Jadonne, with barely any makeup on, wearing sandals that looked like she was barefoot, with a hint of jewelry—always silver—and no real money to her name, and a face that was completely devoid of any Aryan DNA, and real but cupcake sized breasts, was cat nip to every man she met. It never failed, at some Malibu function to save the desert Pupfish, that she'd wind up with ten scraps of paper in the palm of her hand with the phone numbers of the massively married who promised, to a man, to make her his mistress or fifth wife.

"Pretty soon, all the alimony money was gone. Poof? But I had a family to take care of. You take care of blood," she told him through the moistened tip of a breadstick.

She strung together a series of thoughts that segued one to the other in ways that felt like she was carrying him along on her perfect back through a world of her own invention.

"You did the right thing," Harry said, even though he wasn't sure what that was. She poured herself another glass of elderberry wine and went for Harry's but he put his hand over his glass to stop her. "No, I had enough last night," he said. She pleaded, "Please Harry, I don't like to drink alone." He accepted and she poured.

"Shit!" she said as she looked over Harry's shoulder to the sound of a Harley farting into the parking lot.

It was Rick Knox.

He walked in with a very young, nubile, crystalline blue-eyed, blond, former Miss Iceland. She wore short shorts that displayed a wide gap where her thighs met and fat, fluffy Ugg boots that seemed to anchor her to the ground and prevent her energetically upturned breasts from lifting her a foot off the pavement. She was sexy. She was young. She was innocent and wide eyed as people who live on Arctic islands are. She was just like Rick Knox liked them.

Harry couldn't get over how big Rick Knox's head was. It reminded him of the bobble heads at Milwaukee Braves Stadium souvenir shop. This is true of all movie stars. They all have really big heads. Big craniums. Small shoulders. I don't know if they start out with big heads and get famous or get famous and get bigger heads. I'm amazed they don't get tired carrying their heads around all day. Several scientists at UCLA postulate that their heads are the same size as ours, but because we only know them from close-up shots on the big screen, we actually perceive their heads to be bigger than they are. And that goes double for TV stars.

Big headed Rick Knox oozed clichéd movie star. He wore leather pants and a tight t-shirt and chunky boots that gave him three more inches of height. Then there was the walk. The saunter. John Wayne had to be taught how to walk the way he did. Knox had plenty of consultants to help him learn his signature stride; a wide stance, faux bowlegged, walking on the sides of his feet deal that made it look like he couldn't chase you when in fact he could. He thought it looked tough, but with his big head and features that jutted monkeylike from his face from too many years of steroids, he pretty much looked like an orangutan.

Knox spotted Jadonne right away, smiled a big leathery smile and put his walk into overdrive, but not before telling his Viking princess to stand up straight and stick her boobs out more, which she gladly did and without complaint, being from a small island and all.

"Ja ja ja! More de boops," she said. She wasn't stupid, as of the three hundred thousand people who inhabit Iceland, two hundred ninety are PhD's, so even if she didn't have a degree, she was smart by osmosis. Knox stopped right at Jadonne's table and leaned his crotch against it.

"Jadonne La Rochelle Ms. J.P. Buffet and the former Ms. Rick Knox," he shouted so that his words would echo in the little canyon. He leaned over to Jadonne and tried to plant one on her lips but she turned away in the nick of time and all he got was cheek. "That's cold, sugar," he said. Jadonne eyed the Viking princess up and down. She couldn't help being a little jealous. This was the next generation. And they were being manufactured with even fewer flaws than hers.

"You baby-sitting, Rick?"

"You know I like them young. Like you used to be," he said. Then he looked over to Harry, who was about as wide-eyed in star worship as he could be and said, "Who's this? You doing your taxes?"

Harry got up and extended his hand. He was about to shake hands with a true blue movie star. Never mind that Rick was on the downside of his career and looking at a future in reality programming in less than a year. In fact, he was currently considering a deal right now. It was called "Bitch Beach," and had him living in a house on the water with one of the Olsen twins, a fashion model that kept getting arrested for hitting airport security guards, Paul McCartney's one legged ex and the guy who invented the Dyson vacuum cleaner. It looked promising.

"I'm Harry Corvair," he said, almost completely forgetting the story Jadonne had told him about the abuse at Knox's mixed martial arts hands.

Knox just looked at Harry's extended hand like he was giving him a Mackerel. "That's up to you," he said and then turned his attention back to Jadonne. "Heard about J.P. That's good for you, right? Money in the bank."

All Harry could do was pull his shamed hand back, hide it in his pocket and sit back down.

"It's too bad you don't get more roles playing assholes. You wouldn't have to read the script," she fired back, pissed off that her day being threatened by her checkered past and bad man decisions.

The air was thick tension and they all felt it. Except for the Viking princess, who just stood there looking around at the surroundings, mumbling something in Icelandic about the foliage because back at the University of Iceland, she studied botany.

"Ist mostly eucalyptus, yes?" she asked no one in particular. "Ist olt, zees trees."

It was then that Harry decided to become Jadonne's Dudley Dooright. He stood up and gathered the heft of his full five foot ten inches of height and surprised himself as he stood a good inch taller than Knox.

"Good day, Mr. Knox," he said in the best dismissive tone he could muster. But movie stars don't ever hear anything dismissive, except from critics. And Rick had already put three of them in a hospital. It got so bad that reviewers refused to review his movies. Which was a great business move on Rick's part. The studios were always willing to settle with a journalist for a hundred grand and increase the journalists access to other, less violent stars, with perks that included trips to Cannes, comp rooms, bar tabs and the best looking hookers in the world.

"You're fucking kidding me! Right, Mr. Peepers?" Rick fired back. It was so out of his comprehension that this little man—who was an inch taller than him but had no stature in the land of make believe—would possibly challenge him.

He was, after all, Rick Knox. Action hero extraordinaire and winner of the MTV award for best fight sequence two years running. He had his own action figure. His own energy drink, and was about to launch his own after-shave, *Musculare,* pronounced with a mouthful-of-marbles French accent. Harry gathered himself up even more and went nose to nose with Knox, "No sir, I am not." Jadonne yanked at his sleeve and cooed, "Harry it's OK."

"No. It's not, Jadonne," he said, as he turned right back to Knox. And you know he was scared out of his ass but he stared Knox down and somehow, he tapped into the subconscious part of his brain that stored all the useless information gleaned from late night viewings of CNN, ESPN and TMZ. There have been mornings when I wake up and wonder whether the Queen of England was playing for the Lakers.

"Ist alzo many types of succulents, yes? For da fires? Yes?" Miss Iceland said, still amazed at the Topanga native plants.

"I know you're a big movie star but what's really important is how fleeting that can be, especially with you running around screwing minors," Harry told Knox. Then he asked the Viking princess if she was under eighteen.

"Yes, but I move past two grades, yes? Because I wass goot on test!"

The truth of the matter was that the government of Iceland wanted her so desperately to represent the country in the Miss Universe Pageant that they were forever skipping her ahead and changing her birth certificate so she'd list eighteen. And to say she was mature for her age is an understatement. In that, she had a lot in common with Jadonne. "I am two days from birthday!' she boasted.

Harry trudged on.

"I mean, look at Fatty Arbuckle. He was as big a star as you get—bigger than you, in fact. And he didn't even screw that girl! She was just crazy and looking for an easy mark. So one orgy and a coke bottle later and he was out of the business. Wound up directing short films under the name Will B. Good. So what I'm saying is that you have to be careful about who you piss off. What you do to people that's bad can be used against you. I mean, really Rick, Pepperdine isn't far from here. There are plenty of nice college girls, legal age, that would drop their studies for a night out with Rick

173

Knox. We can drop Bambi here off at Gymboree. So. What do you say? Do we have a plan?"

Harry had no idea what he just said. It just came out. He was hung over, tired, out of sorts and away from home. He was standing up to defend the honor of The Most Beautiful Woman in the World against his former favorite action hero, and so the words just tumbled out.

Jadonne covered her forehead. She knew that Rick wasn't going to let this go. Rick was not good at suffering indignities. Rick was not to be insulted and now as much as Harry had defended Jadonne, Rick would have to impress the Viking princess. He leaned back on his right leg, lifted his left leg up at a perfect ninety-degree angle and launched it in a perfect arc towards Harry's face.

Twenty years of Kempo Karate gave him accurate feet. They were finely honed and disciplined weapons. He could kill a fly resting on a soufflé without making the soufflé fall and put the candles out on a birthday cake without disturbing the wax.

His foot stopped one inch away from Harry's nose and delivered the desired effect. Harry flinched so bad he fell backward, crashed through the rickety railing and tumbled head over heels into the stream below.

Knox grabbed Miss Iceland by the arm and did his signature monkey walk back to his Harley. Jadonne got up and threw her napkin at him. "You piece of shit!'

Knox looked over his shoulder. "Get as much as you can, Jadonne. Make sure it lasts this time. Cause the looks aren't. You're old school, baby," he said as Miss Iceland turned to Jadonne and said "Is very nice meet you," and then asked Rick who this "Freddy Carbunkle" was and he told her to shut up.

Harry was wet and covered in burrs. He'd rolled over a couple of cacti on the way down so he had some needles stuck in him, little tiny fuckers you couldn't see but you knew were there and would stay there for the next couple of days until his body pushed them out by itself.

This had been an interesting day so far for Harry. There had been the stripper, the ride in the Ferrari, the deer, the meatless meatloaf, and Rick Knox assaulting him. It was a series of cultural and tactile events that were sure to create their own mythology in Harry's head over time. He would regale his children with these stories in the years to come, except the stripper part.

Jadonne scampered down the hill, Guinevere running to save her Lancelot. Harry was still pretty much in awe of Rick Knox's skill at not smashing his nose into the back of his head. That man's shoe stopped less than the thickness of a credit card from his nose. And even though he could disrespect him for the harm Jadonne said he did unto her, the man had mean control over his body.

"We'll sue him for assault," she said as she plucked burrs from the zipper of his pants. "He developed that move so he wouldn't knock out his co-stars," she informed him, plucking away burrs and at the same time arousing him. "Or the movie critics who hated his movies. They couldn't get him for assault, cause they weren't touched."

"Don't know where I got that Fatty Arbuckle stuff," Harry said, still trying to make sense of the inciting incident that brought on Knox's phantom kick.

"Biography Channel. Two nights ago. Three in the morning. You probably fell asleep with the cable on. I do it all the time. Kind of gets your news and entertainment all blended together," she said, brushing and plucking and arousing away.

"Well, I guess I deserved it."

Jadonne grabbed him by the shirt collar and pulled him close to her, "No, you didn't Harry Corvair. You stood up for me. No one has ever stood up for me. *And* against Rick Knox. No one stands up to Rick Knox," then she planted a hard Perils of Pauline kiss on his lips. She was saved, and her kiss said her savior would have more than just burrs plucked from his zipper.

Harry was stunned. Jadonne's lips were on his, holding his entire body up. Then, like a man about to die whose who life flashes in front of him, a scolding, jealous and domineering Marsha appeared in Harry's head. He wanted her to go away, but he had too many years with her. She was a tattoo he could not remove. But Jadonne smelled good. Her lips were soft and sweet. She slowly slipped her tongue inside his mouth and she tasted like the cream filling of a Hostess Cupcake.

But, dammit! There was Marsha! She swirled in his head like the fucking Wicked Witch of the West flying outside the window of Dorothy's uprooted house. He pushed Jadonne away, and held her at a distance.

"Jesus, Jadonne. We can't do this. I'm on business. I have a girlfriend. It's not right. It's not ethical," he said as he stared into her round walnut eyes. "A girl can show a little gratitude, can't she Harry?"

And she said it like she meant it. She said it like he was a Saint Bernard that just rescued her from being buried in an avalanche. And if a Saint Bernard with a rum cask around its neck ever rescued you from an avalanche, you'd hug it right? You'd kiss it and scratch its belly and let it lick your face. Yes you would and that's for sure.

"Gratitude. OK. That's OK," he said as he went back to letting her kiss him.

And Marsha started to fade from his memory.

20. TELEVISION KILLED THE DIET PILL CZAR.

Doctors suck. They got you by the balls. It's the only job where sticking a finger up somebody's ass is all in a day's work. I don't like going to them. Money made doctors suck and as I said, once the zeros jump the decimal, it's time to break out the Chateau Asshole. My doctor was no different. But, right now, he was necessary.

His name was Hyman Spengele. His last name rhymed with Mengele.

I had my eye on him for about five years. He had an unofficial rap sheet of providing the children of Malibu with all kinds of drugs that always found their way to the floors of their BMWs we were busy peeling off lampposts. He was fond of prescribing every sort of upper and downer and keep-em-quiet kid drug on the market. It made life for their errant parents easier, and it was becoming fashionable to have a child afflicted with the inability to read the cover of Moby Dick in one sitting.

If one of these parents, who had nothing in their wealthier than wealthy lives that offered them any sort of turmoil, could get their kid into the affliction sweepstakes, then they would have something to talk about at a dinner party besides real estate and stocks and bigger and better kitchens.

I like to know my quarry. I like to look them in the eyes while they think they're getting away with something. Hyman thought I was a screenwriter. I said I was a script doctor. That made us both doctors. And we shared professional courtesies. I asked him cop questions that veered dangerously close to revealing him under the guise of research, and he got to stick his finger up my ass, which he knew was de rigeur for the run of the mill Hollywood screenwriter.

Today, I wanted to ask him about diet pills. I wanted to know how many a grown man would have to take to make the heart tap out, what mixture of chemicals would accelerate the process, and what he knew about J.P. Buffet.

Yup. Old Dr. Hyman Spengele was J.P.'s personal physician. And mine.

Hyman stuck a new Otoscope he was trying out in my ear. If Hyman liked it, he'd buy it, and then all the doctors of Malibu would have to have it and the company that made it would go BOOM with sales and PR and an uptick in their stock price and you'd have another million more millionaires.

"I'm not even here for a check up, Hyman." I told him as he probed the sanctum of my inner ear with his new toy.

I called him by his first name. Most people didn't dare. Calling the man who sticks his finger up your ass by his first name changes things.

"This is a new otoscope. It really lights up good. I can see your ear drum perfectly. Oh look, there's Phil Collins," he said. Hyman cracked the stupidest jokes, but his clientele in the entertainment business were always telling him he was funny and that he ought to get an agent. Usually the ones who told him that were agents. When he called them to follow up, their secretaries were instructed to tell him they were out of town. No wonder he wanted to poison their offspring.

"So what do you see, besides Phil Collins," I asked.

"Ginger Baker," he answered. I gave him a look that said it was pretty clear I thought he was thoroughly Catskill. At which point he stuck the otoscope down my throat.

"Ang da fug ong!' I garbled. "Daz foh da eah."

"It's an ear and mouth otoscope. One device, three orifices," he said.

He pulled it out and I wiped a tear from my eye. "What did you see?"

"A man with many secrets," he answered.

"You're not a very good doctor, are you?"

"I won't tell if you won't," he said as he wiped the formerly the sanitary tip of the otoscope and stuck it back into the little plastic bag it came in.

"Trying to leave a small carbon footprint," he said as he put the used tip back in the drawer.

I handed the good doctor a bunch of LifeThin Diet pill bottles. He checked out the labels, unimpressed. "When am I going to get a credit on one of your films?" he asked.

"Promise you. This one. It's a winner. I'm doing the story of a diet pill tycoon who dies of mysterious causes. And it might be the very pills he sells that killed him. We get German financing, I'll get you a producer credit."

"Sounds a lot like J.P. Buffet," he said.

"It does? Gosh, really?"

Hyman just shook his head. "Hey, I make a living sticking my finger up people's asses. Don't kid a kidder."

"So you gonna help me? Or do I go to Dr. Engleberg in Santa Monica?"

"Santa Monica? That's like going to India for a medical opinion."

"The names will be changed to protect the innocent. Now. Can this shit kill you?" I leaned in on his desk, crowding him a little. Most people, when they talk to their doctor, lean back. They don't invade the doctor's space. I'm all about invading spaces.

Hyman pulled out a small bottle of moisturizing cream and spread some of it around his eyes. He just had them done, and needed to keep the skin soft and loose so it would heal right and he wouldn't look like Burt Reynolds.

"Look, Tommy, it's the usual voodoo. Ephedrine. Ma Huang. Guarana. Green tea extract. Caffeine. Fiber. It's speed, with filler."

"Can it kill you?" I asked.

"Anything can kill you, Tommy, you do enough of it. Even fucking. With a bad heart, a latte is dangerous. But you'd have to take a lot. And that's what these yahoos do. They take the dose and because they're fifty pounds overweight and get tired just hitting the snooze button on their alarm clocks, with this shit, it's like a rebirth. So they take more. Double the feeling. And they don't lose weight, cause half of them find out they can drink twice as much and not get drunk. Now they're the life of the fucking party. So they like that. And they take some more."

I summed it up as, "If two work, what would ten do?"

"Exactly." he said. He reached into his desk drawer and pulled out a small syringe of Human Growth Hormone and stuck it into his thigh right through his pants. "The FDA can't control it cause it's not sold over the counter. LifeThin doesn't advertise cause if they did they'd have to get FDA approval. It can put all sorts of questionable things in there, and no one can challenge. I deal with that everyday. I got patients poisoning themselves with vitamins and elixirs. The shit is almost as dangerous as prescription drugs," he said as he showed me his little syringe, "Want some? It'll make your dick two inches longer, which would bring you out of negative numbers."

"So how come you work for them?" I asked. I knew I caught him off guard. He'd been consulting with them for two years now, offering bogus endorsements for about a million per annum and showing up at conventions giving rah rah speeches and sleeping with the neglected wives of distributors who were too drunk to care.

"You know how much malpractice insurance costs?" he said as he threw the little spent syringe on his desk and lit up a cigarette.

"Did it kill J.P.?"

"Tommy, J.P. was a walking laboratory. He was the kind of guy the Nazis would have loved to get ahold of to conduct their experiments. He was pretty much invincible and was a wealth of pharmaceutical information."

"Did it kill J.P.?" I wasn't going to let this go.

"Tommy, J.P. took everything a man could take. Prozac, Ritalin, Vicodin, Tramadol. He had a nicotine chip in his arteries to distribute nicotine every three hours and he still smoked. He took Lipitor for his arteries and Benicar for his blood pressure. He took Aricept for his memory. Adderall to make him smarter. Provigil to keep him awake. He took Mirapex for restless leg syndrome and Detrol for incontinence. I gave him shots of cortisone for his knees. Viagra for his dick. And he swallowed aspirin all day long. He did us all a great service. He was a fountain of information on how much we could medicate our patients before they keeled over."

"Then he keeled over."

"Television. You should check that out first. He kept watching the commercials for all that shit and he came in and wanted it. And I wasn't about to lose a patient like him. He was a gold mine. Paid cash. Television is what killed J.P. Buffet."

"I'm still gonna check out the diet pills," I told him.

"Want a B-12 shot, Tommy? Got a fresh batch in this morning. It's lovely."

I liked B-12 shots.

21. ALL HAIL CAESAR!

Jadonne brushed Harry off enough to make him presentable and deposited him in the chair of a salon in a Malibu mini mall. Harry sat in the salon chair getting his hair washed by the cutest little blond freakazoid he'd ever seen. She had six rings in her nose and her arms were tattooed denser than the ceiling of the Sistine Chapel. I'd give anything to still be alive when these pincushions turned eighty and their skin paint is drooping worse than a Dali painting. That will be an ugly world.

Suddenly, it wasn't the blond cutie's hands rolling around on Harry's head. It was Jadonne's. Harry was almost asleep, but her smell woke him up again. He looked up at her from his squint, slightly out of focus, and her blurred image was even better than the sharp one. He smiled a big goofy smile like a man that never had his hair professionally washed before by the most beautiful woman in the world whose breasts, braless and covered in nipple-revealing doe skin, dangled between his mouth and nose.

And Harry started to cry.

"What's the matter, Harry," she asked as she pulled away. "What's wrong?"

"I screwed up."

"We all screw up," she said. "Talk to me. Let it go."

"I cheated on Marsha. It wasn't my fault. Oh bullshit. Yes it was. I'm an adult. I have no one else to blame. I was out with Tommy. Detective Cox. We went to a topless place. Well, it was bottomless too. I feel terrible." Now he was just oozing tears and guilt, and frankly, I was a bit disappointed. No matter what happens, there has to be honor amongst the brothers when it comes telling the opposite sex about our cheating and fucking around. It's the sacred oath we take for the privilege of carrying around a cock.

"It's OK to go to a strip joint, Harry. All men do. I go all the time," she said, trying to comfort him.

"No, I think I slept with one of the strippers," he said. The words didn't make any sense coming out of his mouth. He could say that over and over and it would still feel strange. He had cheated on Marsha and that made him feel like shit, no matter what he suspected. And worse, he felt like he'd cheated on Jadonne, and the concept that he'd ever be in a position to cheat on Jadonne made him feel like a complete idiot for thinking he could. Then, the weaselness of him saying he "thought" he slept with Starr made him feel like an even bigger idiot. So now there were two reasons for Jadonne to dislike him: one, that he cheated on her, and two, that he didn't know if he had.

Jadonne pushed his head back into the sink and continued to wash his hair and massage his scalp, cooing to him like she was calming a baby, "It's OK Harry. Every man has to have a stripper. Just once in their lives. I've had several and I'm a better woman for it. C'mon, big guy, let's get you some style."

Harry was barely awake when the blond tattooed and pierced cutie finished cutting his hair. All the anxiety washed had out of him. When she spun him around in the chair, there was a stranger in the mirror staring back at him. He had cheekbones. He had organized eyebrows. He had gravitas. What Harry had was a Caesar haircut, just like J.P. Buffet, Welch and Gates. Caesar haircuts were the going style for early middle-aged men of Malibu. George Clooney made them popular and they reduced the gray for those that still had hair.

They didn't require any upkeep, so when you did decide to spend some time grooming, you could make them look damned nice. Jadonne ran her fingers through his hair. Actually, it's not enough hair to run your fingers through. You kind fluff it a bit, like a poodle. "That looks much better. My little Mid-Western emperor," she told him just as he leaped off the chair and ran in circles around the salon floor like his head was on fire.

His pants were buzzing. He forgot I'd given him a cell phone the night before to keep in touch. Harry didn't have a cell phone that worked out here. He was on a short cost leash with Asher. He had more of a walkie-talkie.

"What the hell! What the hell!" Harry screamed as he stared at his buzzing crotch. "What is it Harry? What's wrong?" Jadonne screamed.

"My pants are buzzing!"

"Wow," said the blond clipper cutie. Harry reached in his pants pocket, pulled out the phone and opened it. "Hello?"

I was at a Malibu Coffee shop. It was a beautiful sunset. I'd been listening to the action on the iWire and thought about now, Harry could use some support.

"Harry. Tommy Cox. You OK?"

"No. Yes. I don't know. It's been a long day. Is this your phone?"

"I gave it to you. Last night. Right after you cried in your beer about suspecting your girlfriend was cheating on you and a raft of other hugely boring shit and before you started feeding my singles to Starr's cootch. I kind of felt that you needed to stay in touch if you were going to fuck the stripper. Sometimes they roofie your cocktails and take you for what you have. In Brazil, they cut out your kidneys and sell them on the open market. Knew a cop down there, on vacation, got his kidney cut out by a fucking silly hot twin sister team. Woke up in the bathtub filled with ice and a note attached to his toe. Medics ran him to emergency where the doctors put his kidney back in this body. Apparently the girls sold it to the hospital just two hours before. Third world countries are pretty inventive."

"Ah, Jesus," Harry said as some glimmers of the night before found some undamaged brain cells to occupy. He went on to tell me, in a hushed tone, out of ear shot of Jadonne and the hair cutting pincushion, all about what had happened up to now, which matched nicely with what Starr told me when she came over later that same morning to practice tantric sex with me.

"Relax. Look, I'm going out of town on a case. I need you to go to the Mansion. I got an assignment for you. Your first official one." I knew 'official' would be exciting to him. Almost like he was getting to do an internship with the force. More stories for his unborn children.

I told him I wanted him to scout around for some LifeThin pills, the pink and purple ones. The good doctor had given me an idea. Those pills were the mantra of the company, the way they got you to lose weight. Skip all the other shit they sold, the shakes, the powders, that was fluff nothing. The exploding heart of the program was that you took two pinks and a purple two times a day. The pinks were the real kicker. They had the shit in them. Obscure ingredients from the rain forest and the Serengeti that kept starving native populations so thin you couldn't slip a camera around their necks without it sliding down their twig thin ankles, plus some nastier shit from some off turnpike factory in New Jersey that made them extra potent, being that the natives ate mostly roots anyway, and the stuff needed to be stronger for a society that grew up on French fries and corn. The purples promised to flood your body with all sorts of minerals and nutrients and horseshit. The warning was that if you didn't take the purples, you might shrivel up and die. Three people did just that several years ago. Seemed that a batch got out that weren't colored right. The pinks looked like the purples and those with lesser hearts and eyesight took three pinks at a time and that was a little combustible and their hearts popped. But LifeThin paid off the judge, got a slap on the wrist, temporarily discontinued the formula, and J.P. went on a cruise.

"I'm thinking J.P. might've been taking those," I told Harry. "And I know that's not going to help your case, but I got an idea."

"What idea?" he asked.

"Help me out. Find those pills. I'll take them to toxicology when I get back in town. We'll talk to Welch and Gates about how quiet they might want to keep this. We don't even bother with the department. You go straight to the newspapers."

"Me?" he said, "Why me?"

"Cause you can. I could get in trouble with the department. But not you, you're just doing your job, sniffing around and the like."

"Tommy, if that's true it could blow the whole insurance deal. It didn't rule out death by diet pills. Why the hell should I help? It's such a long shot anyway."

"Jesus, Harry! They don't want it out that their own pills killed their founder! That's the endgame! Can't you see? You have that info, you give it to me, we threaten to go to the press, they'll settle, big time. And not for the down payment on your little house.

Shit, Harry, you'll be able to buy the biggest house in Beloit that hasn't even been built yet. You could take off right now and open your little restaurant on the beach and buy the beach it sits on. Shit! You won't need the insurance deal. It'll be twenty times your bonus. You'll be down in Mexico before the El Niño's."

"If those pills killed them, then they should be off the market. That's the right thing to do," Harry, ever the boy scout, said.

"Damn straight, and as soon as we cash the settlement and get the hell out of town, we'll call it in. I'm the godfather of one of the LA Times top investigative reporters. He'll jump at this. Just get me some evidence."

"Boy, I don't know," he said.

"What part of rich don't you understand?"

"It's all just happening too fast!"

"This is LA, Harry!" I felt like I was working way to hard for what was an obvious attempt at life's jackpot. I needed Harry in on this, and let's face it, there is no love lost between me, the department and LifeThin corp. "We a team?" I asked him.

I could tell Jadonne was getting impatient from the sudden lack of attention as Harry kept saying off cell,'Hang on,' and 'Be right there,' and 'Alright, just a minute.'

"Harry, focus! This is important?"

"I'll check it out. But we gotta talk. I don't like this. It's not on the up and up."

"Harry, if this is the cause, you lose. Unless you do it this way. Pinks and purples, Harry. A rosy future."

21. GOOD PICTURES ARE ALL IN THE FRAMING.

Dick Asher and Marsha came out of the hotel room into the brisk Beloit air at about six at night. After one of their marathon sessions of bumping fat uglies, it was time for Dick to go home and play husband.

Marsha just had a dog and herself to feed. She'd put a DVD in the player, settle into the couch with the mutt and a bowl of buttered popcorn and a frosty mug of beer and pack the pounds on. After all, who was she trying to impress? Not Dick. He'd sleep with her no matter what. And Harry wasn't going anywhere.

They played pinch and grope on the way to the car. Dick was no catch by a long shot. He had man breasts and a hairy back. And as I noted before, she wasn't anything to write home about unless home was as maximum-security cellblock. But Dick wanted her cause she was good on the nob, and she needed Dick.

She was willing to overlook the fact that she couldn't tell where his back hair ended and his nose hairs began for a good paycheck, long lunches and a job she could never lose without her needing another job for a long time, and that's only if she blew her settlement money on Cinnabons.

In all the horseplay, they didn't see the Chevy Suburban in the parking lot of the gas station across the street. They didn't see the man slumped down behind the wheel, snapping away on a long lense digital camera. They didn't see him snap a crisp photo of Dick's hand on Marsha's breasts, Marsha's hand on Dick's crotch, Dick's tongue in her ear. The whole deal.

They didn't see him at all.

And he snapped away, through the slit in the blinds of the room they rented. He saw it all. All the details. If these two dumplings weren't such an assault on aesthetics, it might've been funny. But it was a hippo ballet of fat on fat, plump winter-white body parts finding their way into pink plump body parts, on top, from behind, in the ass, lying down, standing up, against the wall, sixty-nine, thirty-two, French, Italian, Thai and Mormon, all of it, around the world, around Disney World. They temporarily made their corpulent bodies the happiest place on earth, as if in one orgasmic explosion of fiction and body fluids, they would become attractive. These two were like a Kinsey experiment to see just what one human being could do to the other.

Snap. Snap. Snap. Their images ready for upload. Ready to ruin a life.

Back in LA, Jadonne was about to discover that the other shoe had just dropped. Welch and Gates were moving in on her, taking things away, giving her a taste of what they would do full bore if she didn't take it upon herself to have the good sense to leave the premises quietly, without malice or protestation.

They had already offered her a deal. Fifteen grand a month for three years and the first years rent on a two bedroom anywhere but California. They'd up it to twenty grand if she'd just up and move to Wyoming or some other place that once she got there would have a population of two. They knew that she'd be back on the market again and it would be high profile. She'd be out dating either A or B list movie stars, studio heads, agents, or real estate tycoons and she'd give interviews and she'd be paparazzi'd outside of whatever was the place de jour in cars and coats and baubles on her neck and fingers that would piss the hell out of the distributors. Welch and Gates couldn't have that. It would make their daily lives more difficult, and then somebody would call in a forensic accountant and something nefarious would come up, some bonus for a million or an apartment for a mistress that was never reported or shouldn't have existed.

If it was money she wanted, she'd have to shut up and disappear. With the prenup and a questionable reputation, she really had no choice.

That's why she called the insurance company so fast. It was her out, her golden parachute and now, it was disappearing. Just like the Bentley, which she discovered was gone the minute she pulled into the Mansion driveway after taking the newly coiffed Harry home from the salon and saw the cavernous, empty garage.

Lou was my eyes and ears to all things mansion, so he filled me in. He kept me in the loop as to the movements of Welch and Gates. He was my eyes and ears to all things Mansion. One day, I might have to repay him. Or just not bust him for something meaningless that would fuck up the rest of his life. I could go either way.

"Damn him! He took the Bentley," Jadonne said surveying the empty insides of a garage that could've held a snack bar, shoe rental station and ten lanes of bowling. "Who?" Harry asked.

"Lou! They gave it to him as a going away present. Maybe part of his severance package. Or maybe they promoted him. But they took the Bentley! You see what I'm dealing with Harry?"

Harry didn't want to get into it with her. He didn't want to remind her that it was a company car and she was living pretty high off the hog or tell her she should count her blessings and take what she could and go on. He didn't want to do that because he knew that wasn't how the game was played out here, in Playland.

If he said what he felt, she'd look at him and feel she didn't have a friend in the world and that he had abandoned her in her second of need. No. Harry wouldn't do that. This was the man who stood up to Rick Knox. "C'mon inside Harry. Let's get you into some clothes that match your new haircut," she said as she took him by the hand and led him into the house. "I'm sorry about the car. It's damn unfair," he said.

Sure as shit, he wasn't going to challenge her about that now. Not with her holding his hand, her head practically resting on his shoulders, about to enter the place where she walked naked and free.

As they entered the house, they didn't see Lou cruise by, Bentley window wide open, snapping away with a small compact digital camera.

They didn't see him at all.

23. YOU THE MAN, HARRY!

Harry stood in the master bedroom of the most beautiful woman in the world. It felt like a sacred place. The air was filled with the essence of her. She was trying to find him something to wear, something to change his look, match his new haircut and put on the kind of threads that would make him look like a player. He'd been in these clothes for a couple of days now and his pant knees were nubby, his shirt collar rounded and droopy and it all made Harry feel droopy in them and Harry didn't need any help in the droopy department. He could manage that fine all by himself.

Jadonne didn't make Harry feel droopy. She made Harry feel like the Marine you see in the recruiting commercials. He looked at the bed, wide and fluffy and inviting. A bed that could cause a meth addict to doze off mid-dose.

The. Bed. Was. Right. There.

Jadonne sorted through the racks of shiny, flashy clothes. She noticed him looking at the bed, and she caught his eye, and she smiled and made the connection that the bed would be a good idea for both of them, but not yet, Young Master Corvair, you haven't had the appropriate training to embark on the adventure of making love to the most beautiful woman in the world. When Harry saw her seeing him looking at the bed, his eyes shot practically out of his head in another direction, to a blank spot on the wall, and he kept them there like there was something to look at.

Harry shuffled his feet, and you just know *he didn't know what to do.* You just know his mind went to Gettysburg and the diorama. But instead of the battle and the history all he saw in the middle of the smoky field was Harry on top of Jadonne and Jadonne on top of Harry. He saw himself taking Jadonne from behind and the diorama kept spinning and the indelible images of his childhood all started to compete with the one he was inventing. He saw Ulysses S. Grant taking Jadonne from behind and Robert

E. Lee getting a blowjob from Jadonne and Sherman trying to go down on Jadonne and Harry was in the middle of it all, fending off the generals, keeping his woman to himself, waving his saber cock to ward them off as Lincoln jerked off to the scrum.

Harry was General Corvair. General String Bean.

It would be Harry that would free the slaves. It would be Harry that would free Jadonne.

"Harry, what's the matter?" she said, snapping him out of his tour of duty.

"Oh, nothing. Sometimes, I just get to thinking about the Civil War."

"I liked Cold Mountain," she referenced. But Harry was still in the diorama, with Custer on a great white steed, except he looked like Rick Knox, and Custer/Knox pulled Harry off of Jadonne and mounted her himself and Harry stuck him through with his sword.

"You know Cold Mountain?' she asked.

"Yes," he said, "I feed it to my parrot. Marsha's parrot," and that sort of trailed off cause the last thing he in the world he wanted to do was mention Marsha's name in Jadonne's bedroom.

"Silly, that's Hartz Mountain."

"Oh, yeah."

She rummaged around in the J.P.'s four hundred square foot walk in closet.

Like all rich folk, J.P. liked his closets big. The poor could inhabit the streets, but dammit, the clothes of the rich would have their own rooms.

And then there were the shoes. It was the shoes that took the most space.

J.P. had over two hundred pair. From Italy, France, Germany, Japan. From New Hampshire, Texas, New York. He had espadrilles from Mexico and Morocco and wooden clogs from Holland. He had boots made of Yak from Norway and custom-made shoes from shoemakers right here in Malibu. He even had a pair of shoes made by Daniel Day Lewis, a really good actor who one day decided he wanted to make shoes.

Jadonne laid the outfits out on the bed, matching them up like she was about to dress her own real-life doll, which she was. She'd cross a sleeve over a shirt, to see what Harry might look like in the shirt should he cross his arm like that. Then she'd uncross the sleeve and put the shirt back in the closet, apparently not happy with the shirt's gesturability.

Harry mulled nervously over by a table filled with pictures of Jadonne and

J.P. in Hawaii, in France, in Italy, in Japan. On horseback, camel and ostrich. The good life. One he would never have. They looked happy. J.P. happier than Jadonne. He glowed with her on his arm. Of course, he glowed most of the time, because most of the time his blood alcohol level was .20. It was amazing the photographers could keep him in focus. But it was OK by Jadonne. Cause at the end of the day, he'd always pass out. And she could do her own thing.

"You've been around the world?" Harry asked.

"Lots of times. I lost my cherry when I was seventeen. But I was giving blow jobs before that," she answered as she matched up a cashmere top with a pair of black running pants. Harry's jaw just about dropped to the floor. The bed grew a foot in length and width. It was swallowing the room now, like he'd have to jump up on it to avoid being forced against the wall. "High school was all about blow jobs and hand jobs," she continued as she tried to match the Tommy Bahama tropical print shirt with the khaki pants. "It was fun. We were learning. And it wasn't like I was giving away my virginity or anything. And blowjobs and handjobs are just favors you do a man when they're growing up. You have no idea how much calmer they become, how much nicer they are when that sort of tension is released."

She noticed the framed picture of Italy in his hand and knew she got his question all wrong.

"Oh, you mean like in travel. Yeah. Sorry. Guess you know a little more than you wanted about me. But yeah. All over the world. Six, sometimes seven times a year. But, it wasn't that much fun. It looks glamorous, but it wasn't. They were all business trips. Every picture was staged in some spot. Then he'd go back to his distributors. I'd wander off and shop. Maybe go back to the hotel and sleep. I could get real lonely. Real depressed." Then she held up a bright dark blue silk shirt next to a pair of black silk pants. "Here, put these on," she said.

"I don't know, Jadonne. Those are a dead man's clothes."

Jadonne sat on the edge of the bed and covered her face in her hands. Harry knew immediately he had made a colossal error. Almost as bad as Napoleon invading Russia. "I'm sorry. I didn't mean to say that," he said.

With her hands over her face, she chugged through her sobbing and told him the clothes were probably going to be auctioned off to the LifeThin distributors. Gates and Welch knew they'd pay top dollar to have anything that had touched J.P.'s skin. It would be like the Pope being able to make a sweater vest out of the Shroud of Turin. If he could, you know he would.

The proceeds from the sale of the wardrobe would somehow find their way into the direct accounts of Gates and Welch, and no one would know a thing. "And do you know what would get the highest price?" she asked Harry. "The underwear."

The doorbell rang. Berta called up. It was somebody to see Jadonne.

Jadonne gave Harry a peck on the cheek, told him to take it easy and to put the clothes on. She told him she'd make a little dinner. They could watch the beach at night, have a cocktail, relax. Harry could explain about the insurance policy and she'd understand. Right now, she told him, "It's just nice to have someone nice around." Then she left Harry alone in the master bedroom of the most beautiful woman in the world.

24. UNDERCOVER LOVE.

The video cameras were the eyes and ears of what went on behind the thick walls of the house of troubled money. I had about six months worth of footage. I should've just thrown up a website and run them in three minute clips, charged fifteen bucks a month and sold advertising.

My customers would see drunks stumbling around, famous people snorting coke off the asses of A and B list girls and less famous people stealing stuff from the kitchen and living room during parties that got boozy and bloated before the first guest arrived. They would see fights—both verbal and physical—and lots of crying and some vomiting. They would see J.P Buffet getting his pubic haired dyed. They would see couples fucking in the bathrooms, the garage, the stairway, the kitchen, the den and on the deck and in the pool. Man on woman. Man on man. Woman on woman. Woman alone. Man alone. If you squinted hard and had a bit of an imagination, you could catch Jadonne showering. But that girl loved her steam.

With a web site like that, I'd be a rich man. I ran the numbers in my head. Nine bucks a month, fifty thousand subscribers, equaling half a mill a month. But there would be lawsuits and the like, and after awhile, I let that one go. A lesser man would've run with it.

I watched as Harry got dressed in the clothes Jadonne laid out for him. He checked himself out in the mirror: black silk pants and a deep purple silk shirt. He had never worn silk before. It felt like another layer of skin. Cool, slippery skin. He liked it. It made him feel important. It made him feel rich.

He checked out the bed. It had a silk duvet cover on it. He ran his hand over its slippery smoothness. He looked around, made sure he was alone, then got on the bed in his new silk wardrobe and slid around the bed. He made flapping movements. Arms and legs. Up and out. He was making a silk angel. It was fun, something he had never done before and something he might never do again.

He got up, admired his work, then smoothed the duvet to erase any trace of his childishness. Then he started on his quest. First the closets, both because J.P. could have hidden a stash of something in there and just plain curiosity. There was a suit section divided up into types of suits. Pinstripe together with pinstripe, charcoal black, blue, brown, tweed, khaki. All in their own exclusive neighborhoods. Tuxedos had their own exalted status at the beginning of the rack, like a locomotive pulling the train. There was more order here than in the Library of Congress.

He opened sock drawers, shirt drawers, underwear drawers, belt drawers, tie drawers, cufflink drawers, watch drawers. Nothing. No drugs. No LifeThin pills. Nothing but clothes and accessories.

I was proud of him. He did it like on TV. Fast and nimble, not making a mess, just pushing shit aside and then pushing it back and smoothing it out.

He moved to the bathroom, which was just a little larger than the closet. It looked like a marble cave with gold faucet accents. It had a bathtub that could easily fit three people. Three Wisconsonians. It had a shower that you could lie down in, with more showerheads than a car wash. You didn't have to move. Just soap yourself up, raise your arms and they would spray you with a stream capable of giving you a light enema, should that be what you wanted that day.

He checked the medicine cabinet. Everyone has secrets in the medicine cabinet. Some cream for a rash you're not supposed to talk about and can only get if you've had intimate contact with terrorists from one of the 'Stans.' Maybe J.P. had a preexisting condition. A pre-existing condition would rule out the policy as much as anything. Insurance companies were experts at that. They knew everybody has a preexisting condition just waiting to pop up and say "Ta-Da!"

So here was Harry dressed in silk head to toe, in the bedroom of the most beautiful woman in the world, rummaging through the cabinets and closets looking for some evidence that would screw her over. Just to get a bonus. To buy a house in a state that prided itself with its ability to shape cheddar cheese into soft balls and cover them with walnuts.

And he found nothing. No prescriptions. No creams. Nothing but aspirin and deodorant and Band-Aids and floss. Everybody had something in their medicine cabinet. Not J.P. Not Jadonne. It was clean.

He opened a closet. It was filled with towels so cottony soft they looked like clouds stacked one on top of the other. He pushed a stack aside, and behind that stack was a box of Depends. He pulled one out. He'd never really seen an adult diaper. Just in commercials and they don't show you an actual adult in the diaper. That would be too insulting to those who have to wear them and too funny to those who didn't and if those two were in the same room watching that commercial, somebody was going to feel mighty squeamish.

Harry didn't notice Berta standing there, at the bathroom door. Just watching him like a common criminal. Or a cop. She hadn't been let go yet, as someone had to keep the house in some semblance of sellable appearance. She cleared her throat. He looked up. He felt like a fool. No. He felt like a common criminal. Or a cop. "I was just looking for an aspirin," he told her. She reached into the medicine cabinet and handed Harry the bottle. She didn't say anything. She just gave him a look that said 'You are up to no good. I have my eye on you.'

Harry descended the staircase to the living room. He was trying to roll up his sleeves. J.P.'s arms were longer. Probably from years of making grandiose proclamations and hugging his many thousands of admirers, who were all fifty pounds overweight. Every time Harry got the sleeves rolled up, they'd unravel. Silk has no friction. Harry was feeling the same way. Nothing was catching. He was in a frictionless world. He started to button the cuffs when he heard Jadonne's strained voice. Then he heard Gates' voice say, "We don't want this to be any more painful than it has to be."

He entered the living room and saw Jadonne with red eyes. She turned to him, her eyes begging him to save her. Harry pushed his sleeves up, like a man that would spit into his rough, manly palms and lift that wagon wheel off that kitten's tail and give the kitten back to the pretty little pioneer girl, all the while eyeing her beautiful, rugged and husbandless mother.

"Make what not painful?" he asked defiantly as his sleeves slid back down.

"It just like I feared, Harry. They gave Lou the Bentley. They're taking away everything," Jadonne said through the tears.

Welch and Gates could only stare in wonder at the transformation of Harry Corvair. Here he was, fresh cut Caesar hairdo, silk finery and a pair of satin espadrilles made by Martha Stewart from a pattern by Daniel Day Lewis.

"We gave him the use of the company car." Gates said, eyes on Harry and smiling his ass off, "We can do that. We're the company."

"Until he gets his life together," Welch joined in, eyes on Harry and smiling his ass off, "Because he's been a loyal employee."

Gates slid a stack of papers in front of Jadonne and handed her a pen, "You agreed to the pre-nup. Your signature is right there. We need another to confirm that you are not agreeing to anything under duress."

"Hang on there. Just a moment." Harry said as he snapped the papers off the table and started flipping through documents that were completely—linguistically and culturally—alien to him.

It was a legal document written with the sole intent of putting up an impenetrable firewall between Jadonne and J.P.'s money, which was LifeThin money so it was essentially Gates' and Welch's money. Even if she bore him a child, even if she got herself in position to rescue him from the mouth of a great white shark and stitched up his mangled body using only a needle and thread and tube of Crazy Glue, while breathing life into his lungs; even if she was able to bring his dear sweet mother back from the grave in the condition she was in before the bad genome kicked in, she wouldn't get J.P.'s money.

It was an onerous document. It had been constructed by Welch and Gates and slipped under J.P.'s runny nose to sign the morning after the night he wolfed down three grams of cocaine and wound up in jail after getting arrested for giving a blowjob to some guy in a West Hollywood bar and then biting his dick when the joker revealed he was a cop.

J.P. didn't read the document. He didn't read any documents anymore. He trusted Gates and Welch. They had the same haircut as he did, wore the same clothes, listened to the same music—The Eagles, Grand Funk Railroad and Celine Dion—and drank the same wine without being able to appreciate a drop.

They were of a feather, these birds.

And this was Gates' and Welch's plan all along.

They knew the King was flawed, and the High Priests are always more evil than the King. They had already let a lot of money and property bleed out of the company to J.P.'s three previous wives. Damned if they were going to let that happen again. Especially now that there was Ebay.

So, no, Jadonne would get nothing. Walking money, maybe. "And if you try, we'll just bring up your lifestyle issues to the judge," Gates told her, "The drugs and booze, the endless shopping, the cheating."

Jadonne went Taliban. She leapt up on her perfect legs and wagged a long, tan finger at them. "You fuckers. You know that's a pack of lies. I never cheated on him!" So Welch countered with his best online law school talents.

"That's not what Lou says. And it really doesn't matter, Jadonne. You can challenge it in court, and the judge that will preside will be one of the judges we helped appoint to the bench, and in Malibu, we helped them all get appointed, and we'd be willing to spend a million on lawyers, and you'd have to spend at least that much, and you don't have that, do you? You might even win, this being California. But then we'd appeal, and spend another million on lawyers and you'd have to spend at least that much. But you don't have that do you, Jadonne?" Welch had all the angles covered. But just in case he left something out, Gates filled in more.

"And there you'll be, getting older by the minute. And desperate. And every man in town avoids a former A-lister who's getting desperate. Isn't that so, Jadonne?'

She flopped down on the couch and told them Lou was a liar. That he was covering his ass for stealing from J.P. That he was playing them like a flute. All she got from Gates and Welch were stone faces. "Lou's been trying to make it with me ever since J.P. died. I turned him down. So now he's making shit up." That was her last pitch for decency before she covered her face in her hands.

She was too angry to make tears and too scared to cry. That's when her hero rolled up his sleeves, spat in the palms of his hands and got ready to lift that wagon wheel off her kitten.

"You boys are speaking out of school, aren't you," Harry twanged.

For over twenty years he was dying to tell someone that. He had no idea what it meant to 'Speak out of school,' but he liked the sound of it. "Let me get our lawyers to take a look at this, just to see if it's all on the up and up," Harry said as his silk sleeves rolled right over his wrists and covered up his hands, leaving him looking like a ten year old in his Dad's shirt.

"Mr. Corvair, this is a surprise." Gates said, not holding out his hand.

"I don't think your company would be too keen with their boy in the home of the policy holder's wife dressed in the deceased clothes." Welch chimed in.

The boys were chipmunk tag teaming him. Gates: "But we'll let you keep the clothes." Welch: "They fit you so well." Gates: "Yes they do." Welch: "Better than on J.P." Gates: "Infinitely better." Welch: "Yes." Gates: "Indeed." Welch: "Indeed yes."

Harry put the papers down. He wasn't going to figure this out. He had to change the conversation. "OK, cut the patter. Legal get back to you?"

Gates told him that they were still reviewing a copy of the policy; that it took time; that they were very busy. They are launching a new product this month that was a powder that you put in your food to make it taste bad so you wouldn't like it and not eat so much. Which begs the question why you wouldn't just cook up a bowl of dog shit and push away from the table after two fork fulls instead. It'd be cheaper.

"Why does everything take so long? I want that coroner's report. And I want it soon, as in tomorrow. Or I'm just gonna file my report. Drugs and alcohol. And it will hold and it will go public," Harry told them, without thinking that what he just said would sink Jadonne. And Gates knew just what to say. "Now, who's taking everything away? We're not the only bad men in your tawdry little life, Jadonne."

Jadonne ran out of that room like Bambi ran out of the burning forest. But when she got to the stairs, she thought the better of climbing them and got into her varicose vein saving motorized chair.

The cell phone I gave Harry buzzed. It was Marsha. He forgot he had called her from that phone the night before while Starr was giving him a private show.

25. OL'HARRY'S IN A HEAP O'TROUBLE.

Harry turned away from Welch and cupped his hand over the phone. He was stuck. It was Marsha the Mommy calling and he knew he was guilty. Not just with the stripper, he could live that down and bury it way deep in his brain folds, but with Jadonne and he hadn't done anything with her, but he wanted to, he so wanted to, and cheating emotionally is way worse than cheating glandular satisfaction. So he said nothing, waiting for the phone to say something, but Marsha said nothing, waiting for him to say something, knowing that if he didn't he was guilty of something.

Here he was, trying to assert his machismo, feeling like a toreador in his silks, and mommy was calling, and his silk sleeves had slid down over his knuckles, making it look like he was talking into the end of his arm. He didn't remember calling her from this phone. But he didn't remember much after the fourth shot of tequila. He'd have to plow through this, he'd have unpinch his sphincter, deal with Marsha, once and for all. Or maybe just for now.

"Hey Marsha!" Harry said with a dollop of sparkly, bright-eyed guilt.

Harry's ass cheeks clenched together so tight they practically swallowed his butt crack. "How'd you get this number?"

That was about as wrong a thing to ask as there could be. It opened a floodgate of screechings he couldn't shut off. It confirmed how drunk he was the night he called her on my loaner. A man should never call his woman drunk. Let her worry, let her stew, but do not call her on the phone drunk. You say things you can't take back, insults or proposals of marriage or another woman's name. I have known more men who called their girlfriends while drunk and proposed or called their wives and were soon divorced. I've known drinking men who called their mistresses and promised riches they didn't have and wound up ruined when they couldn't deliver.

"Bastard! Shit Head! Bad Boy! Fucker!"

It just wouldn't stop. All I could hear and see was Harry letting out monosyllabic vowels that told me he was getting his pinched-ass chewed out. She accused him of cheating on her with Jadonne. She'd Googled Jadonne and found a bunch of magazine photos from her Rick Knox days. Then a bunch of photos from her Hawaiian Tropic Swim Suit modeling days. Then photo from her baby food label model days. If she had the patience, she would have found her photo from her most fabulous fetus days.

"Son-uva-Bitch! Dick Head! Loser! Wimp!"

Welch and Gates couldn't help but snicker as Harry took the phone out to the deck to get some privacy. He pleaded with her, told her he loved her, but it was hallow, from memory, sayings picked off of anniversary cards.

Marsha probably didn't notice that or care. She was probably in the same position I snapped her in, standing over a naked, bound and gagged Dick Asher, dressed in black leather lederhosen with the suspenders strapped over her nipples, whipping him with a feather duster and spitting on his lobster bib.

"Bastard! Lying Snake! Cheater! Asshole!"

In between insulting Harry and exciting Asher, she managed to tell him to check his emails. "Sure Marsha, I'll go online as soon as

I'm finished with the lawyers. Check it out. No doubt, it's probably the perfect house. Yes dear. No dear. Don't say that, you don't mean that. OK yes you do," he wimped into the phone. "Tell him I'm on it. Closure soon. In the bag," and then, "Yes, I know I'm an asshole."

26. THE HARD-ON FROM HELL.

Harry stood at the edge of the deck of the mansion nursing a gin and tonic, mostly tonic, watching the ocean roll in and out, his silks fluttering in the breeze. He was taking advantage of an awful lot of hospitality considering his end game was to take away the very things Jadonne was being hospitable with. He felt like hell. What the fuck did he think he was doing? It wasn't like he was going to get anywhere with Jadonne. He was Harry. Harry Corvair. Plain Jane Harry. She was a goddess. She wasn't blind. She was just playing with him. She was lonely. He gave her a shoulder. He was a Mid-Western middle manager, no, lower than middle, on his way to the middle, if his girlfriend could grow another finger and find another orifice on his boss to stick it in. He was encouraged by the way she talked to him, but so the fuck what! They all talked like that out here. He had a job to do, dammit! He didn't want Marsha's words to be true. He didn't want to be a loser. He would surprise her. He would surprise them all. But first, he wanted another gin and tonic. The ocean air does that to you. That's when he dialed me up on the cell.

"Tommy," he said. "What the fuck am I doing?"

I got the message later. Long and rambling. Not drunk, just one thought running into the next, out of order and sequence, stream of consciousness, the way they all talk in Malibu. The ocean air does that to you. From his tone, he sounded like a little boy whose Dad had dropped him off at the brothel and he wasn't sure what he was supposed to do with the condom the hooker gave him, and it was an Extra large and made his dick look like a airport wind sock on a still day.

Jadonne strolled out in a long diaphanous beach kaftan with her hair rolled up wet under a towel. Fresh from a shower she told him she had to take after Gates and Welch threatened her with the prenup; a shower, she said, she took to think things through; a shower she needed to take to clear her head; a shower she knew she would emerge from smelling like sweet calmness. He could smell it; her skin scrubbed new by the three hundred dollar loofah under the filtered water from a three thousand dollar showerhead.

Harry told her he was going to call a cab, go back to the hotel and act like this perfect day never happened. It hurt him to say that, so he was glad when she wouldn't hear of it. "Berta just put your clothes in the wash. Let them dry. She'll press them and stitch them up a bit from the fall. It won't take her long." She told him to help himself at the bar. And he did. This time he added a bit more gin.

He also started to pour some splashes of vodka and gin and whiskey into cocktail napkins. I told him to do that. I wanted to send them to the lab, see if they had anything in them, anything that, over a period of time, might accumulate in J.P.'s body and brain and drive him crazy, kill him slowly, and leave no trace.

But he couldn't do it. He threw the napkins away. He wasn't going to help me anymore. He had to make the policy stick. Silk sleeves or not, sweet smell or not, he had to follow through. He didn't have to help a rogue cop on the right side of truth and justice and the American Way investigate beyond where the department was willing to go. The autopsy would come in. It would tell him what he needed to know. If not, he'd challenge it. But the money would not be paid, and any publicity would be shitty for the corporation. Maybe Jadonne would cooperate with the insurance company, offer up some juicy tidbits about her old man, and show a pattern of abuse.

Maybe the insurance company would pay her for that, as it would be cheaper than paying out the policy if my hunch was right and somehow, he had been taken out.

Harry was working the angles. Creating scenario after scenario, each playing out to get Jadonne get something out of this. A taste, a serving, an appetizer. After all, her dead husband had wanted it, and he hadn't thought he'd ever die the way he did. He never thought he would die, that's why he didn't care if he killed himself a little every day. He was J.P. Buffet after all. Rich. Invincible. Loved.

But the corporation would do the minimum of what they'd have to do to keep her quiet, to make her go away. They'd just as soon have her wash up on the same beach as Lars then give her a single dime past what they had to.

So Harry was on his own. Head to toe in silk and satin in the home of the most beautiful woman in the world, who had unwrapped her hair from the towel, and was shaking it back and forth, letting the ocean air blow it back, letting the sun dapple her cheeks, letting her kafkhan open slightly to reveal her left breast right to the edge of her aureole, then pulling the kafkhan closed with a smile to Harry that said, 'You saw it didn't you? Was it nice?'

Harry ran the scenarios through his head again, seeing if he could get her past a taste to a full gulp.

"I don't blame you, Harry," Jadonne comforted him.

Harry caught her profile watching the horizon. The sun was glowing red as half of it sunk into the ocean. The light softened her face and made her more perfect than she already was. It made her teeth whiter, her eyes more azure. Nature and her had a pact. She wouldn't litter and she'd use recyclable shopping bags and Nature would provide the lighting so she always looked good.

She sipped from a big crystal sphere filled with a frosty white wine. She clinked his glass and smiled, as if all was forgiven. As if she knew he had a job to do, and that was that. The more she forgave him, the crappier he felt. The more she looked at him with big, round, Keane painting eyes, the more he felt like the slum landlord, the Simon Lagree, tying Pauline to the train tracks, twirling his handlebar mustache.

He asked her if his clothes were dry. He thought it was time to leave. All his figuring came down to this: He was a little man. Who the fuck was he to fart above his asshole with this woman? What would become of it? It would be better if he tucked in his tail and headed back to what he knew in the land of summer sausage. "I don't belong here," he told her. Big words. Took guts. He could've faked it for a while, at least until he finished his drink or the other breast popped out and he'd have a vision for a lifetime. At least until the sun went down completely and he couldn't see her. "None of us do," she said, face still in profile, eyes to the sea, lost in her thoughts just as the sun went down and the light-sensitive deck lights came on in a slow dramatic fashion.

J.P. had them installed special. They were made by a cinematographer for Spielberg or Lucas or Waters. They were designed to light any actress over forty and make her look nineteen. They worked gangbusters on wrinkles and bags and fatigue. So you can imagine how much better they worked on Jadonne. They put the sun to shame and made it even harder for Harry to take his eyes off her, not to mention turn and leave.

So, faced with not being able to act on his better instincts, his future a blur, his past an embarrassment, his legs frozen in place, with the most beautiful woman in the world willing to forgive his stupidity and selfishness, he did what any modern red blooded American male would do. He started to cry.

"I'm a skunk. I'm such a fucking loser."

"You're just doing your job, Harry. Getting your bonus. So you can go off and have a great life—one you deserve." She pulled out a little handkerchief and dabbed one of his tears. Just one. She could've dabbed two, but she left one on his cheek. He took that as her only half forgiving him.

He could smell her on the handkerchief, lavender and sweet dried mother's milk, mixed with the crisp warm ocean air. It was an aphrodisiac. It sent him back to the womb, with a baby woody.

"It's not so great," he told her, "I'm a phony. I haven't been doing this long. And I never liked doing it in the first place." He was drinking faster now, faced with who he was and trying to calm the wood.

He went on to tell her his life. It was a history of such exceptional lack of interest it could make a full-scale meth addict with an arm full of crystal fall asleep mid tremor. But Jadonne hung in there, nodding, asking questions about such scintillating morsels as how far he got up the pole as a boy scout, how he liked being a counselor at a day camp, and how cool it was that he was employee for two months straight at the dog washing clinic he worked in for a year.

Dogs were his true passion. Dogs don't judge you. Dogs give you unconditional love just for rubbing their bellies and handing them a Milk Bone. He would've been happy at that. He had planned on learning everything he could about running a business that washed other peoples dogs so he could open his own place, maybe even franchise it. He would call it Harry's Dog Washing Parlor. He'd even come up with a nifty little tagline: *Bring your hairies into Harry's.* He started to sing a little jingle but the alcohol clouded his rhyming abilities.

"So what happened, Harry? What happened to the dream?" she asked him like this was the only thing in the world she cared about right now.

"Marsha," he told her. Seems his ambition around washing a dog's balls wasn't sitting too well with Marsha's dad, who was a local real estate machter in Beloit and a member of the Chamber of Commerce and Harry's former scout leader, who Harry had a vague recollection of molesting him in exchange for getting his Wolf Badge without mastering a slip knot.

The old man got Harry the job with Asher, who supported him in his bid to become mayor of Beloit, until some kid came out of the woodwork and accused him of molesting him too. The old man hung himself in his garage in full scoutmaster uniform, sans pants. Marsha was devastated, and so what the hell was Harry going to do, go back to washing dogs? He stayed on with Asher, investigating all sorts of sundry little insurance scams. "Stolen cars. A fireman hurts himself getting a cat out of a tree and is suing for workman's comp. I step in. Pretty soon, firemen were not longer allowed to help people get their cats out of trees. Last fall, the trees were full of stuck cats. That's why I like dogs better. They don't climb trees."

He finished his drink in one fat gulp and Jadonne took it to the bar for a refill. Harry sat down on a deck chair, his head swirling, his mood swaying with the breeze coming off the water. It was quiet. He was calm.

"I'm tired," he said. "Too much to drink."

Jadonne took that as a signal to mix another drink. After all, gin and tonics are like prunes; is one enough, are six too many?

"I'll put more tonic this time. It's too early, Harry. Too early for the night to end. You'll be fine. It's not the alcohol, it's the ocean air."

Harry started to babble. "I need to go online. Do you have an Internet connection? Have to check on some real estate. Have to please Marsha."

"Sure Harry, later though. Let's enjoy the night. Just you and me." and she handed him his drink. "Here's to Harry Corvair. Dog washer extraordinaire!" They toasted. They drank. Harry took a deep pull on the air.

"She's cheating on me. I just know it. But so what, right? I cheated on her."

"Screwing a stripper isn't cheating Harry. It's kind of expected of a man. Like mastering the slip knot in the scouts."

Harry downed his drink. Jadonne brought him another.

"Slow down, sailor. Make the night last," she told him.

The very concept of Harry being in a situation where he might actually be granted access to this woman's body terrified him. He wondered if it was so she'd have a funny story to tell years from now about the night she allowed a milquetoast, middle class insurance investigator from Beloit, Wisconsin make love to her and how he didn't know where to put his hands or even how to do some of the more exotic things to another person's body that was her specialty.

He was right to be nervous. Jadonne had studied the arts of man-manipulation. It gave the extra edge over the other contenders that were part of the competition. So she'd studied the Kama Sutra, the writings of Don Juan, the Penthouse Forum, the pelvic fertility exercise routines of the Tiabapaci Tribe of the lower Amazon Peninsula and took a couple of classes from a German dildo manufacturer in how to perform oral sex and give that real "Girlfriend Experience." She met with a couple of porn stars who moonlighted as escorts and they gave her some tips. She even read medical journals on the physiology of the penis so that she might understand the workings of the vessels and nerves and be able to invent a couple techniques of her own. Which she did.

Harry was trying to find his debonair but the alcohol was spoiling his smooth. He lifted the glass to his mouth and the ice rushed to the lip and spilled all over him. That did it. He'd blown it. He was trying to win her respect and instead became a former dog washer with a drinking problem.

"I'll get you a refill, Harry," she told him.

"You trying to get me drunk?"

"And what if I am?" she answered, "Don't you trust me? I'll take care of you. You're safe here."

Harry handed her his glass. She got busy behind the bar.

"I've been with that woman for twenty years. Since high school. Since eleventh grade," he confessed. "And now she's cheating on me. Or I think she is. And if she was, I wouldn't know what to do."

"Original love," she said as she clunked fresh ice into the glass.

"Tommy told me about that. I never heard that before. I'm so out of it. It's like you people have a whole other language out here. I don't like most of you for the most part, but you guys got everything going for you. Money, weather, big places to live, nice cars with shiny hubcaps. I'm this fish out of water."

"I'm not a big fan of your police friend," she told him. And that made sense. She had been on the bad side of all things legal for a while now. The corporation with lawyers, lawyers with prenups, prenups with accountants, accountants with dandruff, and cops always figured somewhere into the occasion.

Harry stuck up for me in a vague way. Sort of a soft sell he could back off of if it upset her and made her cold to him. "Aw, he's not a bad guy." That's OK. I didn't expect him to have a backbone. Not when his front bone was sapping so much of his energy.

"He thinks J.P. was murdered," he told her.

"And you?"

Harry put down the drink. He was feeling a bout of blood pressure come on. He knew it would get worse if he lied some more. "I think J.P. died drunk and filled to the gills with what ever drugs was popular that day. I think he had a bad history of abuse that isn't as much a secret as LifeThin wants to think it is. And I'm sorry, truly sorry, that his stupidity is going to impact your life."

Jadonne blurted out "LifeThin killed J.P." without even looking at him.

"They built him up. Made him a God." she went on. "Christ, Harry, those pills don't work. They don't do a thing. They're just speed. Natural speed. They make you talk so much you don't have time to eat. And he knew all his money and all their love was based on shit. A scam. Gates and Welch argued with him all the time about him going public, or changing the company into an exercise and nutrition deal. But it cost more, made less, and they were not going to let him kill the goose."

Harry had a hard-on so big it was affecting his hearing and his concentration. It was a sudden ironwood totem. And the crazy thing was, he wasn't aroused. Not mentally anyway. He loved hearing her talk, but right now he was developing a boner that was threatening to tear a hole right through J.P.'s silk pants. The last time he had a hard-on that had a mind of its own was in the eighth grade and he had to walk the school hallways sideways with a loose-leaf binder in front of his crotch. That binder bounced on his boner all day while he crab walked past suspicious and taunting classmates who, most days, beat him up on the playground. So this was not good.

By the time he got home, his dick was black and blue.

"I have to go to the bathroom. Something's running right through me," he said as he slid off the lounge chair and held his drink down by his dick and walked crab like off the deck.

Jadonne smiled, and poured herself another drink.

27. NEVER PARK YOUR BENTLEY IN A TRAILER PARK.

The ocean fog rolled over the beach like amnesia. It crossed the PCH and crawled up a small hill into a trailer park. You wouldn't think there'd be a trailer park in Malibu, but these weren't ordinary tornado magnets. These were double wide and built out from there. The only thing that defined them as trailers was the hitch somewhere underneath the raised hot tubs and chimneys. The park was a remnant of a less populated time, and was ample housing to the infirmed parents or slacker children of the rich folk that lived on the beach.

Lou was in the Bentley. He'd been camping at the park for most of the day, snapping shots of the Buffet Mansion.

He snapped pictures of Jadonne coming home, pictures of Harry walking into the house on her arm, telephoto lense shots through the open bedroom window with Harry and Jadonne in the bedroom, shots of Harry in J.P.'s clothes at the window over looking his new kingdom and lying on Jadonne's bed making silk comforter angels.

Incriminating shit. Bad shit for Jadonne. Stupid shit for Harry.

The fog was too thick to shoot anything now. It looked like someone was pouring Big Slurp vanilla smoothies over the Bentley's windshield. Lou had enough shots for awhile. I told him that if he wanted me off his back, he'd have to keep tabs on the widow. The tapes did a nice job inside, but I wanted more. I figured that if he was involved with her, it might compromise him, turn him, flush him out. He'd be spying on himself and have a tougher time manipulating the plan. It would slow the whole thing down. Take him out of the picture and if he wasn't involved in anything nefarious, then a new player would emerge. I get the truth about how J.P. died. And let's face it, if I could prove he was murdered, that meant a bonus, a promotion and a book deal. Just clock the visitors, the comings and goings. With the right amount of pictures you can incriminate anyone—just keep a camera on them all day. Snap snap snap. We're all guilty of something.

The fog sat on everything like a fat baby in white fur diaper made from clubbed baby seals. Lou put the camera in the glove compartment and pulled out the little bag of coke I'd slipped him at the restaurant. It was just him and the Bentley and the fog. And a full bar in the back. To Lou, that was a party of one. He could sleep in the back, wake up in the morning and be ready to take some more shots. Snap snap snap. Harry coming out of the mansion and Jadonne kissing him goodbye. Ozzie and Harriet.

But the shots were also a bonus for Lou, I figured. If he wasn't involved, and Jadonne was and cut him out of whatever she assumed she had coming to her, he had the pictures to cut himself in. I knew that. He could blackmail both Jadonne and Harry, maybe even Gates and Welch. His mind was racing. He had a head full of coke. And even though he was working for me, he was figuring out his own angles of getting in on the rich.

Lou was slicing up a line on the mirrored bar inside the Bentley. No 'off-the-back-of-the-hand' for this boy. He had rolled up a crisp hundred and was getting ready to huff it back in style, feel the drip, drink some champagne, hell, he might even call up a local escort he knew, join him in the back of the car. He was smiling from ear to ear, thinking of the trouble he could get into tonight when there was a tap on the driver's side window. Lou finished his line, sucked it back into his throat and enjoyed the big numb.

It was probably one of the inhabitants of the trailer park just making sure Lou wasn't up to no good. A Good Samaritan, Lou thought.

The last time an expensive car stayed up here all night was when Sissy Phus and his Peeps were visiting lot 6-D. The woman in that trailer was a dealer, the fucked up daughter of a music producer that wrote a big song for some Africa starvation or AIDS crisis sing along that Sissy sang in. He sat waiting for the deal to go down in his black Escalade; a party float he could've run down Colorado Boulevard in Pasadena during the Rose Parade and gotten applause. Sissy just wanted to chill that night. The girl always had the good stuff and she wasn't bad looking and liked to charge both for the drugs and a sexual favor; a typical value equation. There was a fog up there that night too. A lot of strange things happen in the fog.

One of Sissy's peeps didn't like the cut that night, so he beat and raped her in the Escalade. Sissy watched, even recorded the whole event on the camera he had mounted in the front. The camera was there to record the faces of his back seat passengers to make sure no one was making faces while he drove. Money had made him paranoid and he was a shitty driver because his eyesight left him long ago and he took to wearing prescription glasses that were tinted black and he couldn't see shit when he drove at night.

So it wasn't hard for the cops to find out about the rape and the perpetrators. It was right there on the video. Sissy is still in appeals. His defense is that he wasn't in the car at the time, except that his camera also had sound and had recorded Sissy singing his hit song, 'Escapade in the Escalade' over the rape footage.

After that, the trailer park inhabitants hired a security guard, but trailer parks are transient places, so when one home up and drove off and a new one parked, the new neighbors didn't want to contribute to the fund.

Lou would tell the Good Samaritan he was taking pictures of the house across the street for the Malibu PD. Lou would tell him a version of the truth. That would satisfy him. Then Lou would ask how much it cost to live up here, and were there any lots available? and "Gee you folks sure have it great." That would ingratiate him. At any rate, it was a Bentley, not an Escalade—not an asshole expensive car. It was more an expensive car for assholes.

He'd offer the Good Samaritan a shot of two-hundred-year-old brandy. He'd impress the Good Samaritan with its age and his savoir faire for having it. Tell him that it came from the cellar at Spielberg's house. Then the Good Samaritan would leave him alone, realizing that a man with a connoisseur's appreciation for Spielberg's two-hundred-year-old brandy would not be up to no good. It wasn't like he was drinking Cristal, after all.

So when Lou slid open the window and flashed a big coke smile, he was mighty surprised when a bullet drilled into his perfectly bald head.

28. IT HAPPENS.

Harry's boner bent skyward like it was saying, "Fuck you," to the rest of the boners in the Boner Hall of Fame. He stood sideways in the bathroom mirror, his hard-on jutting out of the pee hole of his black silk pants like the burly arm of an SS in full Seig Heil salute to the Fuhrer.

It was painful. It was an erection that made him sweat. It panicked him, but at the same time, it made him feel like the new emperor with a huge army at his disposal and a great and irrefutable cause. He would conquer Poland, then march straight to the ocean, attach a flag to his boner, wave it on the beach and be drowned in the waving accolades of the boners of the millions of his followers. It was also draining the blood from his brain.

Harry splashed cold water on it. He smacked it against the shower door. He swung it side to side, letting it slap against his hip to punish it. "You OK, Harry?" It was Jadonne. Right outside the bathroom door. Harry turned the bath faucets full blast on cold, pulled his pants off and jumped in the water and sat there as the tub filled with nerve numbing water.

She knocked again, "Harry, you OK?"

His whole body seemed to go into shock. But not his mighty boner. No sir. It defied the laws. There was only one thing to do and that was to try to jerk it into oblivion, choke it into submission, let it know who was boss of the body.

"I'm just going to take a bath," he answered as he looked at his hand, made pruney by the water and he wondered if it was large enough to wrap around his member.

"Do you need anything?" she asked.

"No, no, I'm good. Just going to take a bath here. Nice tub. Never been in a tub this big. Big tub," he blabbered as he stroked himself almost to the point of blistering his hand. His dick felt like the cast he had on his leg when he was twelve. But it was bigger. It looked big enough to get twenty signatures on it in ballpoint and he wouldn't even feel a thing. He could have been jerking someone else off for all he felt, which he would gladly do right now if it would get him limp.

Bath water splashed over the edge of the tub as Harry two-handed his hard-on in a chicken choking frenzy.

Then he heard Jadonne's voice again, this time not muffled by the door.

"Wow, Harry. Water's a little stormy."

Harry went from being a man with a shot at the most beautiful woman in the world to a kid in the confessional. He scrambled to look dignified by crossing his legs and folding his hands on his lap, his hard-on the elephant in the room.

Jadonne stood at the bathroom door, hands on her hips, smile on her face.

"This is so embarrassing," Harry said as every part of him except one shriveled up in shame.

Jadonne stepped into the bathroom and stood right over the tub and looked right into the eye of his boner and told him, "That's nothing to be embarrassed about, Harry. Most men would give anything for a hard-on like that. Most horses, too." Then she pushed the straps of her gown off her shoulders and let it float to the floor.

And there she was.

Harry's head snapped back at the sight of her perfect, naked brown body and hit the faucet with a thud and he didn't feel a thing. The water went still, all was quiet. Even his dick turned itself around to get a better look at Jadonne La Rochelle Buffet.

She put one foot in the tub, revealing more of herself to him as she parted her legs. Harry was breathing heavy, his heart up in his throat. As she descended into the water, she grabbed hold of Harry's dick for balance.

It was the first time he felt anything. But now it was like all the nerves in his body were sitting on top of the skin in Jadonne's hand.

"You are so beautiful," he said. That's all he could think of saying.

She straddled him and slowly sunk his dick into her. Harry shed a tear.

"Be gentle with me, Harry."

"This is wrong, Jadonne."

"I know. But I can't help myself. I wanted you the first time I saw you."

Harry told her "Me too," and then, "Really? Me?"

She rocked forward on him, covering him with her hair. He was surrounded by her scent, deep inside of her. He was back in the womb.

But there was still part of him left that wanted to object. "I shouldn't be here," he told her as he held her in his arms and felt her perfect soft wet skin in his pruney fingers. She breathed deeply and let out her breath and it was captured in her tent of hair and he breathed it in and it was like having oxygen for the very first time.

"But you are, Harry. With me," she told him and before he could say anything stupid, she placed her breast to his mouth and asked him to bite it. And so he did. Softly, as biting a woman's breasts was new to Harry.

"Harder," she told him.

And so he bit harder, and she wanted it harder still, and so he bit harder, and she leaned away from him, even though his teeth were clenched on her nipple and she told him it was good, stay there Harry, bite harder and now suck it and he did and she absorbed his dick even deeper into her body with Harry still attached to her nipple.

"God, you taste good," he told her and it wasn't a line, it was the truth.

Most women spend an ungodly amount of time and money on creams and fragrances to smell good. Jadonne did no such thing. It was all baked into her skin, so she not only smelled good, she tasted good. She tasted better than anything Harry had ever tasted before. Her flavor wiped away all the fond memories he had of summer sausage, cheese balls, Jell-O molds, bunt cakes and bratwurst that are the staples of fine dining in Beloit.

"Did you ever just want to run away, Harry? Away from all the liars, the cheating girlfriends, the assholes who take advantage of you?" she asked with a little whimper that made him want to protect her against the world forever and past that.

Harry was getting more comfortable with this, and he wanted to show some style so he pushed himself into her, felt himself go way deep, and she leaned back and moaned and he could swear he saw a tear.

"Where would I go?" he asked.

He was getting in the groove of this talking and fucking thing. With Marsha, it was straight in and out and some degree of cuddling until she got the remote in her hand and had something infinitely more fun to play with. Up to now, that had been OK by him. But this wasn't fucking. This was transcendent.

"Mexico, Harry. Open a place. Right on the beach."

"Cabo," he said dreamily, then "You smell good."

"I smell horny," she said, which is one of the better talking fucking lines. Jadonne knew them all and had an uncanny sense of timing.

She kissed him, nibbled on his lips, was still able to tell him with one lip in her mouth, "We'll call it Harry Corvair's. We'll sell your own signature fried string beans. 'Harry Corvair's Fried Hericot Vers'," then she sucked on his neck and reached behind her and cupped his balls with her hand.

Harry had floaters in front of his eyes.

"We? Like in me and you? Like in us?" was what he said but he didn't know he was saying it.

"Twenty-million in the bank and a lifetime to get to know each other, every nook and cranny, every part I want you to know. You could teach me things," she said as she gripped the towel racks on the wall and lifted herself up off Harry then descended back down on him from the heavens.

For the next two hours, she showed how to make love to her using every surface, sink and shower nozzle in the bathroom. She was teaching him how she wanted to learn. She was teaching him to teach. She was No Man Left Behind incarnate.

Harry kept up with her, his dick obeying her every command. He did things he didn't think he was capable of. He did things he didn't think humans were of capable of. He wasn't thinking at all. He had amnesia for his past and neglect for his future. It was just Jadonne. She had one foot on the light-switch turning it off and on with every thrust and the toes of the other foot were stroking Harry's ear.

"Did you come yet?" she asked him.

"Did you?" he asked, because you're supposed to.

"Ten times."

Harry was a hero. Fuck Rick What's-his-name!

And with that, she squeezed her vaginal muscles around his cock and brought him to a climax and Harry started crying and then laughing and then crying and she was licking the tears off his face and breathing in his ear and whispering, "Just you and me. Every part of me. And I will fuck you every day and we will live forever."

Images of a row house in Wisconsin and a pasty wife making Bunt Cakes went through his head and slammed into those of a sunset drenched restaurant on the beach and the most beautiful woman in the world feeding him his own signature string beans.

He had been infected by perfection.

And then he came again, which made him worship her even more.

"Bow-fucking-wow," she whispered in his ear.

29. POOR OL' USEFUL LOU.

Lou was a mess. Whoever shot him wasn't content with just one perfect shot. Lou got plugged seven more times, the whole clip. It could have been the Russians. Lou had had a run in with them a couple of years ago. He tried to open a bar and they shook him down. Then they kept upping the split so he took what was in the till, got in his car, drove to a recruiting office and signed up for the first Gulf War. He figured that Iraq in the midst of a shelling was a safer place than LA after taking money the Russian mob thought was theirs, and he'd be right about that.

It could have been the Gangsta's. It's my bet that's where he was getting his drugs and who knows might have gone wrong there. And those guys are such bad shots and watch such bad movies; they always fire the whole clip.

Or it could've been Lifethin. Maybe he'd out served his usefulness and was now the last man on earth who knew the sordid history of J.P. Buffet, and Gates and Welch wanted to close that chapter permanently and burn the book.

He was covered in coke. The inhabitants of the trailer park peeked out at the Bentley, smelling something wrong. The open window let the scent of blood out, and it stands up pretty well to ocean air. I waved my badge and shooed them back behind their curtains, and they'd shut the windows and pull curtains tight, thanking their lucky stars that there by the grace of God they weren't going.

I knocked on a couple of trailer doors, but they all had the same story. It was foggy. They never saw the car. They didn't hear anything. They all asked the same questions. Who is he? What did he do wrong? They all made the same comments—This place used to be so safe and nothing happens like this in Malibu and how times of changed and everything is more violent and TV and rap music is to blame. I smiled. It happens all the time, I told them. But the ocean just drowns out the sound and washes away the blood and the next day is so impossibly sunny that we all move on, not missing a moment to enrich our tans.

The squad cars had surrounded the scene. Sergeant Lucas got out of the lead squad car. You could tell that with the Lars' "drowning" and now this, he was feeling Full Serpico. Finally, some action. He was trying hard to make detective class, and it didn't hurt that now he had two grizzly cases on his docket.

He'd built up a bunch of resentment against me. I'd made detective before him, even though we were at the academy together. He thought it was on account of my wardrobe. Hell, he might've been right. His mistake was in thinking these two dead enders—Lars and Lou—were going to take him up the ladder and mint him a badge he didn't have to pin to his shirt. This wasn't going to get him anywhere, and he wasn't smart enough to turn the death of a couple of dead enders into something more imaginative. I, on the other hand, had broken plenty of cases that might have led to an option on a story that would've led to a synopsis on a screenplay that would have led to a development deal on a series as a consultant. But this being Malibu, the Brazilian waxed pussy end of the movie business, it never did. All the cases I broke were always too close to the guys I could make deals with. Their rejections were always the same: The public will never believe it. This they said as they sealed the deal on the third Spiderman movie.

"Christ, look at him," Lucas said when he saw Lou's blood muddied head. He picked up the bag of coke, took a sample to his tongue and said, "Well, at least we got a motive."

"What motive? A gram bag of coke? You can buy that at Ralph's."

"What the hell you doing here anyway, Tommy? You should be sleeping in. You not getting any from the porn star?" He looked at me and I could feel his resentment. No. Lucas would never make detective.

I was supposed to meet Lou this morning, supposed to get the shots he took and another video he snuck out of the mansion. So I had to be discreet. And Lucas' questions were deserved. I was always late to a crime scene. It allowed me not to get caught up in the flurry of opinions fueled by the rush of adrenaline that the smell of fresh blood sends your body into. I was known to be the coolest cat behind the tape, able to logically access the circumstances and layout a rational construct of motive and suspect. Rookies were in awe of my abilities. Lucas hated that.

I picked up Lou's camera before the others got there and started going through the pictures on the little screen. There were foggy images of Jadonne and Harry, Harry and Jadonne. It was incriminating shit for sure, real conflict of interest shit, as Harry had stopped just listening to her and was in the touching phase of young love. He'd gone beyond my contract with him. He was on his own now.

I also pocketed the videos, even though it was a crime scene and nothing should be touched. But these guys were dead enders to everyone but me, and I sure as shit didn't want a department I couldn't trust to be as smart as I was now and the other thing, the thing that proved to me that Lifethin wasn't involved in this parade was that the video's were there at all. So that scratches one group of suspects off my list, and that's too bad because I liked having them on it.

If the Russians had taken Lou out, they might not have bothered with the tapes, but would've taken the camera, the car, and Lou's watch, being that they liked things. Period.

So, I was figuring, it must be the Gangstas. Might've been Sissy Phus. Maybe it was Bubba Rub's last chance to stay on Sissy's good side and out of the In and Out job. He wouldn't have taken anything, because he would've just shot Lou and run like crazy, with his track suited thighs rubbing together making that nylon whistling sound.

"Did you hear about the Israeli producer?" Lucas asked.

"Does it have a punch line?" I answered, full on thinking he was about to tell a joke and hoping like hell he did.

"No. They found him cuffed to his electric meter outside his house. Or the skeleton anyway. Coyotes ate him. His name was Avi Harrad, Arrad, some original Jew name like that."

"Shit. He made King Arthur and His Nights on the Round Table," I said.

"Must've lost money," Lucas chimed in.

"Hard to see how, with you buying so many copies."

Lucas and I just stood there staring at each other until my eyes crawled over his forehead and cap to the red dawn sky of Malibu. The air was heating up and the smell of eucalyptus was starting to punch the air and cover the smell of blood and coke.

There really isn't anything like it in the world.

"Gonna be a beautiful day," I said.

30. NEVER READ EMAIL WITH AN ERECTION.

Harry couldn't sleep. Even after spending himself at the altar of Jadonne for three hours straight, he still had an erection. He tossed and turned, trying to get comfortable on the huge Eastern King bed that was created and calibrated to make even people with bedsores comfortable.

Jadonne slept like an angel. She looked like an angel. Harry didn't want to disturb her. He was getting worried. Having an erection this long wasn't normal. He'd seen the warnings on TV about seeing a doctor if your erection lasted more than four hours after taking one of the ED drugs. And since he didn't know that Jadonne had reduced his will power by slipping him a crushed up tab of Viagra in his gin and tonic, having a four-hour erection without cause was cause to either rejoice or repent.

She wanted to do that to a man for a long time. More out of curiosity than anything else. Nothing nasty. A man's sexual organ kind of fascinated her, which was why she studied the art of seduction like she had. Harry was ripe for the experiment; healthy, Midwestern, non-smoker, no drugs, didn't drink much. Shit, she thought, that drug would turn into a randy sixteen years old with some experience. How much fun would that be?

Harry got up and wandered around that big house. He went to the refrigerator and wrapped a paper towel in ice and swaddled his erection with it. In two minutes time, the heat from his missile melted the ice and all he held in his hand was a soggy paper towel. He tried to jerk himself off but it got too painful. He dunked himself in the pool on the deck, but the warm water just made it worse. His balls felt like they were hanging onto his dick for dear life. They felt like Christmas ornaments. They felt like they could smash into a hundred little pieces if he just flicked them with his finger.

With an erection lasting more than an hour—and I read this so I know—you get to wondering whether you'll be at full salute the rest of your life. There have been men who have committed suicide due to the condition brought on by these drugs. A life with a tyrannical, mindless erection is too hard to contemplate, and it can drive men as crazy as a toothache.

Harry went to the library, sat down at the desk and booted up the computer. The head of his dick pressed against the edge of the table like an Irish Setter begging for table scraps. He pushed it aside and it sprang up again. He had to push it under the desk, and as he moved around in the chair typing in his username and password, it was like his dick was sniffing the underside. He went onto his email account. He told Marsha he'd check out the pictures of the houses she liked. He'd honor that pledge. But it was an empty honor. There wasn't a house in the world he wanted to live in with Marsha. Not after being with Jadonne. He had 'How-ya-gonna-keep'em-down-on-the-farm' syndrome. He wanted to be back in bed with Jadonne. And he damned well would've been if he didn't fear impaling her on his rod.

Marsha had sent him a six house pictures in all. Each priced a hundred grand over what he could pay. They were plain little ticky-tacky houses with little lawns, little fences, little windows, little backyards and little style. Perfect for his little life. He pictured himself and Marsha in the little front yard, waving their little hands, two kids on tricycles. It was an image that only a few days earlier would've made him smile, before he landed at LAX, drove in a

Bentley, stayed at The Four Seasons, met me, met Delpin, met Starr, met Carlos Prima, met, fucked, gotten oral, given oral and had one of Jadonne's scones. He sat slump shouldered at the desk, dick chafing against the underside of the desk and opened a shitty email from Asher. All warnings and insults. He deleted them right away. Email lets you get back at those more powerful than you. You just delete them. Then he opened an email from somebody he didn't know, with a subject line that said, 'U been wronged.' That was intriguing.

He opened the attachments and his body language changed. He sat upright and studied the monitor like it was about to reveal the secrets of the grassy knoll. He clicked through the attachments. There was picture after picture of Marsha and Asher coming out of a motel room, going into a motel room, playing grab ass by Asher's car, kissy face inside the car, even one with Asher at the wheel, a smile on his face, his hand on what looked like the top of Marsha's head.

There were pictures of inside the hotel room, through a slat in the blinds, Marsha and Asher on the bed, on the couch and on the floor. My guy did a good job of capturing their shameless and hurtful hypocrisy and their unbridled and almost superhuman horniness. By now you know I am no boy scout, but just a day earlier, Harry had been. And he'd been fooled. Asher did it cause he didn't have to pay Harry much and he could have Marsha. He was a small town powerbroker and needed to see how close he could get to being caught, especially by someone who couldn't do anything to him even if he was. Marsha did it because she resented that the best she could get in life was Harry. With Asher wanting to deflower her on a regular basis, she felt somewhat sexy, even though he had the back hair to rival Sasquatch. And she had a job for life or she'd have a settlement just as big.

Harry's whole body went back to slump shouldered after the initial shock of the pictures. His fingers hung on the keyboard, his dreams shattered, his ego smashed, his erection gone. And all his suspicions verified. He was both relieved and depressed. The pictures wiped away any guilt he was feeling. The pictures made him feel like a fool. Jadonne entered the room and saw the state he was in and asked him what was the matter. She stood naked at the doorway of the library. A pane of stained glass window spread the morning light over her body in hues of orange and red. Harry looked up to see her, and his erection fought its terrible way back through the fog of his depression and almost pushed the desk over.

Jadonne sat on him, put him in her, and moaned.

"I've never made love in the library before, Harry. All these books, makes me horny," she said as she rocked gently back and forth.

He looked around the room to the bookshelves. There were only six books on them. They were thick ones, the kind no one reads.

31. YOU CAN'T GO HOME AGAIN.

Jadonne insisted Harry carry her back to the bedroom with her attached to his boner. For the next hour or so, she pleasured him some more. And he fucked with all the anger and disgust and revenge he could muster on his little potato princess back in Beloit. He fucked her to get back at Marsha. He fucked her to get back at Asher. He fucked her because when he fucked her he knew he was still worth fucking. He fucked her because she was the most beautiful woman in the world. And he fucked her because there was a about 500 milligrams of Viagra coursing in the veins of his dick and couldn't connect his newfound virility to the dose he took without knowing.

After two more orgasms, Harry's dick went into a coma, which was no small relief to Harry. He was starting to think he'd have to live the rest of his life with a permanent erection, that he'd need pants custom made with a built in holster.

"I haven't had a man touch me like you have in a long time," and that reassured him as she snuggled to his side, like a little girl protected by her mighty daddy. "What about J.P.? You said it was pretty sexual."

"J.P.was gay," she said as if she was saying, "I like Tater Tots." Harry got up on his elbows and ruined the perfect spooning symmetry of their bodies, not knowing quite how to be incredulous. That J.P. would commit suicide when he had all the money in the world was hard enough to believe, but that he would be gay when he had Jadonne was way off his believe-ohmmeter.

"That's why he was wearing the Depends," she said as she fluffed out her morning hair that didn't need any fluffing really. "I shouldn't tell you that. It's too . . . . controversial."

"Do gay men in Los Angeles wear diapers as a fashion?" he asked, but not like a rube. He asked it more like a cultural anthropologist getting the lay of the land for a documentary on cable. He'd been in LA for three full days now, and he'd given up on being shocked by anything anymore. He'd gone over to the side of just being infinitely curious about this alien place. After all, he just went around the world and then some with Jadonne. He earned his Wolf badge. He had peed on the floor of his room at the Four Seasons, watched a stripper give him a private show, faced down Rick Knox and was in a consulting position with a member of the Malibu PD. He'd been vetted. It was time to understand the habits of the natives like an objective anthropologist who just got his pipes cleaned by the best of their own. It didn't matter that he just saw pictures of his life partner screwing the man he thought he'd work for the rest of his own life. Right now, that was water off a duck's ass. Duck's that he was finally getting in a row.

Jadonne told Harry that J.P. had to wear the diaper cause he was losing control of his bowels due to the amount of times he had taken it up the ass. She told him J.P. liked her to put objects up his ass, like cucumbers and zucchinis and that's when she suspected he played for the other side. And that was on the honeymoon. "Are you hungry, Harry?" She was going to feed him and complete the trifecta.

"I gave Berta the day off," she said as she slid out of the bed on her aerodynamically perfect ass, slipped on a satin robe and didn't bother to tie it shut so half of her nakedness peeked through.

She kissed him on the forehead and told him she felt like sausages and that she was going to make him the best omelet he ever had.

Jadonne was the picture of efficiency in the kitchen. She broke eggs without spilling, and whisked the bowl with the same rhythm she fucked him with. Part of her beauty pageant training was in the kitchen. She had to be the perfect woman to win: Glamorous in a formal gown, able to hold at least a passable conversation with Steven Hawking, Play a decent 3rd Movement to the Moonlight Sonata while wearing a thong bikini, and cook at the very least a decent omelet. But of course, Jadonne went further. Her omelets actually won awards—from Steven Hawking.

She had brought in the morning paper before Harry got to the kitchen. She had made him a cup of the best coffee he ever tasted and told him to read the paper on the counter while she cooked. She told him she liked when a man read the paper in the morning. She told him she thought it was sexy. She told him she liked the way men took out the ads and the inserts and knew exactly what they wanted to read and then would get all silent as they read the paper while they drank their coffee. Harry sipped his coffee and flipped through the paper like he was reading it. Every now and then he'd run into an insert and he'd pull it out and put it aside and smile at her while she was skinning portabella mushrooms with the mushroom skinner and extracting seeds from heirloom tomatoes with the seed extractor.

He saw a small article about a body found in the ocean off the pier. He saw an article about a man cuffed to his electric meter who had been eaten by coyotes. He saw lingering news of J.P.'s death and business stories about how that might affect Lifethin and stories about how J.P.'s widow was seen tooling around town in the

Ferrari. He saw an article about the Green Bay Packer game and that one, he read.

The oven beeped and Jadonne pulled out a tray of scones. From the videotape I will vouch for Harry when I say there is nothing sexier in the universe than the most beautiful woman in the world—who's naked under a robe that won't stay shut—wearing an oven mitt and holding a plate of fresh baked scones. Not on this or any other planet. She turned them over into a basket like Derek Jeter would throw out a guy at first and put one on a small plate right on top of the Packer story.

"I made them with butter. They don't break when you dunk them," she said. Harry looked up from an article announcing Brett Favre's retirement to her holding the perfectly browned fist-sized scones—with blueberries—to the small separation in her robe that allowed the edge of her nipple to peek out.

"I can't go back," he told her.

32. EVERYBODY FREEZE!

It was a little past noon when I knocked on the door to the Buffet mansion. I'd spent most of the morning taking what I needed from the scene at the trailer park and making fun of Lucas as best I could. He finally ran me off, getting real territorial. I hit the queer coffee shop awhile, went over the pictures from Lou's camera, had a laugh and a latte. Jadonne was up to something. Funny how the last picture was taken at 10 pm. Funny how they guessed at the scene that Lou was shot at around midnight.

Jadonne opened the door.

She smelled like omelets and bakery and damned good coffee and she looked freshly fucked.

"Ma'am, I have a few questions," was all I said. She stood at the door and looked past my shoulder across the PCH to the entrance of the trailer park. She saw a bunch of squad cars, one TV van, and a bunch of looksees and paparazzi. Then she looked back at me and I could tell that I might be close to the bottom of the list of people she wanted to see today.

"You gonna be a smart girl and let me in?" I asked. She turned away and left the door open. I followed her terry clothed robed body into the living room, breathed in her scent. It was exciting, I will say that. The inside of the Bentley had smelled like blood and shit. It's always hard to get that out of your head, but smell could. It was on the good side of primal.

"Won't take long. Just a couple of questions for you and Mr. Corvair." She spun around on me at the mention of Harry's name and told me he wasn't there, "Why do you think Mr. Corvair is here?" was how she asked. I smiled, took out Lou's camera.

"Great. Now I'm being followed," she said.

"That's not new for you. Being followed, I mean."

"Coffee?" she asked, cause she knew she wasn't going to win at this game, so a little hospitality was in order.

"If it's coming from the same pot as what I smell. But I don't eat donuts," I added, trying infuse the moment with a little clichéd cop lore.

She turned into the kitchen and I got comfortable in the living room. She asked me what I took in my coffee and I told her I took it with milk.

"I have Silk Soy cream in French Vanilla, Hazelnut and Irish Cream. What'll it be?" she asked.

"That's soy, right?"

"Heart healthy," she said.

"Taste shitty," I said.

"Black?" and she didn't wait for an answer. She just poured.

"And you wouldn't happen to have any scones?" Knowing Harry was here, scones were going to be in pretty good supply.

Once I got settled, I got down to business. She came over and sat opposite me in a long, thick, terry bathrobe with her leg peeking out. It was a treat to see her dark olive skin against the white of the robe. Of course, I knew she was naked underneath. It made the coffee and the scone taste that much better.

"I think what you need to be able to do, Ms. Buffet, is vouch for your whereabouts last night," I told her.

"Am I under arrest?"

I get that all the time. I ask a vaguely potential suspect for the time and they ask, "Am I under arrest?" I sit in a coffee shop asking a couple of innocent questions of one of my informants and I ask him to pass the sugar and it's "Am I under arrest?"

"No, not yet. Not if you have a real good alibi?" I said, "And another scone."

Those fuckers were good. If that girl would've invested in her own scone business instead of the Inside the Toaster Toast Butterer, she would have made a fortune. She got me another, sat back down, stirred her own cup, looked up at me and said, "Why are you playing games. You know where I was last night."

"I know that you were probably with Harry. I don't know how long. I have pictures of you and him coming into the house, but none of you coming out." She looked real shocked at that. Legitimately shocked. Like she didn't have a clue.

"Lou took those pictures, Ms. Buffet."

She buried her face in her hands. And then Harry came down the stairs.

He was fresh out of the shower, his hair going every which way, in the His robe of the His and Hers matching robe set. He was singing and acting like he'd lived there for years and that he and Jadonne were about to be profiled on 'E' as the most perfect couple in the world.

His little feet danced down the stairs like he was George Clooney at his Villa in Italy and knew how lucky he was to be George Clooney and have stairs in a Villa in Italy to dance down.

"Cupcake, I was thinking we could take the Ferrari up the coast today. I'd like that," he said and then he saw me, soaking my scone in the coffee.

"Hello, Harry."

Harry looked at me like he was a kid that just got caught jerking off in the bathroom by his Mom. He looked at Jadonne, face still buried in her hands, then back at me, and he didn't feel so "cupcake" anymore.

"Sit down," I told him. Jadonne looked up from her period of mourning and told him, "It's Lou. He's been shot," like it was a big fucking tragedy for her.

"Oh my God," Harry said as he sat down next to her, and I don't what it was about those damned bathrobes but his leg peeked out too. His white, red haired leg, and suddenly the coffee and the scone lost a lot of their appeal.

"Shot dead?" he asked.

I loved that. "Shot dead?" That's like, "Was it a serious coma?"

"I'm not here cause they missed. But more importantly, I didn't say anything about being shot, Ms. Buffet. I didn't say anything about him being dead. I said he took some pictures." I had her. I fucking had her. This was gonna be easier than I thought.

My mind went off on her going to one of those women prisons and having all those women-in-the-shower-lesbian encounters. I stayed there for a while. I liked those movies.

"There were six squad cars out there. Six! And the press!" she shot back.

When the press is there, it's a murder scene. Damn. How the hell are we gonna catch people anymore when there's fucking twenty two shows on TV telling people how it is we catch people. It is the end of civilization, as we know it. Now in HD.

"Wait a second. You just wait one second. What are you saying?" Harry interrupted.

"Lou used to ask me that. I can't believe he passed it on," I said.

"You can't think we did it," Jadonne said.

"Is that why you're here?" Harry said.

"What I think is that you two are sitting mighty cozy with each other. I think that's your dead husband's bathrobe Harry is wearing, Ms. Buffet. And it looks comfortable for sure. Lou Mellini's outside with his brains pasted against the dashboard of the Bentley and with half an ounce of cocaine floating in the air like it's a snow dome. And I know how much you hated giving up that car."

"I wouldn't kill a man for a car."

"You've killed a lot of men for cars, in your own way."

"Now just hang on one minute!' Harry said, sort of in a threatening way. I looked at his pale, freckled little leg sticking out of the bathrobe and I made a face that told him to back down before he embarrassed himself. Then I gestured to his leg and he covered it up real fast.

"So I'm thinking you didn't just come over here this morning to take a shower, Harry, and get the best scone I have ever tasted."

"Thank you," Jadonne said and I nodded and told him, "I'm thinking you spent the night. And calling Ms. Buffet here 'Cupcake' tells me you didn't spend the night on the couch. My boys told me you've been driving around in the Ferrari for a couple of days now. And even if they were lying Harry—and they're not—you rode around with her with the iWIRE on full blast and I heard every little detail. The rest you told me yourself on your copious phone messages. And I'm thinking that I have to put you two under house arrest until I can think some more."

"Jesus, Tommy, we're partners," Harry reminded me.

"I just dissolved the partnership."

"We didn't kill Lou, Detective. You have to believe us!" Jadonne pleaded.

"Where'd you get the shiner, Ms. Buffet?" Jadonne hadn't done any makeup time this morning and there was the tiniest remnant of a little bruise under her eye. She covered it up, embarrassed at her temporary imperfection.

"Lou did it, right? He was a known hitter. Did you two have something going on? Some relationship, either carnal or of the business kind? You didn't wake up extra early, sneak across the street for a little back seat action in the Bentley with Lou, you know, to keep all the players worried about your welfare, keep all the potential partners on board and blow his brains out cause you had Harry here and it was getting easier to twist this rube than to play the GI Joe."

"You're out of line, Tommy!' Harry said.

"Harry, I'm a cop. Telling me I'm out of line is out of line."

Harry got up, went over to pour himself a cup of coffee, took a big sip to fortify himself, and went off.

"How can you call yourself a cop when the answer's sitting there right in front of your eyes," he said, and I swear I got a tingle up my spine. I was just waiting for how he was going to follow up now that he had committed himself so completely to telling me something I did not know.

"It's the pyramid, Tommy. It's collapsing," he kept going as he poured himself another cup and grabbed a scone and dunked it and filled his mouth with it so he had a damned good excuse to not say anything anymore. His wheels were turning. He just plucked something out of the air, and now he had to make good. I didn't know whether to have another cup of coffee or crack open a beer. This was going to be a good show.

"I'm all ears, Marlowe," I told him.

"Too many people at the top making too much money. And the people underneath them, in the down line, get resentful. And the corporation hates giving so much away to the top, since the top doesn't do much more than collect checks after awhile. And that collapses the pyramid. It cheats the promise. So what do you do . . . ?" and with that he ate another scone and drank some more coffee. He was working up a pretty nice mash inside his mouth.

"I don't know Harry, you tell me?" I said and waited till he swallowed that mash and thought up an answer.

You could almost hear his esophagus battle the scone and coffee mash down his throat. "Two years ago, one of their biggest guys in South America was gunned down on the street right outside his home. And no one knows who did it. Last year, the biggest guy in Germany gets found with his head bashed in on a ski slope. And no one knows who did it. And a couple of days ago, J.P. Buffet is found dead in his bed, and I can't get the coroner's report. And please don't tell me that's Los Angeles."

"You telling me the corporation took him out?"

"No. He was a drug-swilling freak who liked to take it up the ass. But I bet Gates and Welch kept him like that. Drunk and drugged. They used Lou to supervise and provide. They knew it was just a matter of time. And they knew there was a prenup, so not a lot of corporate money is going to leave the safe. Except to them.

Because if you bothered to look, to do a little investigative work, you'd see that they were the biggest beneficiary's of his death."

I didn't like his tone with me, but I didn't know how to react to his newfound confidence. Jadonne's pussy worked magic on men, is what I was thinking.

"Don't dig yourself a hole you can't climb out of, Harry," I told him. He waved me away and he went on . . .

"Because now they run the company, and they can do anything they want as no money goes out to J.P. Buffet anymore. Shit. These guys just quadrupled their salaries. So it all fits real nice, doesn't it?"

I have to admit, he was on fire, pouring coffee and drinking coffee and pouring coffee and drinking coffee. He was sweating like a pig under that bathrobe, but he kept going. I took out my pad and started scribbling.

He went on about how Gates and Welch got threatened when he showed up. They didn't even know there was a policy. To deny it, all Harry had to prove was drugs or suicide, but they couldn't have that. J.P. couldn't die like that. The P.R. alone would sink the stock. It would be like Walt Disney getting caught with a Filipino boy. That'll make you think twice next time you waited in line for *It's a Small World*. So they kill Lou and Lars. They knew too much. Harry being here, snooping around, was making it hot. Maybe they saw too much of Harry and me together. Maybe they had us followed. Pop pop pop. Harry on all cylinders. "They're fixing the autopsy right now. Another donation. Anybody can be bought, right?" he said.

"Including you, Harry?"

"Christ, you disappoint me, thinking like that. I do things 'cause I think they're right. And right now, there isn't much that is. 'Cept for her."

We both pinned Jadonne with a look.

"Mimosas?" she said as she got up to go to the kitchen.

Harry told me how he loved Jadonne and how she loved him, "Isn't that right Cupcake?" he asked and Jadonne said "Yes" as she downed a goblet of champagne before it had a chance to meet the orange juice.

Then he told me about how he caught his dumpling Marsha red-handed outside a Comfort Inn with his boss.

"I have you to thank for that, don't I?" he asked and it was true. I offered to satisfy his curiosity by getting one of my boys from the other coast to follow Asher and Marsha. Harry turned me down. But I did it on my own cause I saw the pain he was in, and not knowing was killing him. I had his email. He had the pictures. He had the info he needed to save his life. And all it cost was airfare, meals and five hundred dollars.

"I didn't kill Lou and Lars. Neither did Jadonne. For what, Tommy? What's the motive? Huh? What's the motive? There's a coroners report that'll shit all over the policy. It doesn't matter to me who knew what!"

"My head's spinning, Harry," I told him and it was. He was in control. And even though Jadonne's coffee and scones were good, her mimosas were better. The orange juice was fresh squeezed and she topped it with a shot of Triple Sec and that made them potent and potentially patentable.

"Yeah, well watch this," he said as he picked up the phone and started dialing. Then he waited as it rang, and then waited some more.

"They're out screwing again," he said as he dialed a different number and asked me, "Are you in?"

"In what?"

"Are you in?"

We looked at each other for awhile as the phone kept ringing, and I thought, I don't know what I'm in, but I'll play. If I don't like it, I won't be in. It's not like he was an Israeli. Not like he was a Russian. Not like he was a Gangsta. No money had changed hands. And to see him through on this, I had to let him think I was on his side.

"Sure, Harry. I'm in."

"Good. I was getting worried about you," he said and I was getting more and more impressed by his new found self-confidence. No surprise. He had just fucked the most beautiful woman in the world. That puts a certain snap in anyone's step.

The call answered. It was Asher on the line. And he was screaming. You could hear it across the room. And Harry was smiling. Harry waited until Asher finished and told him calm as a big cat who senses the prey is napping to put the policy through.

Asher screamed some more and Harry told him that, "No, he died of drugs and alcohol, and that will either come through or not and you can challenge it, but you can't challenge the photos I have of you and Marsha outside and inside that dingy cheap motel. Jesus, Dick, that's a shitty place to fuck! Even I would've taken her to a Courtyard by Marriot!"

Then Asher's voice changed and got all civil and Harry told him to put the pay out in Jadonne's bank account and gave him the account number then he told him that he knows the policy is insured, as all insurance assholes insure a big claim in case it pays out, BUT try explaining the shots of you groping Marsha outside a motel off the old highway to your wife and by the way you shoulda done a better job of closing the blinds you egg sucking clam and then he gave Asher Jadonne's account number again, this time real slow and deliberate, like he was talking to a retard. Good move, Harry.

Harry covered the mouthpiece to the phone and said, "We'll cut you in for a hundred grand, OK Tommy?" And he looked to Jadonne for approval and all she could say was, "Harry," and look down at his crotch.

He had a boner sticking out of his pure white terry cloth bathrobe like a snorkel coming out of a cloud.

33. HARRY IS A RICH MAN, YA HA DEEDLE DEEDLE, BUBBA BUBBA DEEDLE DEEDLE DUM.

The Malibu sky was a deep pure cloudless blue. You could see Catalina clear as a postcard. There was a light ocean breeze. The surf hit the beach softly. It was as perfect a day as nature is capable of providing and humans are capable of screwing up.

Harry undulated on a polystyrene pool mattress floating in piss temperature water. He sipped from a frozen marguerite glass with just the right amount of lime and tequila and ice. He didn't even have to lift his head. Jadonne had straws that bent right into the mouth when the body was completely horizontal.

Jadonne floated up to his mattress on a mattress of her own. They bumped mattresses. The water sloshed around them. They giggled. They drank.

Here he was bumping pool mattresses with the most beautiful woman in the world who made the perfect marguerites and who was waiting for the payout to clear so she and Harry could take off, take off to Paradise, bags packed, tickets bought, plan perfect. Destination: Cabo San Lucas. A month reservation at the Twin Dolphins. They would spend that month looking around for a place to rent or build, look for a place to open their restaurant. They would spend that month drinking tequila, not wearing shoes, and making love to each other. She told him there was so much more she wanted to do with him sexually, so many more ways to achieve mutual pleasure. She told him she would unveil her secrets to me. Harry's brain couldn't even contemplate it. He was a poor farm kid that was promised a visit to Disneyland and there would be no lines. He could ride as many rides as his little heart desired, no waiting, eat as much ice cream and candy and Minnie might fuck him on the flume. He was practically jumping out of his skin in anticipation. It would be Perfection. Then after that, more perfection. They had the money to fuck up. They had the money to wait. They had twenty million dollars, each other and all that money would bring, and to top it off, Jadonne accepted the offer of fifteen grand a month for three years from Welch and Gates. She told them she was moving to the Baja and they were so excited she was leaving the country they raised it to twenty for four years. She was gone, out of their hair. They made her sign a document that said she couldn't talk about LifeThin in any disparaging way, which meant she couldn't talk about it at all. She told them she didn't care. She was out. They didn't know about the insurance money. They didn't ask.

"You know how they say money can't buy happiness?" Jadonne said to Harry.

"They're wrong. It sure as shit can," he answered.

Jadonne slid off the mattress, gave him a fat, wet and tongue full kiss on the lips. It was a kiss that had meaning beyond lust, it was a kiss that said, "You are of me now. We are one together." She held his face in her hands and smiled, sincere and good. The look in her eyes nearly brought tears to his own.

"You'll never leave me, right?" he asked her, "I mean, this isn't a dream or anything. You're my girl, right?" His eyes were full of newly adopted, just washed and combed puppy.

"Every nook and cranny," she told him as she got out of the pool and toweled off, then wrapped the towel around her. "I'm going to shower, get ready for dinner. I'll check the account and see what the progress of the payment is. Stay here, enjoy the last hours at the Buffet mansion. We have two small lobsters for dinner. A terrific Fume Blanc. I want to make love tonight, Harry. I want you to make love to me like you never made love before. Let me get myself ready."

She scouted Berta in the living room window shaking her head in disapproval. Jadonne gave her a cold stare as she walked through the French doors and disappeared into the dark insides of the mansion.

Harry's eyes went back to the sky. He thought he could see the planets. He thought he could make out Pluto. He felt like the entire universe was rotating around him.

A dog ran the beach. Harry watched it play in the surf, shake off and get a big hug from a very attractive woman in a sarong. She locked eyes on Harry, and smiled. Harry smiled back. Suddenly, beautiful women were smiling at him like they never had before. Harry knew that Jadonne gave him something. Something to replace what Marsha had taken away. Jadonne had filled him with brightness and hope. Jadonne made him feel like a man.

The cell phone buzzed. He had his own now, a real beauty. Silver, thin. Not a Blackberry. Not a workingman's phone. This was the phone of a man of leisure and wealth and 20 million about to be his and the perfect woman to spend it with.

He closed his meager little bank account in Beloit. He cashed out of that life and invested what he had into this one. He didn't leave a trace. There was nothing for Marsha to search for. He didn't care what happened to her. She wasn't original love. He knew—late bloomer that he was—that Jadonne was his original love.

He knew he would love her forever.

I called Harry just to check in. I was having a mocha frenziatti at a Coffee

Bean and Tea Leaf. A good time to check in with my buddy.

I had a post-dated check for two hundred grand from Jadonne and I just wanted to see what the status of the funds were. That money would come in real handy. Sell the condo and move to somewhere with a better class of people. Los Angeles had gotten old. And, I was a tad worried about the Israelis. I figured they'd find out who got to Avi Arrad sooner or later. Put it together. They avenged their own pretty thoroughly. And he had made a bunch of them a lot of money and Lucas would love to catch my ass doing something on the other side.

"Hey, Don Juan," I said, "You should've seen Gates and Welch's face when I mentioned your theory. Of course they denied it. But it wasn't like they hadn't thought of doing it. Question is, did they?"

"Gotta be careful about that, Tommy. The department hears you're poking around, they could cause trouble for you," he said like he could give me advice. But he was right. But the two hundred grand gave me some fuck you money. I negotiated up from the original offer of one hundred, and Jadonne and Harry were only too happy to oblige. In a way, we were in this together. It was hush money. And I was glad to have it. I told you I'd hit my mark. I just needed a little help. And Harry came floating into Malibu on the wings of cheese angels.

"Hey, Harry, hear anything about the deposit? I want to cash the check and get out of here. Change of scenery."

"Jadonne's checking on it. Should be clear. Where're you going?"

"Where ever the new BMW takes me," I told him.

"Why don't you come to Baja with us?"

"Harry, you're about to head off into the sunset with one of the top three most beautiful women in the world and you want a third wheel? Are you fucking kidding? The spaces between your fingers were created so that another's could fill them in."

"Jesus, Tommy, that's beautiful."

"This is your time," I told him. "Maybe one day I'll show up at your shrimp shack and you can buy me a round or two. Maybe you'll have some senoritas down there as waitresses that I can fall in love with. Maybe I can be as lucky as you."

"Ok, Tommy. Ok," he said in a kind of sad way. Like you get when one adventure is coming to an end you don't have the next one planned yet.

I don't know why but my eyes had been glued to the shelf at the Bean reading the insipid little sayings on the souvenir coffee cups. They were better than anything I was thinking at that moment, so I channeled them right at Harry.

"Never frown because you never know who might be falling in love with your smile," I read into the phone to Harry from a cup that had a sweet little drawing of a child sitting on a tree stump with cartoon hearts around her head.

"Tommy, you're the best friend a guy could have," he said and I could tell he was getting choked up.

"Meeting you was fate, becoming your friend was a choice, but falling in love with you was beyond my control," I blathered and was a little bit embarrassed as soon as I said that as it was kind of gay, but I wasn't reading ahead and my eye caught the cute drawing of two kids holding hands on a swing set. The rest of the cups had

'Have a Nice Day' and 'Cup of Joe' on them, so I had to go back to improvising.

"Enjoy yourself. Drop me a postcard. Save me a seat at the bar," I told him and I knew this would be the last time I ever talked to him. I wasn't going to be big on making new friends in my new life. All I needed was one and I had that already.

"And Tommy? Thanks for helping me out."

"I didn't, Harry. What you did you did on your own. And frankly, you helped me more than you'll ever know."

Enough gushing. "Have a nice day, Harry," was the last thing I told him as I hung up and went back to finishing my coffee and scone, which wasn't even close to being in the same ballpark as Jadonne's. Then I went up to the counter and asked the barista for another Cup of Joe.

34. WOE IS HARRY.

Harry slid off the mattress into the piss hot water and lolled around like a seal. He let the water creep into every orifice of his body. He was cleansing himself of his past and baptizing himself for his future.

He imagined being inside Jadonne on a bed of butter and lobster tails, quaffing an outstanding Fume Blanc, deciding on some of the appetizers for his shrimp shack menu.

Jadonne wanted a ceviche, but Harry thought it too much an insurance risk, being raw fish and all. She goosed him on that, saying he was forever the insurance agent. They laughed and made love in his mind again.

Harry was leaning on the edge of the pool. Steam rose off his body. He had a wide grin on his face so pronounced it made his eyes tear. He sat there for a good half hour, just dreaming away. He looked at his fingers. They were about as pruney as could be. He didn't want to disturb Jadonne in all her preparations, but he was wrinkling up bad. He swam some laps. Felt his muscles getting strong, his lungs expanding. He wanted to be strong for her. Ever since that first night, he hadn't had a hard on like that again. She never told him about the Viagra. Why ruin it for him? Why not let him think he could maintain a seven-hour erection without complications? Why not let him think she might be magic to his erectile tissue?

The light was turning orange. The wind was kicking up. There was a small cloud on the horizon, a rowboat of a cloud. Harry got out of the pool, wrapped himself in his bathrobe, and looked out to the beautiful woman with the dog. They were running back the other way now, probably on the way home. And she smiled at him again. But why would he be interested in hamburger when he had steak at home?

Harry walked up the stairs to the bedroom. The house was quiet, save for the sound of the shower in the master bath: Jadonne soaping up, Jadonne getting clean, Jadonne shiny with the water running off her body, Jadonne getting ready for Harry. Maybe he'd make love to her before they left. Just to christen the moment.

Harry put his ear to the bathroom door. He thought about going in, but didn't want to cross a line with her, didn't want to be overbearing, over eager. But he wanted her. He wanted her bad. All the thinking about her had aroused him. He wanted to take her, under the water, washing each other, exploring each other, kissing her with the water on their faces. He opened the door and took off his robe.

But she wasn't there. Just the shower, still on, steaming up the bathroom. No Jadonne. He put his bathrobe back on and called out to her, "Jadonne? Where are you?"

He walked out to the hallway, "Jadonne, sugar. Where you hiding?"

His voice echoed in that big dumb house. He could hear the antique clocks ticking, the digital clocks buzzing, the DVR whirring, the ice maker in the frig dropping ice into the tray, all mixed in with the white noise of the ocean.

He went outside again, out onto the beach. The woman and her dog were long gone. No one was out. The beach was empty.

He stared back at the house and yelled her name.

He walked to the neighbor's house. It was as big as the Buffet mansion, but modern in the colder than cold style of beach modernism influenced by the architecture of shopping malls. All white concrete and hard angles and metal staircases and lounge chairs by the pool that screamed 'Don't sit on me and ruin my symmetry.'

It was empty. The owners were away at their other house in Colorado. Probably scouting for rocks. He looked into the huge sliding glass window of the living room. The furniture was all white leather. There were sculptures and art all over the place and the carpet looked like no one had ever set foot on it.

He ran back to the mansion. He ran out the front door. He ran to the garage.

The Ferrari was gone.

He ran back to the kitchen. It was untouched. Nothing taken out to prepare a meal. No lobster pots. No wine. He opened the wine cabinet and pulled out a bottle of the Fume Blanc. He grabbed the bottle opener, wrestled with it for awhile until it defeated him and then opened the refrigerator and took out a beer.

She must have gone out shopping for the lobster, he thought to himself. That's what she did. Last minute deal. He figured she started the shower to get it the right temperature and realized she didn't have any lobsters. So she got in the car and thought she could just run a mile to the Ralph's, pick up the lobsters and make it back just as the water hit its perfect temperature.

Or there was a problem with the money. And she panicked and drove to her bank to sort it out and make a scene.

Or Gates and Welch got to her. He shuddered at the thought. It put him in a cold sweat at the thought that while she was in the shower, a flunky of theirs took her, put chloroform gauze over her nose and then put her over his shoulder and took her away. Another flunky took the Ferrari. They could stage an accident. Put her behind the wheel unconscious, put her foot on the accelerator and let her go over a cliff. Then they wouldn't have to pay the twenty a month. Now they too were free of the last remnant of J.P. Buffet's fucked up life.

He ran up the stairs to the master bedroom, looking for traces of a struggle.

Anything. A towel out of place. Footprints on the floor.

He looked for her bags. Hers were gone. His were still there.

He looked for the plane tickets. Hers were gone. His were still there.

That's it. They took the bags with them. Better for a story, he thought. She was running. Whatever they thought they could pin on her, she was running away. Running away with her settlement money. She was drunk. She drove off the cliff. She was a wild girl so this wasn't unusual. The press will pick it up as the end of the sad Buffet saga and then everybody will move onto the next thing, which in Malibu, would be the rights to a movie of the week.

Maybe she didn't level with him. Maybe she demanded more of the settlement. He didn't understand why she would demand a settlement in the first place, what with the twenty million coming in. The settlement was chump change. She said she was doing it cause she had to hurt them in some way. And the extra cushion would keep Harry and her away from the big funds for awhile, until they figured it all out. In the mean time, it sat in a high interest account gaining beaucoup of interest. Smart.

The images were running through his head. He even saw the car explode in his mind as it hit the rocks. He picked up his cell phone and dialed my number. But I had closed that account. Harry called the Malibu PD. He asked for me, said it was an emergency.

What they told him was that I had turned in my badge just over a year ago. Harry didn't believe them. He said he saw my badge. They told him they would be interested in that, as that would be impersonating an officer. Did he want to file a complaint?

Harry guzzled another beer then wrestled with the cork on the Fume Blanc and managed to push the whole thing into the wine. He poured himself a tumbler and ran back up to the bedroom and scoured through the closets.

He was wondering when he should call the police, place a missing persons. He was wondering if he wouldn't be laughed at. "How long has Ms. Buffet been missing," they'd ask. "Thirty minutes," he'd tell them, then he'd hear them laugh at him. He'd hear them laugh at him like he so many laugh at him before.

He'd tell them about his suspicions. How he sensed she might have been kidnapped by two top executives from the multi-level marketing company that just donated money to their pensions. That he was a friend of Tommy Cox, who claimed he was still a cop, but wasn't and maybe he was up to no good. They'd laugh at that too. They'd tell him that everybody was a friend of Tommy Cox, that's why Tommy Cox is no longer a cop. That's why they made Tommy Cox turn in his badge. Tommy Cox was a cop in bed with the conflicts of interest. Tommy Cox was busted for shaking down too many people with too much power and influence. Tommy Cox had taken too many envelopes from people that could fill them with special favors.

And by the time they got there—if they got there at all—he'd be a little drunk. They'd ask if this was his house, and he'd say no it wasn't and then they'd haul him in for questioning while Jadonne struggled with the locks on the Ferrari doors while flames leapt up all around her and the engine exploded, burning her perfect beauty alive.

He touched all of her clothes. She was going to leave most of them behind. She told him she hoped the only thing she'd wear for the rest of her life would be a sarong and a bikini top when she had to. Same with him. Sandals and an old blue work shirt and a pair of cargo shorts and that's it.

When the restaurant was up and running they'd make funny collector T-Shirts and make a couple special just for them, maybe long sleeves and a tweaked design and people would beg them for those and they'd charge a bundle.

He saw what looked like an old high school yearbook on the bed. He opened it. Inside, there was an envelope. He didn't open the envelope, because the page it was jammed into had some pictures that would change him. Pictures of Jadonne in High School. A lot of them. He turned the pages. She was all over the place. Cheerleading squad. Social Society. Most Popular Girl in School and of course, Best Looking.

The yearbook was written in. Tributes by guys who never had a chance with her and girls who were jealous of her. Best wishes stuff. Here's to the future stuff. Can't wait till we come back and party together after our first year of college stuff.

He saw Jadonne's picture as part of her class. She was exquisite. She made every other girl on that page look like a hag, or worse, inbred. She glowed.

The picture of the guy next to her on the page looked like he was pleased as punch to be so close to her in the lineup. He wasn't a bad looking guy. In fact, Harry thought he even looked familiar. There was writing next to his picture that ran over to Jadonne's like he was trying to connect the two. He wrote about the beach party on prom night and the ski trip and the football tailgating parties. He wrote that he loved her more than anybody had any right to love another person. And how she was his original love. His name was Alfred Thomas Coxwinkle.

35. SO SUE ME.

The Amanpur Resort in the Philippines is arguably the finest resort in the world. And that's only because I like to argue with myself. It's all rattan and fans and fawning service. It smells like pure air tinged with mint and vanilla. It's white sand and lush vegetation and ocean water that goes beyond most human's concept of what water is capable of.

The minute I checked in, I ordered the best champagne they had, and it wasn't Kristal. This place knew better. It was a Krug, '95, and it cost over a grand. Fuck it. I maxed my credit card to come to this place, as I had no intention of paying it off. I had long been looking to stick it to credit card companies, and you should too. All the cards are dealt in their favor and they are lying cheating scumbags that in other times would've been hung for usury from a low tree so the citizens could whack them with a stick while they suffocated to death on other peoples debt and they'd shit their pants doing it.

I got naked as a jaybird in the room, which was made out of floor to ceiling teak and bamboo. When the room service guy came with the bottle, I greeted him naked, handed him a two hundred dollar bill, and smiled as only a naked man with fuck you money and not a care in the fucking world could.

I took the bottle out to the terrace, which was right over the water, and took a swig from it. It had a fine bubble content so it came right out of my nose and dribbled off my chin into the ocean, which was tinted baby blue and clear as K-Y jelly and full of happy fish. Fish with rainbow colors that danced like they were auditioning for

Finding Nemo 4. And I heard their happy tune too. And they were just too pleased to perform for my pleasure.

I looked out to the beach and the ocean. Jesus, it was beautiful. They had built a white sand path that ran about a hundred feet into the ocean and ended at a little man made island. Enough for two rattan couches and a small cocktail table. I saw the shape of a woman in one of the chairs. Well heeled. Good pedigree. She had a big hat on. Big sunglasses, no top, body oiled and shiny. The sight of her made me somewhat hard. I could bring my hard on to her, lug it out to the beach. Just being here said we were equals in the sexual agar dish and she looked like the type that was born to wait for my hard on. I could take this bottle of Krug '95 out to Jadonne.

As I walked out on the man made sand bar, I thought about ol' Harry. Right about now or somewhat earlier, not sure anymore as I don't care to be accurate anymore with the lie, I bet Harry was face down, arms spread, on an Eastern King bed wearing nothing but a pair of soiled Depends. His skin was yellow. His muscle tone flat.

Hundreds of one hundred dollar bills lie scattered all over the room. A breeze lifted the curtains by the open bedroom window. It ruffled his Caesar cut crop of hair that lost its luster hours ago to sweat and desperation and pain. He had a letter in his hand. Crumpled up, but still locked in the grip. It was a letter I wrote him, gave to Jadonne to put in the yearbook. It was what I knew. It was what we did. It said:

Dear Harry,

I'm sorry it had to be you. I wish it would've been somebody I could hate. It would've been easier. But you really have only yourself to blame. So don't go through the rest of your life thinking others fucked you over. You fell for beauty. You fell for money. You fell for shit you did not earn. And that is why you are got fucked.

You didn't totally deserve it. You're not a bad guy. You're a patsy, but not a bad guy. It's just that you happened along and gave both Jadonne and me a wonderful opportunity. An opportunity of a lifetime, really. If it weren't for you, Jadonne would have to go back to the salt mines of having to hook up with another rich fuck so that she might have a nest egg for her retirement. And every time she did that I'd have to wait and see if the guy would die, or cheat on her, or that she'd have to go out of her way to make his life miserable so he would divorce her. But here you were, delivered by God from the belly of American Airlines Flight 992, with a folder full of papers and a head full of nice thoughts about the human race. And you didn't even know how fucked over you were. By your Boss, by Marsha, and I guess, ultimately, by us. But we had a reason. Ours was practical. Ours was about the money. Nothing personal. You were a conduit for our dreams. And I think, at the end of the day, we saved you from a terrible fate. That of marrying wrong. To an ugly woman to boot. Fat too. And didn't you feel just a little bit of heaven with Jadonne? Didn't you feel like you could conquer the world? It's in you, Harry. You can do it. Just don't think that your fellow humans are honest or square. Or that they'll cut a guy wearing Kirkland khaki pants a break. And remember, when it comes to big money, somebody has to get fucked over. That's always the way it's been.

When the railroads were built, it was the Chinaman that got fucked over. When the automobile was made, it was the horse that got fucked over.

And when Jadonne and I created a situation that made you hand over twenty million in payout from a policy that should never been awarded? Well, you fucking end the sentence.

Don't bother looking us up. We've changed our names. Don't bother coming after us. What would you do once you found us? Punch us in the nose? Shoot us? It's not in you. You don't want to go there. Not with me.

You just go on with your life know. You find somebody to love. Go down to Cabo. Open the restaurant.

Jadonne has a heart as big as her ass is small, so she left you fifty grand, cash, under the mattress. That should be enough to help you on your way. It sure is enough to cleanse our conscious. So take it. And remember what I said about original love.

Truly yours,

Tommy.

So this sort of brings me to the end of my story. And I'm sort of sorry I had to take you along for the ride, fun as it was for me. Don't get all haughty with my ass as I don't fucking care. Not with a bottle of one of the finest champagnes in the world in my hand, walking out to a white sand island where the most beautiful woman in the world was just waiting to suck my cock.

We had been planning this since high school. We had to work it. I told her we had to earn it. She was always set to cash out at the next divorce. But it was chump change. She married well, but not that well, and the fuckers always had top of the line lawyers and prenups and hidden accounts off shore.

This was all a lot easier than we made it out to be. But, then, it wouldn't be any fun. We wouldn't have EARNED IT. And I told you how important that was. And I told you about original love. Jadonne had been poisoning J.P., but so fucking slow I thought it would never end. We were thankful he was so self-destructive.

She even insisted on installing the stairway chair under the guise of helping him up the stairs when he was three sheets. But this much she knew: Offer a drunk the easy way and they'll take the hard way just to spite you. So we hoped and prayed that every night he went up to his bedroom out of his head, feeling the cumulative affects of the dioxin, vodka, and whatever other shit he ran his blood system with, he would go all Slinky down the stairs. Bang bang bang. Land. Head on marble. Crack. Dead. Jackpot!

But the fucker had the balance of a twelve-year-old Chinese gymnast. Until that last night. The week before his timely demise, she'd upped the mix in every bottle in the bar. She poisoned the little airplane bottles he kept in his inside suit pockets. She even crushed some Vicoden in his cocaine. Everything was a heady, confusing mix. Delpin would have had a field day, if he was an honest man, and if Lifethin hadn't offered to back the ghost written screenplay of his life with 5 million in development money.

Yeah. I killed Lars. I killed Lou. They were a risk. They knew too much. They would've wanted a cut. And Lou came on to Jadonne one time too many. And that I would not stand for. They were both assholes. They both had a criminal records. And you think it's your taxes that keeps the peace? Every cop has a corpse he can lay claim to. I did society a favor. Like I did with the Israeli. Your daughters might have been the next innocent souls he conned into gang banging for commerce.

I imagine Harry hung out at the mansion as long as he could. I imagine he had no idea where to go, what to do. I was hoping he'd call Carlos Prima, sign up, become a distributor. He had enough money to give it a year. He'd be OK. Who knows, maybe one day he'd be a million bonus earner selling shit nobody needs that doesn't really work.

Who knows? Who cares.

I approached Jadonne from behind and put my hands over her eyes. I could feel her smile and she took my hands and led them down to her satin smooth and oiled breasts and kept them there. Her nipples were hard. They were warm. I was amazed at their dexterity. Their design. God was capable of great things, I thought.

I could feel her heart beat. I could hear her breathing quicken. I could smell her excitement.

"We did it, Tommy," she said as she kissed my hands and sucked on my fingers. "We finally did it."

I leaned over the top of the chair and kissed her on the mouth.

Our lips slid against each other. There was absolutely no friction here. These were two perfect surfaces about to fuse into one.

Our mouths were made for each other. They fit together perfectly and she always tasted sweet to me. And when we kissed, we breathed each other's air, we took each other's scent. When we twined our tongues together, I couldn't tell which was mine and which was hers.

I poured a little of the champagne on her body.

She giggled at the coldness of the liquid and the snap of the bubbles on her skin. Then I came around the chair and licked it off her, mixing her own fleshy oils with the coconut oil she used to keep everything soft and moist and brown and it tasted like nothing the finest chefs in New York or San Francisco or Paris could ever whip up in a million years.

Jadonne was all live nerve endings, arched back and hands behind my neck, pulling my hair, then she reached down and pulled my cock out of my bathing suit, spreading the oil from her hand onto me, stroking and pulling, guiding it toward her, into her, like she was committing a form of sexual Hari Kari with a sword that was hard but round at the tip and wouldn't kill her but by pleasure.

And the sun got hotter. And the light got blindingly bright. And we were all alone. On a man made white sand bar. In the middle of a clear blue ocean filled with happy stupid fish that would never spill our secret. And a bottle of the best champagne in the world.

We had twenty million in the bank, cleared, cash, in the Caymans, tax free, earning massive interest, getting fat waiting for us to lick its ink.

I told you what this was going to be about. I told you it was going to be about me making my money. My shot. My opportunity. And did I disappoint? Does it matter how I did it? Now get lost.

"Fuck me, Tommy," she said.

I intend to, Jadonne. I intend to.